WAKE OF THE WEREWOLF

GEOFFREY CAINE

DIAMOND BOOKS, NEW YORK

WAKE OF THE WEREWOLF

A Diamond Book / published by arrangement with
the author

PRINTING HISTORY
Diamond edition / September 1991

ISBN: 1-55773-578-6

Diamond Books are published by The Berkley Publishing
Group, 200 Madison Avenue, New York, New York 10016.
The name "DIAMOND" and its logo are trademarks
belonging to Charter Communications, Inc.

PRINTED IN THE UNITED STATES OF AMERICA

10 9 8 7 6 5 4 3 2 1

This novel is affectionately dedicated to my wife, Cheryl, a strong person who has stood by me after twenty-four years of struggling; she has shared the double-edged sword of the writer's life that cuts with both pain and pleasure. She has done so with forbearance and a constant wisdom born of love and patience, even during those periods when I turned into something of a werewolf . . .

PROLOGUE

He had to be as cunning as an animal. He had to be an animal.

There was a time when the howling in his ears had been still, but Kerac couldn't recall how that felt. He'd been hearing the cry of the creature for too long now. What? An hour, a day, two . . . maybe a week, two weeks . . . double that? A month? Many months? Couldn't tell.

The cries told him he had to escape. If he didn't escape, he'd die.

The howls told him what to do. He fell dead away in the cafeteria at Merimac, the state-operated prison for the criminally insane. He had no idea how long he'd been here, or what he had done to deserve being put away, but the cries told him clearly how to faint by restricting his own air supply.

It'd worked and he'd been taken to the infirmary. There the cries told him even before he'd fully recovered his senses that his disorder must be made more complicated if he was to be taken to a real hospital, outside the great walls that held him here.

Kerac dug for the piece of glass he'd held beneath his tongue, grateful he had neither swallowed nor choked on it. He waited for the prison doctor to look away before he reached down into his pants and slit his penis near in two with the glass. He made not a sound, just listened to what the noises inside his head instructed him to do. He lay back and let the blood fill his pants with a dark, purple splotch, a kind of "stigmata," the buzzing in his mind told

1

him in an indecipherable tongue that somehow was translated into self-mutilation.

He wondered again what he'd done to deserve imprisonment alongside madmen. The pain in his privates was the price he must pay for escape. To keep from thinking about the pain, he concentrated on his laugh. He'd thought a great deal about laughter since coming here, and how important laughter really was. He let out with a laugh now which seemed to percolate in his diaphragm and erupt with the force of a volcano. It was a raw, naked laugh. The laughing slowed the cries, the howls and the mournful wails of an animal inside his brain.

When the doctor looked back at him, quaking from Kerac's laugh, he had a look of horror on his face. Kerac's eyes dimmed over with a thick, gummy substance, and suddenly he was seeing everything in a kind of 3-D, everything in clear perspective, angles and depths jutting out and in, nothing hidden in the dark shadow-covered corners. It was like seeing for the first time. It was wild and exciting. It was mind-blowing, like being on a heroin high, but without the color, because everything was in grays, blacks and shimmery whites.

His hearing had also become incredibly acute. He could actually hear the orderly's sneakers on the floor as he inched toward the door. He could almost hear the other man's heartbeat. He could hear someone in the TV room snoring. He could hear a fly breathe. It was a power he'd not ever expected to possess.

All this as well as his intensified sense of smell. In fact, he could smell the other men as never before, and in his brain he distinguished each man by his smell. The orderly sweat heavily and exuded a goatlike stench; he used no deodorant, while the doctor's perspiration was a cold, sweet scent; there was the faint scent of anise escaping his pores along with the disinfectant on his hands.

The look on the doctor's face, the look of shock and puzzlement, must be due to the cut and the blood, reasoned Kerac. But Kerac then caught sight of his own hands in the now colorless world around him, and he saw the extended claws and the hair and the nestling parasites in the fur covering his limbs. The realization that he was mad only now dawned on him, seeing himself this way.

He lifted off the table and the doctor and his orderly backed away in fright. Kerac saw his gray reflection in the doctor's glass cabinet. Like his mind, his body was all a tangle of knotted confusion. His eyes had dropped below the brow into a deep recess of dark circles created by folds of leathery skin from which prickly, whiskerlike hairs sprouted. His nose had enlarged, the nostrils flared. His jaw was snoutlike and the pain that racked his body made him shout, but the shout came out as an inhuman howl, the cry of a beast that had been raging in his head for as long as he could remember, which seemed to be the last few hours.

The orderly tore open the door in an attempt to race from the room, but Kerac's reaction was quick and instinctive, pouncing on the man in catlike fashion, ripping away at his face to stop the screaming.

"Kerac! Kerac!" shouted the doctor, pleading.

But Kerac's claws came down in rapid-fire fashion, turning the young orderly's features to mincemeat before he slid dead to the floor.

Screaming, the doctor tried to escape, but Kerac's hairy arm caught him about the neck, a deadly claw sinking deep into the man's throat, severing the jugular. Kerac tore a limb from the man as he was bleeding to death. He did so with playful ease, amazed at the strength he possessed. He wanted to try his strength again, but something cunning deep within his mind opted for escape. But not before he ripped apart his prey. He left nothing recognizable as human in a matter of minutes. Kerac lapped at the blood, crawling about the carrion on all fours. But hearing the shouts and footsteps of others, he tore away another limb, and taking his two prizes, he leapt through the window to the sound of sirens and the flash of lights.

One of the guards sighted Kerac, drew a bead on him and hesitated, realizing that the escaping form was some sort of animal. A second guard arrived just in time to see what looked to him like a large dog—maybe a bear—leap over the ten-foot fence, dropping something in its wake. The two men went to inspect what the creature had dropped at the foot of the stone fence. The flashlight told them it was a large man's bloody leg.

"Get the dogs!" shouted one of the guards to the other.

In an hour guards and dogs were scouring the woods surrounding Merimac, but they found nothing when the dogs refused to cooperate.

—1—

The scene in which two men were literally ripped apart by some kind of bloodthirsty animal kept coming back at Abraham Hale Stroud, wanting—*demanding*—clarification from his subconscious.

Twice now it had run on the "silver screen," his playful term for the steel plate in his head which had some years before become a kind of psychic antenna, somehow combining with what had apparently been in his makeup all along: extrasensory perception. The combination made for something the experts called second sight, but for Stroud there were no words that fit the peculiar "gift" that seemed to be initially inherited, in the genes. In a sense his own body chemistry had been wed to a kind of electromagnetic pole at the cranium that sometimes sent and sometimes received messages from far away. He'd been visited by his grandfather's ghost and others on more than one occasion. Typically, the visits were, while shocking and heart-stopping, benign in nature. Often, they were meant to "guide" him to answers not readily perceived by any other means. They'd certainly been beneficial in the case of the Andover Devil . . .

Just the same, he was often confused as to the meanings of his visions. He'd once been a soldier hunting the enemy in a tangled jungle in Southeast Asia, and this was before the metal plate in his head. With his abilities he'd located the enemy where nothing mechanical could. In fact, he was so good at locating the enemy that over half his company was killed in an ensuing engagement. He was himself left for dead on the field for two soul-searching days before he was found and brought out. He was then shipped home after a Hanoi hospital stay where the doctors stabilized the rest of his body, but could do very little for the missing shards of his skull. They then packed him off like a mailbag into a cargo plane and got him stateside where a "real" hospital outside Chicago replaced part of his skull with a metal brace. Curiously, the doctor's name had been Bracewell.

Later, as a cop on the Chicago Police Department for some thirteen years, he became known as the "psychic detective." During those years he'd also completed his work on a doctorate in archeology at the University of Chicago, working nights, weekends and holidays to do so. He had retired from the arena of the policeman when his grandfather died, leaving him an estate in Andover, Illinois, on the Spoon River, along with full ownership of Stroud Bank of Andover and the family fortune. It had all seemed like any man's dream—winning the lottery—at first, but now Stroud knew there were stipulations, even a real live "curse" associated with the wealth of Stroud Manse.

He'd had to rid Andover of what the locals had for years whispered about in the pubs and coffeehouses as the Andover Devil. As a result there'd been a great loss of life, including a good friend, Dr. Jacob Magaffey. And although the immediate threat of the vampire colony that'd held Andover in its collective grasp for generations had been broken, Stroud knew that he'd be called on again to use his wealth and his "gift" to fight evil in whatever other form or guise it took. And right now, it seemed to be taking on the form of a ghastly monster of the night that left men lying in flesh heaps the way a lion on the Serengeti left its prey to the vultures, scavengers and maggots.

Just exactly what the creature resembled in appearance, Abraham was unprepared to say. The images and visions that'd come to him of this overwhelming evil gave him the feelings of the monster far more than it gave him the appearance. The creature hungered. It hungered not just for blood and flesh to fill its stomach, but for the exhilaration and adrenaline high of the kill itself. It was a hunter, a predator of the first order, but the purpose of its hunt was love of the kill first, feeding second. Its instincts were those of the jaguar. It was large, ferocious and powerful and it delighted in its own attributes.

But Stroud had his hands full with his work. The dig at the newly discovered burial mounds at a well-established and well-known Cahokia Indian village here in southern Illinois was disproving some long-held notions about the Cahokias. He was having a wonderful time with it, feeling like a boy in the toy department at Macy's. It was taking up most of his waking hours. The evening hours, however, were being given over to fantastic visions of a creature roaming the countryside. The "disturbance" had not gone unnoticed by colleagues and friends here, including Dr. Cage, the expedition leader.

"You feeling all right?" was a constant question put to him lately down at the dig site.

He had plenty of time to think there on his hands and knees beside students—children—a third his age. He meant to get dirty, to grind the dirt into his jeans, sift it through his fingers and get it under his nails. He meant to learn firsthand what Cahokia must have meant to the Cahokian people. He meant to unearth another set of bones for Cage and the others to marvel over. Meantime, he was truly soaking up the field experience and learning the newest techniques. The game of the bone hunter had advanced rapidly in the past few years; so many new toys at the scientists' disposal, like the Earthscan, a device that told the archeologist where his best chance of finding buried earth formations lie. With the help of the Earthscan, time, energy and backaches were saved, not to mention the integrity of the dig itself. Who needed a useless slag heap?

It was all good experience for Dr. Abe Stroud, newly appointed assistant to Dr. Cage. Stroud knew best that he needed the invaluable experience before becoming involved in an overseas dig.

With work and focusing his attention on the artifacts and bones the earth reluctantly gave into his hands, Stroud had felt he could fend off the nagging nightmare that had now returned for a third time like a bad penny. So long as it remained a nightmare, however vivid, Stroud remained uncertain of the meaning of the vicious killing played out in his mind. It might be nothing more than a simple and meaningless nightmare, and yet he knew that he wasn't like other men who had bad dreams and could wake up and forget about them or blot them out entirely. His dreams sometimes predicted the future, and sometimes were replays of incidents already in the past. That was how he had first met the missing boy, Timmy Meyers, who had eventually led to the discovery of an entire vampire colony that had learned to cohabit with humans by day and night so closely it was impossible to tell them from ordinary humans. Maybe the dream was trying to tell him something. Maybe the dream was brought to him by his dead grandfather . . .

How did the old Celtic prayer go? *From ghoulies and ghosties and long-leggety beasties . . . And things that go bump in the night . . . deliver us!*

Maybe he was just being foolish, letting his imagination run wild . . . maybe the stress and excitement of the work weaving itself into his night and turning into a garden worm when it hit the plate in his head. Maybe . . .

Dusk was coming on, and Abe feared going to sleep again. He had tired of the shaking, heart-gripping scene that'd played out in his tent and in his mind thrice now. He prayed it wouldn't return. He clamored to his feet, his legs numb at first and then shooting with pain, especially the knees. A young fellow named Jack offered him a hand up out of the pit, and he took it gratefully.

"You've been at it since noon nonstop, Dr. Stroud," he said.

"Guess I didn't notice the time. Happens in a flash when you enjoy what you do."

"Everybody in camp's talking about you."

"What?"

"About how you pitch in, how you work, get your hands in . . . not like some I've worked with, believe me. Last guy I worked with, real old, ugly, skinny fart—"

"Dr. Sturdevant?"

"Yeah, sorry . . . didn't know you knew him."

"Only by reputation."

"Reputation, hah. All he was interested in was getting the freshman girls into bed with him."

Stroud laughed and said, "*Archeology and Sex.*"

"That's right . . . bartered grades for it, the old weasel."

"I meant his book, *Archeology and Sex.*"

"Oh, oh yeah . . . Well, I'm off to mess. See you, Dr. Stroud."

"Thanks, Jack, for the hand up and the lesson."

He looked back over his shoulder and said, "Don't mention it to her, but Tammy Wymes thinks you're a hunk, Dr. Stroud. Might help you sleep, you know what I mean?"

Stroud dropped his gaze and shook his head. "Yeah, maybe that'd set things right, all right."

Stroud then wandered off from camp as was his habit, to spend a little time along the brook the Indians had no name for. For the Indians, where the water flowed from and where it went as it moved past their village was of no consequence. It was enough that it was here and that it gave of itself to them. Stroud wondered how the world had become so complex and difficult.

The night was coming on fast, a chill in the breaking wind. Young saplings twitched and the bugs were chattering. It was the sort of night a man could see forever, the stars flirting with the imagination, a high, near-full moon blinking around a stray cloud; when the moon moved over, it flushed the land around Cahokia with a sandy, silvery hue. Then it dawned on Dr. Stroud that he'd stood here in a near-catatonic state so long that he'd missed dinner. He was left with the prospect of going to his tent where he'd log a few notes, catch up on his reading and try like hell to get some deserved sleep. Maybe tonight it wouldn't elude him.

"Dr. Stroud? Is that you?" A female voice made Stroud turn. It was Tammy Wymes as if on cue. Everybody in camp must know she'd come out here looking for him. She'd been flirtatious since the day Stroud arrived, but he'd chalked it up to a schoolgirl's interest in one of her teachers. She was wearing a sheer blouse that showed her midriff, her stomach heaving a bit with the cool night air, puckering her belly button first open and then closed as if it were a third eye, winking.

Stroud calculated her age at nineteen, possibly twenty. He was in his early forties. He began to wonder about her motivation in coming to him like this.

"You must be cold, Miss Wymes," he said.

"A little, but here you are in your shirt sleeves."

Stroud seldom wore a coat or jacket even in the worst of weather if he didn't have to. He'd normally leave it tossed in the back of his jeep. Coats made him feel cramped not only physically but mentally; they reminded him of the heavy army issue loaded down with canteen and gun belt and grenades that he wore all through Vietnam. He hated sweating underneath the weight of a parka.

"Yeah, well, April can get nippy, but not for me, Miss Wymes."

"Can't you call me Tammy? Wouldn't you like to?" She came closer as she spoke, her arms opening, inviting him into them. "I could keep us both warm, if you'd let me, and maybe, Dr. Stroud, I could chase that awful nightmare away."

"Christ, has everybody in camp learned of my sleeping disorder?"

"Dr. Stroud, you'll soon learn that everyone in a small camp knows about everyone else's . . . ahh . . . sleeping arrangements."

"So I've heard, but tell me, Tammy, why're you interested in an old man like me?"

"You're sharp, Dr. Stroud . . . really. Everybody says so, and . . ."

"And what? I remind you of someone? Your father, maybe?"

She laughed at this. "Couldn't be further from the truth, Dr. Stroud." Her honey-blond hair fell over her left eye, and her right took him in again. "My father's a bald, fat man. Look at you. You're trim and tall and powerfully built. No, Dr. Stroud, you'll have to do better than that."

Abraham Stroud's eyes radiated his own desire, reflecting the moonlight in the deep, sincere pupils that were an ice blue in this light. His hair was peppered with silver strands. Stroud was a big man at six four, and his hands were large like the flats of two skillets. She took them in her own, her hands made miniature by his. Stroud had drawn her attention the moment she'd laid eyes on him. "The way you talk, your voice," she said now, "and the way you walk, kind of princely, regal . . . like . . . like no one I've ever known. That's what first attracted me to you, Stroud."

She reached up on her toes and kissed him full on the lips. Stroud started to resist, but he didn't have enough reason to resist. Her passion was searing through her pores, and her warmth was like a fire of churning embers. In his ear she whispered, "I just like you, Stroud, because you do remind me of someone I loved as a child, a fictional hero."

"Gary Cooper, *High Noon,* maybe?"

"Try James Bond . . . double oh seven, Sean Connery."

Now he laughed, and it felt so good and natural to do so. He'd had little to laugh about lately.

"Some people say your bad dreams are a result of the war . . . that you have bad memories. Let me give you some good memories to . . . you know"—she dug her hands into his shirt and wound them around his wide shoulders—"chase the pain."

Her next kiss was returned by Stroud forcefully, and then their kisses seemed to transfuse each other with a lust that Stroud hadn't felt in a very long time. It made him think of innocent days in college when he would try to capture the girl's breath by swallowing it, feeling a high from the experience that he learned much later had all to do with a carbon dioxide high.

Tammy was very sensual and Stroud found himself on his knees along with her there below the moonbeams that cast their shadows into the wood and beyond in what seemed an infinity of its own.

A jolt of immortality rose in Stroud's veins, and this led him to lift her into his arms. He plucked her from the earth like a prize, carrying her to his tent.

There in the darkness she took her time removing her clothes before coming to him and undoing his clothing. Abe lost himself in her attention, in her caresses and kisses. She treated him with great tenderness which seemed beyond her years. She whispered, "Let me come into where you live, Abraham Stroud."

He knew that was impossible; that no one could ever truly know him, not fully, not without fearing him. Still, he let her believe she could, and he let her continue to touch.

He lay now on his back as she explored him, a scent like magnolias coming off her perfumed body. Stroud lost himself in her corn-silk hair. They made exquisite, exhausting love and the act itself was to Stroud wondrous; each of them found infinite pleasure in the touch and warmth of the other. Stroud found magic in her, and without further words between them she sensed this and delighted in it.

Afterward, exhausted and chilled from the mix of cool air and sweat from his body, Stroud dozed to her final whisper, "Connery's got nothing on you . . ." Stroud felt replenished, sated, happy and calm.

He fell asleep thinking that in the instant they shared their bodies with one another they had vanquished a terrifying foe; that passionate love somehow kept the darkness and the evil of his dreams at bay.

"Alpha Charlie" was the soldier's code for stand down, all clear. "Alpha" was the cop's term for all's well. But Stroud wasn't sure there was a lover's term to match, or that there ever could be a word to describe the peace he felt at that moment. All he knew for certain was that tonight he wouldn't be at battle with his own brain which spawned hellish nightmares without apparent reason. Tonight his worst nightmare had been banished by a teenager with the capacity for irreverent and beautiful lust.

Nothing disturbed Stroud and he slept through the night to awake to the morning noises of camp. Tammy Wymes had gone. He breathed a deep sigh of relief for both her discretion and the fact he'd shaken off the nightmare that'd haunted him now for several nights. But his contentment and his thoughts were rudely interrupted by his friend and associate, Dr. Louis Cage. Cage, a burly, lumbering man with spectacles too small for his huge face and a walrus mustache but no hair on his head, burst into Stroud's tent flapping a newspaper.

"Look at this! Abe, look!"

"I came out here to escape newspapers, Lou."

Cage looked momentarily stunned, but then went on. "This is your dream, your nightmare, down to the last detail. It's made page one in *USA Today*."

"What?" Stroud grabbed the paper from Cage's fumbling fingers. He glanced over the cover story, scanning for details below the photo of a Dr. Harold Perotto and a second man. The two men were wearing the normal look of medical men standing for a photo, but in another picture, there was nothing left of either man, save the bloody torso and a scramble of limbs about the floor. The paper said that a criminally insane man named John Kerac had butchered the men with some unknown weapon, leapt through a glass window and had eluded guards to escape the state facility for the criminally insane near Merimac, Michigan. Kerac remained at large.

"I'm right, aren't I, Abe? Isn't this the nightmare you've been having?"

"Premonition . . . the first time and the second. Happened last night."

"You couldn't've known it. Now, don't go blaming yourself. You didn't even know the men were medical men, or that the monster you saw was an insane fiend. You didn't know the time or the place."

"But if I'd let it come, instead of fighting it . . . maybe."

"Damn it, Abe, you're not a sorcerer. You're only human."

"Thanks, that's great comfort, Lou."

Cage took in a great breath of air, seeing a familiar look come over his friend's features. "You're going up there, aren't you?"

Some of the guys at the watering hole outside were laughing over something. In a paranoid moment, he wondered if they were discussing Tammy and him. If he knew anything about paranoia, he knew it was quite often an early warning device as accurate as a Timex. His instincts marched along the epidermal layer of his skin to alert the brain that was, like a slow cursor on a computer, half a pulse behind this morning.

"Maybe it wouldn't be such a bad idea," he said. "Around here, I seem to be stirring up more curiosity than what's out there in the Indian mounds."

"That's nonsense."

"Really?"

"Damned straight it is."

"Damn it, Lou, you're the best detail-man in the pathology business, and you're an excellent paleontologist, but you've got a hell of a lot to learn about the *living*."

"I take that as a compliment. What the hell do I really want to know about the living?"

"Enough to keep these not so angelic broads out of my tent."

"Hold on there, Abe. What goes on in the tents at night is the business of consenting adults. I'll be damned if I'm going to pat you on the back or send you off for such nonsense."

"I'm going, anyway, Lou."

"Fine, go! Good riddance, as you say. And what'll you do in Michigan once you get there?"

"I'll offer my help."

"And if they refuse it?"

"Then at least I can say I gave it my best."

"To convince whom? Your dead grandfather or yourself?"

"Both, maybe."

"Dead set on this, are you?"

"I have to, Lou . . . you know that."

He frowned and slowly nodded. "Get back as quick as you can. Give me a holler if you need me."

"Thanks, and will do."

"Taking your new chopper up?"

"I figure to fly, sure. Sooner I get there, the better. Lou, I think I understand how this madman, Kerac, thinks. It could be helpful to the authorities up there."

"Well, if you should find yourself butting heads with a backwoods geek who thinks he's God, then turn yourself right around and leave them to their own stupidities." Cage stood up and took his hand. "It's been a delight, these past weeks with you here, Abe, you know that."

"All but the past few days and nights, you mean."

"All of it, my friend. We'll be here when you've finished in Michigan."

With that, Cage left abruptly, not a man for lengthy good-byes.

—2—

Kerac awoke naked and bloody, the pain in his penis shooting a searing rod of fire through him. He had blood encrusted over his lips and chin. He had a foul taste in his mouth, coppery and greasy. He felt he might wretch at any moment. He crawled about in the cold, high, dead reeds and grass all around him, trying to determine where he was and how he'd gotten here. He felt numb from the cold, so numb he could hardly think to recall anything. Then he crawled up toward a bone from which some fleshy strings clung; it was all cushioned in a nestlike place in the high thatch. He realized he'd stumbled onto the lair or sleeping place of some sort of animal that had been feeding on the large bone. He looked around instinctively for whatever it might be. When he saw nothing, he calmed a bit, going closer to the bone and lifting it as much from curiosity as anything, and yet . . . something about the bone and its smell, and the smell of the flesh clinging there like a wet noodle brought on images that made little sense to John Kerac.

He saw himself at a hunting camp, sitting by a warm fire, a few friends without names or faces with him. He saw the flames blind out the image and replace it with his running madly through the woods. He tried desperately to remember, fighting with his mind for the right to his past, to access more than mere images flashing on and off in the manner of a wino. There was more . . . much more, he knew. If only he could tap into it.

Then he saw the doctor's face at Merimac; he saw it torn from the man, reduced to a gelatinous mass. He saw it being done by a creature of immense power, and as he watched he saw the creature's eyes, and in the eyes he recognized something else. He saw that the eyes of the monster were his eyes.

He found himself cradling the bone again, realizing now what sort of bone it was and where it had come from. He also realized that the nesting animal had been him and that it was he who had fed on the flesh of the bone.

He trembled at the cold around him, and he trembled at the power of the *other* within him.

They must be scouring the countryside for him this instant. There must be an APB out on him. He must run and he must hide. But which way? Indecision and fear could get him captured or killed. He'd be crucified for killing the doctor and his orderly. What had he done before this to warrant his being locked up at Merimac? he again wondered. Then he saw the fire and the camp once more, and he saw the dark shape in the nearby trees leap down and run ahead of him, as he and his friends chased after it with guns.

Something had happened out there . . . but what?

Something was drawing him back, too . . . back to where this all started, to where his nameless, faceless friends had . . . had all . . . all dead . . . they were all mutilated by some *thing*. He saw the bone in his lap, and he wondered if it had been he who killed the others in a brutal spree of madness. He thought he recalled feeding on them as he had on the doctor's arm last night.

He dropped the bone and bent over, vomiting up chunks of the doctor's flesh, crawling to escape the sight and the smell and himself, but he could do none of these things.

Kerac heard a dog's braying. Alert to the danger, he raced away from the thatch lair, searching for something safer. In another direction he heard the call of a cock and he went instinctively for what he prayed would be a farm with an automobile somewhere on the premises.

Something told him he had to go back, back to the area outside Grand Rapids where it had all begun, but he feared it terribly. He had friends in Chicago and he knew the city like the back of his hand. Maybe there he could get straight somehow. Maybe there he could beat this insanity thing.

He fought back the pain in his lower parts, rushing wildly toward his future.

—3—

Stroud stepped out of his helicopter to a waiting patrol car driven by Merimac's own sheriff, a lady sheriff named Chief Anna Laughing More. The name alone had intrigued Abe, and he had wondered about its history during his flight to Michigan via his newly acquired Mooney XE6000 chopper. He'd had breakfast in the Cahokia archeological camp, and he was in Merimac, some fifty miles southeast of Grand Rapids, for lunch. But the reception he got from the lady cop was as cutting as the cold wind that rippled across the small airstrip in Merimac, a town founded, it seemed, on the economy created by the state facility from which John Kerac had successfully escaped.

Before the rotor blades on his shiny new helicopter had slowed to a stop, Chief Laughing More indicated with a gesture that he was to get into her patrol car. She was dressed in a tight-fitting, strangely seductive brown and beige uniform that showed off her tall, elegant figure. Her hair was a jet black, severely cut like a man's, perhaps to fit beneath the Chief's cap, perhaps to gain acceptance and respect? But this was the only feature that detracted from her femininity, he thought as he got into the vehicle. Without a word, she tore off the tarmac, using no siren, but clearly no one best get in her way. Immediately, Stroud got the feeling she didn't want him here. It was as cold inside the car as out.

The chatter of the radio car buzz recalled his days as a police

17

officer in Chicago. "I'm Dr. Stroud, and you must be Chief Laughing More?"

Her Ojibway ancestry showed in the high cheekbones and her proud bearing. She was beautiful to look at. He imagined she'd worn her hair long all her life, up to the point she'd become a police woman. She was as tall as Stroud, and he guessed her to be in her early to mid-thirties. The skin was a smooth, tight, coppery color and her eyes were as black as the darkness on a blank computer screen, giving up nothing.

"I know who you are, Dr. Stroud."

"You understand why I've come?"

"You've come to"—she paused, considering her words carefully—"help out, as I understand it."

She spoke exquisite English, despite her exotic features. "Yes, any way I can."

"You say you saw this man, Kerac, in a dream, kill our Dr. Perotto and Carl Holms?"

"I didn't know their names at the time. Read about it later in the papers, like everyone else."

"But your dream—"

"More a nightmare than a dream, a premonition."

"Premonition, yes . . . well . . ."

"I fully understand your reluctance to believe me, Chief Laughing More."

"You can call me Chief More," she corrected him. "Everyone else does." She didn't appear in a laughing mood, nor, Stroud guessed, did she display laughter very often while in uniform. "Listen, Dr. Stroud, I'm not much of a believer in your . . . in powers of precognition, is it called? Nor do I much hold with psychic investigators. You may as well know it."

"Refreshing," he replied cryptically.

And for a long moment, she tried to decipher his meaning without benefit of explanation. Finally, she repeated the word in puzzlement. "Refreshing?"

"I only wish everyone were as honest around me, Chief."

"Oh, you will find me honest, all right—honest Injun, as they say, Doctor."

He managed a weak smile at this, unsure how to take her remark. "I've fought very hard to get where I am today, Dr. Stroud."

"I can see that you have."

"Can you? Really? You have any idea how entrenched the KKK

is in Michigan? The Knights of the Baldies? Ordinary redneck mentality? Any idea how hard it is for an Indian in Michigan to beat the reservation system, the inadequate school system, the poverty, the prejudice? No, I suppose not."

"Perhaps not . . . Certainly not firsthand, but I'm here to learn."

"I thought you came to provide us with lavish information on the crime and the killer, Dr. Stroud. I had no idea you were here to gather information. Are you writing a book?" Her sarcasm came full to the surface now.

"I used to be a cop, Chief More. I know how you feel when an outsider steps in, but—"

"Chicago cop. What do you know about Michigan?"

"I know serious crime is on the rise here, like most places, 686 murders in Detroit alone . . ."

"This isn't Detroit. This is—"

"And 6,458 serious crimes reported statewide."

"So you've done your homework, and now you know how Merimac works?"

He frowned and scratched his ear and moved uneasily in the car seat beside her. "I don't pretend to understand the people or the politics, but I had expected a little common courtesy after flying here at my own expense to look into this matter and offer—at no expense to Merimac—any assistance I can render. What the hell is it, Chief? Election time in Merimac?"

"Why, you are very perceptive at that, Dr. Stroud."

"Election's coming up, huh?"

"It's always election day in Merimac. You may think Michigan is cozy, Middle America, the hunting and fishing paradise in the brochures, and all is beautiful and serene in the Michigan forests, that all's right in the world. What bad could happen in Michigan? How about we begin with a red population that is still treated like animals?"

He could see she had a large chip on her shoulder, and that he wasn't about to dislodge it here and now. He was a white man and she was a red woman; he was an outsider, and she was an insider. He was a civilian while she was a police chief.

"Is Kerac . . . is he Indian?"

"He *was*."

"What do you mean, was? Has he been shot?"

She looked across at him. "No, he is still at large, but he is also *Ninatoo;* you might call it banished."

"Banished?"

She swallowed hard. "When an Ojibway Indian murders, he is cast out of the race of the *first people*, the Ojibway. Kerac was a guide. He led several men into the Manistee National Forest a month ago. He slaughtered all three of the other men."

"Three white men?"

"On holiday . . . Hunters. Anyway, he was apprehended and sent here to await trial. He had been judged completely insane. He'd . . . he had eaten the flesh of the white men."

"Cannibalized them?"

"Yes."

"All three?"

"Yes, like a wild animal might."

Stroud breathed deeply, his skin crawling with the image. "Autopsies were done on the dead men?"

"In Grand Rapids, yes."

"And here, with Dr. Perotto and the other dead man?"

"Our town, the hospital pathologist performs any autopsy."

"I see." Stroud knew that hospital pathologists were not the most reliable people where autopsy was concerned. "What about Grand Rapids? Do they have a municipal pathologist?"

"Dr. Henry Sands, but he's second-rate at best."

"Why do you say so?"

"Let me put it this way: I've worked cases with him before. I know."

"Good enough for me."

She gave him a quick gaze. "What do you hope to find in a pathology report, anyway?"

"Connections, patterns . . . not sure."

"Oh, you'll see patterns, all right—patterns on the bodies, gashes. Whatever Kerac used on these men—" She shivered involuntarily. "I've never seen such brutality before, I'll admit that. I'm sure it's nothing to a Chicago cop. Want to swing by the morgue first before going out to the pen?"

"Is it on the way?"

"Have to go through town, then on to the other side."

"Fine, whatever you say, Chief."

"Funny thing about Kerac and me, Stroud . . ."

"Oh, what's that?"

"We grew up together on the same reservation . . . went to the same schools—"

"Ever figure him for this?"

"He was nothing but a shy, sweet boy when I knew him. Big

and clumsy and shy, like a bear up here," she said, pointing to her head. "Not very smart, but keen as a tracker and a guide. We have one other thing in common, Dr. Stroud."

"And what is that?"

"I'm also banished from my tribe."

She fell silent, and Stroud sensed that it would be unwise to ask her why she shared this fate with Kerac.

She turned on a local radio station, the announcer speculating on the deaths at the prison. She turned it to another station that was obviously Indian-operated, the music being distinctly American Indian. It made for an unusual chorus between them for a moment before she said, "You see, my people live in the past. Songs, myths, religion, all strong medicine . . . so why do they hurt for food and clothes and doctoring? They resent me because I'm a traitor in their eyes, twice over. Number one, you don't take on the work of a warrior—a man's job. Number two, you don't stand with the white man. 'Fraid I did both."

"How close is the reservation?" he asked as the car passed shacks and delapidated mobile homes.

"You're in it. Have been the entire way. Merimac is largely reservation land. The whites left the scrub grass and rocks for us."

The land around was dry, arid and brown, the grass still dead from winter kill; no amount of sunlight could heal this area or ever hope to revive it, or so it seemed at the moment. Ashen woods, thick with naked branches, touched the sky all around. The timid homes had the requisite broken-down car, children's toys, trash cans and tottering fences. It was a sad, drab place, filled with evidence of poverty and the typical Indian ills. Gambling was a way of life here, as was drinking. Every business establishment sported a whiskey sign alongside a lottery sign and a banner proclaiming one-armed bandits inside.

The car rambled past a general store that was falling in, the proprietor's name illegible with years of weathered paint and peeling. "Not exactly Palm Beach," she muttered.

You grew up here? he wanted to ask her, but he didn't bother forming the words. She could read it in his gaze. Instead, he asked, "How about the prison? Has it put any of your people to work?"

She laughed. "Most on the inside—as inmates, I'm afraid."

He decided to drop the subject. She turned the patrol car onto a side-street going for the hospital. "Our morgue isn't much, but we do the best we can, Dr. Stroud." The hospital itself is small by modern standards, the construction early sixties."

"Please," said Stroud, "no apologies necessary."

"You sure about that? Might want to wait until you meet our so-called coroner. He wears several hats: M.D., pathologist, coroner. Unfortunately, he doesn't wear any one very well. Name is Cruise. Came up here from New York City several years ago. Strange sort of guy . . ."

"Strange?"

"Exception to the rule, you might say."

"What rule is that?"

"For what we call an outlander, he fits right in on the reserve. Friends in high places in both the City Council and with the elders—"

"In the tribe?"

"No, the church! Yes, the tribe. What else are we talking about here?" Her voice sounded like the rock singer Cher, especially when she was angry.

"No one else from outside ever fit in so well. And you're a *home girl*, and you aren't allowed in . . . Yeah, begin to see what you mean."

"It's not like that. Not like I dislike him because of my situation. Don't misunderstand. There's just something sleazy about our Dr. Cruise."

"Maybe it's just that he's from New York, and you don't have much tolerance for people from big cities coming into your town. Correct me if I'm wrong."

"You're wrong."

He wondered if she was asking him to read between the lines, as one cop to another. Small towns, as a rule, were tight as balled fists all over the nation; some may as well be villages in Europe for all they knew of world events, geography. They were that insular and parochial. Most people in such places as Merimac still believed that the moon landing had been a fake, created by the wizardry of television. No, they didn't as a rule take kindly to strangers. He knew this from his own experience in relocating to Andover, Illinois, from Chicago. There, to this day, he was still considered an "outlander." Here, in sleepy, little Merimac, which had its own tight social structure and levels and little political intrigues to do with school boards and zoning laws, taxes and taking care of business, anyone not born down the street must surely be suspect and might live a lifetime here and still remain unacceptable. This category ought to fit a doctor moving in from the Big Apple, as well as make room for those "excommunicants" banished from the "tribe."

She radioed ahead to the hospital.

Studying her, Stroud figured Chief Laughing More as a hardworking, tough-minded cop than anything else, and that she would love nothing more than to drag John Kerac back here by his heels to stand trial for multiple murder. Maybe such an act would reinstate her with her people as well as boost her in the general population of whites. He was not sure. He thought she'd be a good cop anywhere. This led him to wonder why she hung on here. Was it the money? Not likely. Family? Could be. Or was it simply the usual fears that small-town girls grow up with? Typical small-town mentality held that you didn't abandon your roots, no matter how shriveled or dead they were.

Stroud understood roots perhaps better than most, but he also knew that some roots confined, strangled, or twisted people.

Maybe she'd just worked too hard to give up her rank here, to start over somewhere else. Maybe she'd convinced herself she could not make it outside Merimac, or ever escape her roots.

Finally he asked what he hadn't earlier. "You grew up near here?"

"We're here," she said, averting the question.

She pulled into a no-parking zone and stopped the engine. "Come on, I'll introduce you to our evidence."

Her tone was set in the concrete of a dare. He merely frowned and climbed out. At the door someone was there to meet them, a gofer for Dr. Cruise. The young resident droned on endlessly as he directed Stroud, Chief Laughing More dropping by the wayside to catch up with a nurse friend who offered her a cup of coffee and some gossip.

—4—

The lacerations—approximately twenty-four hours old now—were still filthy—vile, in fact. Stroud had to concentrate on the ghastly wounds so intensely as to not think of the remains lying before him as ever having been human. The ugly, puckering holes left where Perotto's shoulder socket dangled amid a myriad of jagged edges and matted blood were not the work of anything—*anything*— Stroud had ever seen. And for a second or two, he felt almost relieved. His first fear had been that here in Michigan, as in Illinois, he might have to face another vampire outbreak. And yet, vampires he understood; vampires had some reasoning and logic behind the killing. This creature they called Kerac was not like that. His murderous impulses were not motivated by the desire to feed, or even the desire to live. His killing instinct rose from the need to kill. Perotto's body alone told Stroud this in no uncertain terms.

"Here's the leg the two guards located just inside the gate," said Dr. Cruise, carrying the limb in a cushion of white linen. "As you can see, there are several unusual marks on the flesh aside from the rent itself. These, in my estimation, are tears where the guy did what he did to the others—took out several bites."

Stroud swallowed hard, feeling his morning's breakfast welling up. He held on, taking a moment to look directly at the fetid white flesh of the thigh. He examined this parcel of flesh in silence until

Cruise said, "Left arm was not found until much later by the dogs . . . in a clearing about six miles from the prison. Picked almost clean."

"You ever see anything like this in your experience, Dr. Cruise?"

"Never. What this man did . . . it defies the senses."

"How did he do it?"

"Best guess?"

"Best guess."

Cruise paced, the sign of a man who didn't want to answer directly. He picked about the cold, clinical room, avoiding Stroud's eyes. "I don't pretend to know what kind of weapon the man used or how he got hold of it, Dr. Stroud. All I'm certain of is that he cut these men up and gorged himself with their flesh. He's a madman, a maniac."

"The Merimac Maniac," said Chief Laughing More, who stepped through the door. "That's what the press is calling Johnny Kerac now. I've got to get into the field, Doctors; seems my men have located more of Johnny's work, a farmhouse down at Green Lake."

"Damn," said Stroud while Cruise dropped his head.

"When're you people going to apprehend this fiend, More?" asked Cruise.

"We're doing our . . ." Stroud saw that she wanted to swear, but she swallowed the foul words. "Don't worry too much, Dr. Cruise. If he's true to form, he's trying to get as far from here as possible, maybe to the lake."

"Lake Michigan?" asked Stroud.

"He has family in Chicago. My guess is he'll try to get there. I've already alerted the police all along his route. Contrary to public opinion"—she stopped to glare at Cruise—"we're doing our jobs. We didn't lose Kerac. It took the idiots at the pen to do that. Now, are you coming out to examine the crime scene, or are you too busy, Dr. Cruise?"

"Damned straight I'm too busy. What the hell would a crime scene investigation of this cannibal tell us, More? We know all we need to know about this creep!"

"Not exactly," said Stroud, interrupting. "We don't know the murder weapon. We don't know how he concealed it. We don't know if he worked alone, and from your reports, Dr. Cruise, we don't even know the depth of the wounds inflicted on Perotto and Holms, or for that matter if they match the wounds up in

Grand Rapids. Didn't it occur to you to send for a copy of those reports?"

Cruise was momentarily stunned, surprised by Stroud's sudden attack. Then he said, "Do you know how goddamned shorthanded we are around here? How much is on my shoulders? I practically run this place. Hell, they don't pay me enough to take abuse from an Indian girl playing police chief, and . . . and . . . what'd you say you were? Some sort of rich playboy archeologist? What goddamned right've you to come in here and tell me how to do my business?"

"Negligence, stupidity and a drug habit in a medical man, Dr. Cruise, is everyone's business, and whether I'm a possible donor to your hospital or not, ought not to enter into the picture."

"Drug habit?" he shouted.

"And negligence and stupidity."

"You have a fucking nerve, Laughing More, telling this man stories."

Stroud stepped in front of him as he approached her. She'd instinctively placed her left hand on her weapon, prepared to draw it.

"You come in from New York to a nothing place, after graduating Princeton Med?" said Stroud, who'd seen his degree on the wall in his office. "Makes a former cop suspicious, Doctor. Also makes me suspicious about the dope connection on the reservation."

"Now, look here!"

"No, you look here," said Chief More, stepping around Stroud. "One of these days, *Doctor,* you're going to find yourself needing medical assistance."

"I want you two out of here now! And as for you, More, the city councilmen and the tribal elders'll hear about this."

She turned and glowered at him with those black eyes. "In the meantime, Dr. Cruise, I want Perotto's and Holms' bodies held here. Do you understand, *Doctor*?"

"What the hell for? The families are already in enough agony over this. The sooner we can release what's left for burial, the better."

"You've got my request, Doctor, and in matters of murder, you take orders from me." She'd taken the gloves off.

Stroud left with Chief More, and they pounded down the hallway. "That man makes my skin crawl. If *I* ever murder someone . . ."

"Easy," said Stroud. "Look, can I go out to the crime scene with you?"

She stopped and looked at him queerly. "Are you one of these guys who get his rocks off looking at gore or something? Hey, I like what you said in there, and how you read Cruise—tells me a lot about you, Stroud—but every time I think I've gotten you figured out, you say something like this. I thought you wanted to visit the pen, talk to the guards and the duty people."

"The pen isn't going anywhere. I just think that maybe, just maybe, I could be of help out there."

She frowned, unsure. "You miss being a cop or something?"

"Something like that, yeah."

She considered his request a moment longer. "You stay back, out of the way . . . don't touch anything . . . I guess, if you're a glutton for this stuff . . ."

"Thanks, you won't regret it."

"Promise?"

"Promise, yes."

John . . . John was his name . . . Johnny to his friends. Johnny Indian to the whites around the reserve who sent him business. John Kerac, he kept telling himself over and over as he sped down Interstate 90, trying to keep calm, trying to keep hold of his mind and personality, to identify himself to himself. At the same time, his hands—or someone else's hands—shook on the wheel, and he stared at the strands of thick, coiled, brown to black furlike hair covering much of his knuckles and the back portion—hair that'd not been there before. Or had it? He could not even recall having grown up, much less how much hair covered his legs, his body, his arms and hands. Was he a hairy man?

His head hair was long and sleek and black, an Indian's mane. It went with his past, his notions of self, his image of Johnny Indian. The tufts of hair in the crooks of his arms and behind the knees, the long strands on his forearms and thighs . . . this wasn't Indian. And his face in the rearview mirror of the battered old farm pickup wasn't right. The eyes were swimming in a pool of liquid like those of an animal staring at nothing; the nose was flared and flattened like that of a Flathead Indian maybe. He was Ojibway. He fought to hold on to that fact by concentrating on the sound of the word, repeating it to the strange, whiskered face in the mirror. John Kerac had never had a facial hair in his life before; couldn't grow a goddamned beard if he'd wanted to, but now he was itching with the checkered, uneven patches that were only partially formed there. His face looked like a scruffy, old white man who'd been injured by one of their barbers' clippers. The result was a patchy growth of matted hair, filled with debris and blood.

Kerac's tongue, of its own accord, snaked out past his teeth, and then it coiled up and back, licking at the filth in the hair beneath the nose and about the chin. As it did so, he felt the sharpness of his teeth cause a laceration in the tongue. Nothing about his mouth or jaw seemed right. His jaw protruded too far out. All over his body he felt an additional weight in the muscles of his legs and arms, back and shoulders. He'd had to take some of the old farmer's clothes, because the prison garb was a dead giveaway, but it also didn't fit.

Who was he?

What had they done to him in that asylum? Had they stuck him with needles? Experimented on him with weird drugs? Who was responsible for this man that stared back at him in the mirror? Where had this person come from? Where had the hair come from? The tongue that seemed to breathe for him like a dog's tongue? Where was Johnny Indian, the guide who worked out of Grand Rapids? Maybe *he* wasn't John Kerac. Maybe John Kerac was some madman he'd met in the prison where they had kept him, and he, too, was just mad enough to have come full circle and had taken on the belief that he was this other man. For the sake of God—the Indian god or the white god, or both—he prayed he would find out soon, that his senses would return to him.

His trembling hands increased their agitation on the wheel when he thought about what had happened at the farmhouse. He could only recall bits and pieces, broken images that were so horrifying that they were instantly short-circuited as his conscious mind tried to focus on each. An elderly woman . . . leathery-faced . . . screaming . . . instantly silenced, blood everywhere. Old man, near unable to get up, so sick in bed. Something leapt onto him and ripped out his throat with its teeth, its long snout pushing into the wound, tearing . . . lapping at the blood there. Feeding . . . a creature feeding on the flesh of the old people. He could stand no more of it, shutting it out.

He wondered how he had come by the battered old pickup. He must've stolen it, but he could not remember locating the key. He had a very bad memory. Johnny Kerac had had a good memory, he thought . . . but he really couldn't remember for sure. In fact, he was having a hard time remembering Kerac.

Maybe he was a madman.

The images of fields, fences and animals grazing on hillsides rushed by on either side of the interstate as he somehow remembered how to drive. Perhaps there were some things that he must forget and others he must recall in order to survive, or just to steady his quaking hands and shaken mind; some things a man must deny even to himself, he told himself. He saw the first sign for Chicago, 113 miles to his destination, although he wasn't sure why.

The farmhouse they drove toward gave off an aura of terror long before Abraham Stroud and Chief More got to the front door. It was absolutely isolated, a perfect Edgar Allan Poe setting for death's visit, Stroud thought. The wind in the trees even now, by day, whistled a warning here as it dipped and scurried through the tall, wild grass all around. The house was delapidated, weathered gray and lifeless, looking like a large, wounded elephant; its porch was falling in, held upright at the steps by a makeshift support of masonry bricks turned green with mold. Even Chief More knew that the scene inside was going to be hell. She felt it from the start, as did Stroud, from the moment they entered the dirt driveway that meandered up to the house where two uniformed police officers awaited them, the two men smoking, one sitting in a straight-backed rocking chair on the porch.

"I know this house," More had said the moment they took the turn off Highway 11 and onto county road 1748. "I know the old people."

"Indian?"

"Yes. The old man's name is Kinewskoo-wee in his native tongue. His white name is Maclin. Maclin was once an elder, but he got tired of the politics at the longhouse—retired. You can see from his house that he was an honest man. Some say he was aware that others in the tribe were stealing from the people, and that he was threatened, along with his wife, if he did not step down and forget about what he saw at the longhouse. I've investigated some of the rumors and talk, but I've gotten no proof. They have their own ways, you know. They've got their own bookkeeping, and it never sees an audit. Bingo money, business donations to the tribe . . . all of it unaccounted for. This old man tried to take them on once alone. That was before I became sheriff."

The admiration she had for Maclin was evident in her tone. "I talked with him about the situation a couple of times."

"You sure you're up to this?" Stroud asked.

"It's my job."

She got out of the car and introduced her two deputies to Stroud. Both men were Caucasian and there seemed some hard edge on the three-way relationship.

"Tom Shanks," said one of the men, offering his hand to Dr. Stroud.

"Nice to meet you, Tom."

"Miller," said the other man, who didn't offer his hand. "Gavin Miller." He went instantly to business. "Got a call from the old sister, ahhhh—"

"Miss Maclin, Rae Maclin," said Chief More.

"Yeah. Said her kin weren't answering the phone, got worried and called us, asked us to check it out—like we haven't got anything better to do with a cannibal on the loose."

"We were in the area, anyway," said Shanks, cutting in, "on the lookout for that crazy Johnny Kerac. Farmhouse . . . Well, it was smack in the middle of the manhunt, so we came over . . . and found . . . Chief, it's an awful sight inside."

"Real messy," agreed Miller, "and we did just like you said, Chief."

"We didn't touch a thing."

Miller added, "We didn't want to."

"Dr. Stroud going to help us?" asked Shanks. "Tell you, we need all the help we can get with this nut case."

More didn't hesitate at the door, pushing it open on its rusty hinges, the noise like a radio broadcast of a creep show. Inside the dark interior, she found a light switch and turned it on, causing her to instantly gasp at the sight of Mrs. Maclin, whose body had great chunks stripped from it where John Kerac had fed his inhuman lust. She almost vomited, drawing back. Stroud took hold of her, but she pulled away, seeing Miller looking in on the scene.

"Told you it was bad, Chief."

She couldn't find words, fighting back bile.

"The old guy is in the bedroom."

It was a small house, not much more than a shack. Stroud, too, fought for control, but he could see what lay on the bed in the other room, and the stench of blood and animal leavings threatened to overwhelm him as well. The old man's body, half on, half off the bed, was also brutalized, but the neck wound struck Stroud with a vengeance, the sight not only awful in itself, the head nearly severed by the wound, as was one of the man's

mangled arms, but sending a horrid memory along the pathways
of Stroud's mind, a memory he had successfully hidden from
himself since Vietnam.

Miller said, "Sonofabitch went for the old man's throat like
some kinda goddamned animal."

It mirrored Stroud's own thoughts. *Wild animals go for the
throat.*

The woman had died of injuries to her face, torso and limbs.

"You want to get some air?" Stroud asked Chief More.

"Place smells so bad," she agreed, but she didn't take a step
toward the outside.

Miller said, "That's shit."

"What?"

"Kerac . . . he shit all over the place while he was here."

"Why don't we get a man in here who can take this place apart
and learn something from it?" said Stroud. "I know a forensics
man who—"

"We can call in the guy from Grand Rapids," said Shanks, who
hung near the door, not wanting to enter again.

"Look, Dr. Louis Cage is a topflight professional in this area,
and frankly, you people can't screw around with this anymore.
You've got to get help, and—"

"We only have what we have," she said.

"I'll pay for Cage's trouble. I'll fly him up here. He's the
best."

"Why'd he give a damn? To come to a place like this?"

"For me . . . he'll do it for me."

Miller and Shanks knew to keep out of this. "I'll call for an
ambulance," Miller said as he attempted to disappear.

"No," said Abe Stroud. "Hold on that. Cage will want to see
everything as it is."

"We can't hold these bodies until your friend shows up," she
disagreed loudly. "These people have close ties here, relatives
who will want to see them properly . . . properly taken care of."

"Chief More," he pleaded, "I can get Cage up here in a few
hours. I can make arrangements."

She looked from him to Miller and back again, taking a handkerchief from her pocket to cover her nose. "You really think this
man Cage is that good? That he can help here?"

"You'd be getting the best pathologist in the business—no
hospital hacks. Do you really want Cruise to come in here on
his own sweet time and put together a useless, half-assed report?

All I ask is that you keep the crime scene intact, and Cage'll be here by nightfall."

She dropped her gaze, her mind still on the people lying about in various stages of disgraceful debauchery. There was the sister and other "brethren" to consider. It was obvious she cared about this family. She considered his offer, stepping out to the porch, taking in that much-needed clean air. Stroud looked once more at the bloodstained sheets and discolored gray walls where the red stuff had fired from severed veins. He, too, needed air, and he followed her out. Shanks was once more in the rocker; Miller was searching about the grounds, and he called out that he had found some tracks, but they weren't human in appearance.

Tom Shanks got up quickly and joined Miller, staring down at the footprints, proclaiming them those of a bear.

"Where's Kerac's prints?" asked Miller. "I've scoured this whole damned place, and not a single sign of his entering or going, but these come right out of the wood and up to the back porch, where they end."

Stroud studied the prints. "Don't disturb them."

"What?"

"Cage'll take casts of them, and we'll see what we can make of the prints."

"Cruise could do that."

"Cruise could also screw it up," said Chief More, staring at the prints. "Either way . . . those are not Kerac's footprints. There's no shoe impression, for one thing, and look at the size of it."

"What is it, then? A bear or a cougar, maybe?" asked Miller snidely. No one said anything as they stared at the impression. "Now we're going to look to Indian superstitions for answers?" he added, tossing stones down at More's feet and walking off to his squad car where he sat in sullen silence.

She turned to Stroud and said, "All right, bring this Dr. Cage here, and the town, or the tribe . . . someone will pay the bill."

"I'll foot the bill," he replied.

"Why? Why should you do all this?"

"I'm connected to this . . . this slaughter somehow, as I told you, and I'll be damned if I'll take a backseat to it, at least not until I'm satisfied that I've done all in my power to end it."

Tom Shanks' eyes went wide at the first time he had ever heard Chief More compliment a white man, "You might have made a good Indian, Stroud."

"My grandmother was a quarter-blood Cherokee."

"Uh-huh . . ."

"But why do you say so?" he asked.

"You're stubborn."

"Stubborn, really?"

"Bone-headed, like an Indian."

If you only knew the half, he thought, but he cared not to tell her about the metal in his head.

—5—

It was no easy matter to convince a distraught Dr. Louis Cage to abandon his hard-won vacation at the Cahokia digs in southern Illinois to come to Michigan on Abe Stroud's urgent request. The medical examiner didn't often find time to be away from Chicago, and when he did, he meant to relax, and like Abe, nothing relaxed him more than roughing it on an archeological dig.

But Abe was firm over the phone, and he was so certain of Lou that he had already sent his private plane out of Andover, Illinois, for him.

"I know it's a lot to ask, Lou."

"Christ, you have a gift for understatement. You do this to me, Abe, and I swear, you'll owe me for . . . for . . . well, for*ever*!"

"I wouldn't ask, Lou, if it wasn't important. Things here are not right, and I need a man of your talents to bridge the gap between what we know and what we don't know. Only you can provide that for—"

"Only me, only me. Don't they have an M.E. in Grand Rapids?"

"Nowhere near your caliber, Lou."

Lou sighed into the phone in resignation. "This better be worth the ride, pal."

"You ever see a man's arm ripped off, Lou?"

"Sure, in industrial accident victims, and in the war—"

"But as the work of a mad killer?"

"Cut off limbs, sure. Too goddammed often."

35

"I'm talking ripped off, Lou. Real nasty. Using no saws, only maniacal strength."

Cage considered this in silence before saying, "Jesus, you sure of that?"

"I'll only be sure when you look over the bodies."

"Bodies?"

"Enough to keep you busy, yeah."

Lou cleared his throat and then said, "Sounds like you're in over your head, pal."

"I think I know that. So, you begin to see the need, Lou? I need the best, and I'm willing to pay your going rate for the assistance."

"Damned straight you will," he muttered.

Still, Cage did see the need, particularly when Stroud described the condition of the bodies he had seen, and followed this up with the fact that the police in Michigan believed the killer was on his way to Lou's city.

Lou was on his way.

In the meantime, a police barricade had been placed around the old farmhouse, and with nothing left to do there, Stroud had gone with Chief More to learn what he could from the authorities at the Merimac asylum and prison. Stroud was disappointed, however, learning very little at the prison. Memories had faded, or had been softened by time to ease the horror. Perroto's office had been cleaned. It still smelled of disinfectant and fresh paint.

But something in the room was eerie . . . as if Stroud could sense the odor of the animal that had killed Perroto, also covered by the paint. He asked the director who showed him around if there had been any unusual animal odors left in the killer's wake. The director looked as if he had aged a year at the question. "Yes, a strange, alive, animal odor like musk . . . like an animal."

Stroud talked then to the guards who had reclaimed Dr. Perroto's leg in the yard. They told their story without inflection or much embellishment and very little imagination. They'd decided what they saw was either a mad dog or a wolf that had somehow gotten into the compound. They did not see John Kerac that night.

Later, Stroud took a room at the only hotel in Merimac, a god-awful place called the Nomad, where the carpets crawled, and the window shades had never been cleaned, and the curtains cast out spores from the deep, green pile and caused him to sneeze. Still, it offered a bath and running water, giving Stroud a chance to clean up and shave. From the hotel, where Chief More had left him, he arranged for a rental car, and at dusk he drove out to greet Lou Cage at the small municipal airport.

They exchanged a handshake as Cage asked, "Why me, Abe? Couldn't you make do with the local guys?"

"When you meet them, Lou, you'll see why."

"That bad, huh?"

"That bad."

"Well . . . I brought everything I could think of, under the circumstances . . . from what you said over the phone."

Lou was like a plumber, carrying with him several suitcases filled with the tools of his trade. Stroud asked his pilot to carry these bags off the tarmac, and they were deposited in the waiting car, a large white Lincoln.

"You can fly back anytime that's convenient, Warren," he told the pilot. "We've got the helicopter."

Sooner the better, Warren was thinking as he looked over the area that displayed so little, a one-room airport terminal, a stand of naked jack pine that went off in all directions as if forever. But he calmly replied, "After some coffee and a sandwich, sir, I'll take her back to Andover. Oh, and good to see you."

"Real conversationalist, that one," said Cage, who'd had enough of Warren.

"Hell of a pilot, though. Come on, we'll get you organized, have dinner, and then out to the farmhouse."

"From what you tell me, I think I'll hold on dinner, pal."

"Fine . . . Sooner we get in and out, the better."

"Locals already want your scalp, huh?"

"You might say so."

"Quite a place you picked to vacation in, Abe . . . quite a place."

"Thanks again for coming, Lou," he said when they reached the car.

Lou shrugged. "What was I going to do?"

They got Lou settled as well as possible in the not so accommodating accommodations and then sped out for the crime scene. Along the way, Stroud filled Cage in on all the details, including those that seemed bizarre, from the nature of the wounds ("I've never seen anything like it since Nam, where guys were blown apart") to the strange tracks found by Miller ("We'll want to make casts of these prints, Lou").

Lou listened politely but held himself in check. He was a born Missourian who'd been replanted in Chicago at an early age, and this made for a no-nonsense, cynical "show me" kind of man. It wasn't that he doubted Stroud, but he knew that people often saw more in a mutilation murder than was there; that it took a trained M.E. such as himself to determine the exact nature of the mutilation.

Lou had seen headless, handless corpses—torsos—fished from lakes and rivers; he had seen what a real chain saw could do to real flesh. Lou had sixteen years with the CPD crime lab. He'd hold his judgment until he saw the corpses.

Stroud soon realized what was going through his friend's mind at the moment. A kind of silent truce was struck between them, and Lou closed his eyes to the unimpressive scenery of a nasty winter that'd turned the area to hard mud and devastated vegetation. He wished that he'd brought a warmer coat.

Cage was stunned, standing there on the steps above the rickety masonry blocks that held it. It was the third time he had had to come back out of the weathered old place to catch his breath and reel in his spinning mind. He had seen brutality before, but this was beyond anything he had ever witnessed, and he didn't mind saying so for the benefit of the others, Stroud, Shanks and Miller.

"I tried to prepare you for it," said Stroud.

"Abe," he replied, sitting down on the stoop, his apron dirty from his work inside, "nothing you could have said would've prepared me for this."

"Then you agree? There's something unexplainable at work here. The weapon he used?"

"Nothing yet . . . Nothing I can point to, but Abe—" He was staring directly into Stroud's eyes when the flash of headlights from the car turning in hit him, and Abe saw something in Cage's eyes he had never seen before: fear.

"It's the Chief," said Miller, and the emphasis he placed on the word *chief* was such that it was insulting.

"More?" asked Lou.

"I want you to meet her, Lou," said Stroud.

Lou stood as the policewoman approached.

"Anything on Kerac?"

"What's happening in the rest of the state?" her deputies wanted to know.

"Nothing . . . no sightings . . . APB out on the truck hasn't helped." She then turned her gaze to Stroud and Lou Cage. "Dr. Cage, I presume."

"That's me, all right."

"So, Doctor, can you help us with . . . with what's inside?"

Lou nodded several times and pulled out a small flask of whiskey, taking a long drink, before saying, "I can tell you this much: you've got one hell of a maniac on the loose."

"Tell me something I don't already know."

The whiskey seemed to be a bad idea, a last straw for Lou's empty stomach, his mind filled with the sight of the flesh heaps left inside by Kerac. He rushed to the side rail suddenly and vomited over it. This made the deputies and Chief More stare, and Stroud knew that they'd all become skeptical of Lou's ability in this moment of weakness.

"Dr. Cruise wouldn't've done that," said Miller to Shanks.

"Stroud," said Lou, "crank up that generator you got out here. I'm going to need floodlights in there."

Cage went to work, displaying his meticulousness, an attention to detail which fascinated Stroud. Chief More relieved Miller and Shanks. She'd lit a cigarette and was pacing the boards outside.

Inside, under the harsh lights, the wounds of the victims came into sharp, disturbing focus, but Cage remained silent and uncommunicative as he worked, so much so that Stroud had quit asking him questions or interrupting. He merely stood by, handing tools and items from Cage's bag to him, should the M.E. request it. In his gloved hands he'd passed small plastic bags, slides, fixatives, sprays, tweezers and a huge magnifying glass. Cage studied the minute details of the flesh and the rents with his keen eye and deft hands.

Occasionally, Cage broke his silence with a hum or a cough. He'd covered his face with a white surgical mask and had offered one to Stroud, which Abe had taken without hesitation. It helped cut the stench. Cage took sample after sample, and he took photographs from every angle. He followed this with measurements in millimeters of the depth and width of gashes and wounds, trying his best to determine the size of the carving knife Kerac had used on these people.

"What kind of meat grinder's tool could do this, Lou?" Stroud had asked at one point, but he'd gotten no answer.

Stroud realized it had to be something Kerac could easily carry and as easily conceal. No high-powered tool or electrical saw could've been used on the men at the prison.

Finally, Cage was finished. It was three in the morning. He got up from his kneeling position over the woman's body, his knees wobbly from the effort. Stroud asked, "Are you all right, Lou?"

"Are any of us?" he replied, leaving the carrion to the room and to those who must come in and carry it out.

Outside, Chief More wanted immediate answers, but Lou put her off with an upraised hand and a statement. "I need a lab where I can work."

"Grand Rapids," said Stroud as he, too, left the dead behind him. "They've got the autopsy reports on Kerac's first victims, anyway, and we can buzz up there in the chopper after you've had some sleep."

"That suit you, Chief More?"

She frowned but said, "They're more likely to welcome you into their labs than our Dr. Cruise."

"Settled, then. If you'd give them a call, pave our way . . ."

"I will be happy to. I could see from your labor that you . . . that you are competent and—"

"Well, thank you."

"—and, Dr. Cage, that you care about those people's lives."

"Yes, well . . . of course, I do." Cage then looked at Stroud, his voice breaking when he said, "Do you really have any evidence this madman is heading for Chicago, Abe?"

"According to Chief More," said Stroud.

He looked at her, his eyes imploring a moment, as if to ask her to take it back, to tell him the trail was leading elsewhere.

"It's my guess," she said.

Lou started for the car, carrying his black valise, filled now with pieces of the victims, the minutiae of murder. Chief More looked at Stroud for some kind of answer, and seeing he had none, she chased after Cage. "Wait, Doctor, you must have learned something in there you can share with me. Anything at all that might help us?"

"Only this, Chief More," he said hesitantly. "I've seen all kinds of brutality, every imaginable wound made by every conceivable weapon that might inflict such horrendous lacerations, tear an arm from a socket, rip a man's head off, but . . . but—"

"Yes?"

"I can't . . . at this time . . . account for this. Not yet, anyway."

"Maybe the plaster cast will help," suggested Stroud. Earlier, they'd taken a break from the torture of the horror show under the harsh lights inside and had come outside to take the cast. It was now solid as a rock and in the trunk of the Lincoln.

"You're not telling me everything you suspect," she said, angry with Cage. "We invite you in, we expect cooperation, Dr. Cage!"

Cage was staring off into the darkness beyond the house lights. The surrounding world might just as well have been a black void, so intense was the country night.

"Lou, Lou," said Stroud, placing a hand on his shoulder. "You okay, Lou?"

Cage turned to More and said, "I'd only be guessing in the dark, Chief."

"Then guess, damn you!"

"All right . . . if I had to guess, I'd say that the wounds inflicted on these people were done by some superhuman strength—"

"Superhuman strength?"

"Something possessing much more power than you or I."

"Madmen are known to possess great strength," she said, "and we know that Kerac is mad."

"This goes beyond that," he replied. "Don't you see, no man—no one—can tear out another man's arm with his bare hands, and those marks . . . tears, rents . . . like talons or claws and teeth—definite teeth marks, but so much deeper than any human teeth, more like . . . fangs."

Stroud's stomach turned over with the mention of fangs.

"Animal . . . like the footprint," she said thoughtfully.

"Animal, mechanical," said Cage, pulling back on his wild diagnosis. "Who knows . . . but a bear, perhaps a panther could rend flesh and bone this way . . . tear a man's leg from its socket . . . but another man?"

"Are you saying it could not have been the work of a man?"

"That is what I am saying, yes."

"This is what you call *expert*?" she said to Stroud.

Cage confronted her quickly, raising his voice. "I mean that my eyes—not my microscope—are this moment telling me that what happened here was not the work of a human being; that this . . . this thing that fed on these people—literally ate parts of them—is not a man. If he is a man . . . he should be shot like a dog."

"Lou, we have to believe it was Kerac. It lines up with what happened at the prison," said Stroud, "and the manhunt had him in the vicinity, and—"

"Here, goddammit, here!" shouted Cage, offering Stroud his arm and elbow.

"What? What, Lou?"

"Take my arm in one of those commando holds they taught you in the war. Take it, take my arm."

"Lou?"

"Twist it, pull it up!"

Stroud went through with the charade as More looked on.

"Harder, go on!"

"Lou!"

"Think you could twist it off, Abe? Think you could for a moment tear my arm from its socket with your bare hands? Did you see that woman's severed leg? Did you see the old man's throat? No, as strong as you are, Abe, and as helpless as I am now, you couldn't physically separate my arm from my body. No man could, not even Lou Ferrigno. To wrench my arm out like it was a goddamned chicken leg? Answer that, Chief More, Abe. Answer that with your second sight!"

Stroud let Cage go and Lou found some peace in the car, closing his eyes on the horror of the day, laying his head back. He was completely frustrated by events and questions. Cage, like Stroud, couldn't abide a question without an answer. Stroud knew it would drive Lou to distraction, and that like Stroud now, Lou wouldn't sleep well until he got a usable answer.

"I'm calling in the paramedics now," Chief More said, turning from Stroud and going for her squad car. "Sounds to me like this has all been a waste of time."

Stroud's hands went up in a gesture of one part exasperation, one part confusion and one part anger. "Don't sell us short yet . . . not until we've gotten the lab work done."

"Yeah, sure," she replied, and kept walking.

Stroud didn't want to leave her alone here with the macabre house and the black night, but she made him so angry, and he was tired, and Lou deserved a shower and a bed, even if he didn't get More's thanks. Stroud got into the Lincoln and backed from the drive, stopping beside her at the squad car where she was in the midst of the call to town.

"Would you like us to wait here with you until they come?"

"Sure, and you can hold my hand, too. Get the hell out of here," she shouted.

Stroud didn't bother buckling his seat belt or rolling the window back up. The Lincoln fired up rocks from the gravel drive, pinging at the oil pan and the muffler and the underside, each pellet's sound coming together in a stinging chorus for the Chief.

"Be damned glad you only had to spend the evening with her," Stroud said.

This made Lou's eyes open and his head turn. "Oh, I didn't think she was so bad; certainly not so flinty as McMasters in Chicago. What, you letting her get under your skin?"

Stroud recalled the bear of the Chicago Police Department that he'd worked under, Captain Phil McMasters. It gave him a moment's laugh. Lou tried to laugh as well, but it sounded hollow and forced.

"Not on your life is this Indian cop getting under my skin, Lou."

"Sure, and I can see that, too."

Stroud turned onto the highway, the dim light of the ghostly old farmhouse framed in his rearview mirror. He thought of her for a moment, there alone; he wondered if they shouldn't go back, but in the distance ahead he heard the racing sirens. "Tell you what, Lou. I'll just be glad to be rid of the Nomad Hotel, Merimac and the Chief tomorrow when we fly out of here."

"You can't blame the woman for being skeptical, Abe. Hell, what I said about a creature breaking in there and eating those people alive . . . hell, I don't believe it myself . . . don't believe my own findings."

Never in all the time that he had known Lou Cage had Stroud ever seen the other man so confounded. Stroud's words seemed feeble even as they left his lips, and he was a little sorry for having spoken them. "You need some rest, maybe, huh? Lou?"

Cage said nothing, the look of confusion still there.

Stroud tried to soften his words, hoping that his friend would not take them wrong. "Lou, soon as you have a lab to work in . . . get that old magic working . . ."

"I'm no alchemist, Abe. I took scrapings on the feces left behind. I made all the usual tests—hair samples, fiber, nails, you know—but I'll be honest with you, Abe . . ."

"Yes?"

"I've never seen a crime scene like this. Something, I don't know . . . is wrong. I know that sounds like a sick joke, an understatement to anyone hearing it—something wrong here!—but, I tell you, it's downright . . ."

He let it go. Then Abe said, "I know it's a weird case, Lou."

"Can't put my finger on that odor, rank like . . . I don't know."

"Hey, when you get to that lab in Grand Rapids—"

"Don't count on the doctors in Grand Rapids to be any more excited about having us than those you found here, Abe."

"They'll cooperate. They'll have to once they know who you are."

He frowned at this, his round face pinching inward. He took down his glasses and rubbed his eyes with both hands, the spectacles dangling from his big fingers like an oversized praying mantis. Cage was clearly beat.

"And don't," Cage continued, "count on my findings confirming anything you've presupposed about this killer of yours, Abe. Jesus," he moaned. "Just got my ulcer under control, and now this."

Stroud sensed it was time to leave Lou to himself and ask no more of him tonight. The ride through the black countryside back to the sad little hotel finished in silence and frustration. Abe Stroud felt a great weight over him, pressing downward, and he realized it was the weight of not knowing.

Chief Anna Laughing More had stared after the big car with the two strange men inside, wondering once more if she had done the right thing. The *Enquirer* could do a lot with this Dr. Abraham Stroud and his traveling troupe of weirdos who came in Lear jets and helicopters in a mad rush to look over the goriest crime she had ever been associated with.

What's worse, she thought, was the pronouncement of the coroner from Chicago, Cage. Did he honestly think that she or anyone was willing to believe that Johnny Kerac had come into this old house and had torn these people limb from limb without the use of some kind of butcher knife or saw?

She had seen the same results at the prison. Somehow Kerac had gotten hold of some sort of battery-power tool that did the damage. There was no other answer. No one could pull a man apart, Cage had said, but in the saying of it, he had opened the door, left it ajar to the wondering mind.

"It sounds crazy," she said aloud to the surrounding night. At the same time, with the wind causing naked branches to scratch one another over her left shoulder, Anna Laughing More caressed the gun on her hip. The solidness of her .38 police special made her feel a little more secure.

She wondered how Stroud could just leave her here alone. The bastard.

—6—

Kerac had seen one too many state patrol cars along his route to remain long on the interstate. He had been on a county road for several hours now, going without sleep, when he saw unsteady lights in the distance. As he approached, the lights became flashers, strobing atop squad cars, and he realized it was a roadblock. Unsure of what to do at first, he continued toward the lights. There were several cars being held up ahead of him. They'd be looking for the pickup. They'd catch him and return him to Merimac, lock him up again.

He wondered if he should turn around, go back. But if he did so, he would have to go thirty miles out of his way and in the wrong direction, and there was no guarantee a roadblock hadn't been arranged elsewhere, and they must have a description of the missing truck.

But it was dark, and if he was cunning . . .

Kerac cruised easily toward the line of cars ahead of him, but the moment he got to within striking distance of the vehicle just ahead, he wheeled out into the opposite lane and put the gas to the old Ford, going directly for the too-small opening in the road. He saw uniformed men racing to get out of his path. He saw their eyes in his headlights, and he saw a flash of fire erupt when the truck tore into the front end of a squad car.

The truck threatened to run off the road as Kerac struggled for control. Behind him gunshots rang out and the rearview mirror was shattered by a bullet that continued through the windshield. He then heard the sirens blaring in pursuit. Perhaps two cars.

Kerac saw the steam rising over the hood where the punctured radiator spewed forth its hot liquid into the air. He felt the power of the truck draining away as he pumped and pumped with his bare foot, but it was useless. A tire blew, the result of a bullet from behind, and the truck careened off the road and into a thicket, where it came to a jolting stop, sending John Kerac's head into the dash, causing a nasty wound.

Semiconscious, he heard the approaching cars, men jumping from them and clamoring down from the roadbed; he heard each stone as it skittered toward him ahead of the men with the guns who wanted to kill him, or worse, take him back. He found a reserve of strength he didn't know he had, along with an incredible sense of hearing and smell. The smell of his own fear, perspiration and blood lifted him from the cabin. The instant the door swung open, bullets rained into it, and he leapt out the other side, landing on all fours, dirt and debris pinging and exploding in his eyes as the gunshots continued.

He disappeared into the underbrush.

They were still coming.

Which way? What should I do? he wondered, no longer conscious of any conflict within him. No identity crisis now. Only one thing was important: survival.

He must either be killed or kill those who came for him.

He heard their voices, saw the moving lights, blinding in their intensity, freezing him in place. He saw it all in black and white, their forms complete and detailed in the surrounding darkness. Then he ran.

More gunshots, one ripping into his ankle, causing him to trip and roll down an embankment toward the sound of rushing water. He got up, fell with pain, rose and forced the weight on the ankle, making him howl. Gunshots responded. He stifled another howl that went guttural and choked in his throat. The searing pain in his ankle was worse by far than the self-inflicted wound to his privates.

He found himself standing in water—icy cold and paralyzing. But it stopped the pain in his ankle long enough for him to think. He had to use what he had; he knew where they were, each one of them. He could smell them. He could see them clearly in the night, and this amazed him. He could feel the displacement of air around these men. It was a kind of power he had never consciously known before.

He knew what he must do.

Kerac went across the water, leading them further into the woods. One of them would still be on the road. He didn't know how he knew this, but he did. He must get back to the road first, and there kill this sentry.

Kerac circled, moving on all fours, crouching, silent and at peace with the pain in his ankle. He then smelled one of them nearby, very close.

He leapt upward, caught a branch and silently pulled himself up. He lay there like a serpent, waiting. His patience was soon rewarded when one of them stepped beside the tree.

Kerac fell on him, using his own weight to crush the man senseless, flipping him over and tearing at him with his claws and teeth. It was natural and calm, a thing he had done before and would do again and again. He no longer questioned the hairy hands, the enormous claws or sharp teeth. This was him. He was not mad or a freak anymore. He held no such thoughts. He was a thing of beauty, a thing of nature, and the blood that matted his chest hair was what he lived for.

But he hadn't time to feast. The man he left bleeding to death was paralyzed with shock. He must get to the other on the road. He sensed that this one posed the greatest threat. The others were still beating about the woods. Kerac's attack had been swift and silent.

He made his way deftly back up to the road, but he came out some hundred yards from the strobing lights, skittered across the highway and came around from behind. He watched the movement of the large man who had remained with the two vehicles. The man went to the interior, got in and came out again. Kerac lifted from his crouching position and started across, the man's back to him. Just as he did so, two bright lights hit Kerac, and a car came right at him, tires screeching; in that same instant, the policeman wheeled, turned and was about to fire. But the driver of the car veered off Kerac and toward the police car. The car went straight into the lights of the police car, crushing the man who was standing before the grille.

Kerac, sensing more danger now than ever, silently disappeared into the woods on this side of the road. As he ran for deeper cover, his body felt powerful and strong and invincible. Behind him, he heard the sounds of human concerns at the site of the wreck.

He was on foot again, but he smelled water nearby and he'd kept Lake Michigan in sight most of the trip along the road he had taken. He knew there was another way to reach his destination.

Stroud was awakened by the telephone's insistent ring. It was a blessing, even at four in the morning, because it shook him loose from the nightmare of a re-creation of events at the farmhouse where the Maclins had died so violently. When he grabbed for the phone, it was like grabbing for a lifeline.

"Yes?"

"Chief More," she said. "Thought you'd like to know that Kerac has struck again."

"When? Where?"

"Broke a roadblock near the Indiana border."

"Any deaths?" He knew the answer.

"Two officers dead. Details are sketchy, but I'm going, and from there I'm going to Chicago," she said emphatically.

Her voice had taken on the timbre of a driven woman, Stroud thought. He worried for More. He'd seen enough carnage attributed to this Kerac fellow to fear for her life as well as the lives of anyone that might come into contact with him. Yet it was her job to come into contact with him, and to make every effort to either apprehend him or kill him if need be.

"Why don't we travel together?" he suggested.

"You're going to Grand Rapids."

"I can leave Cage there, and you and I can go on to Chicago . . . together."

There was a silence at the other end.

"Come on," he urged her. "Why not? I've got the bird, and you've got the juice. When we get to Chicago, I may need a favor of you."

"Do you really think you can buy my favors, Dr. Stroud?"

"I didn't mean it that way."

"And how did you mean it?"

Stroud took a deep breath and chose his words more carefully. "It would be convenient for both of us—advantageous."

"I suppose you're right. I'll meet you at the airport."

She almost hung up. "Wait," he stopped her. "Cage, he's really fagged out next door."

"I can't wait for you, then."

"Hold on. Meet you at the airport in one hour."

"Done."

She hung up, and even in the dial tone, Stroud sensed her coolness toward him.

Stroud's chopper pilot had gone on a drinking binge for which he was fired. Stroud would pilot the chopper himself.

Cage slept in the car to the airport and later in the backseat of the helicopter. Chief More had made all necessary arrangements with the town and its mayor to make the trip in pursuit of Kerac. By eight in the morning, Dr. Louis Cage and his findings from the farmhouse outside Merimac were in a laboratory in Grand Rapids. There, Lou would also match up anything he could to the earlier killings attributed to Kerac. From Grand Rapids, Stroud and Chief More flew for Chicago's Meigs Field.

Already in Chicago, at least along the airways of the police band in Stroud's helicopter, mutilation deaths were being attributed to an escaped madman from the Merimac prison facility. But both More and Stroud doubted the reliability of the reports, since Kerac had been in Indiana at dawn. It seemed highly unlikely that a death the night before and one that morning could be the work of the same madman.

"Chicago has its own madmen," Stroud assured her, speaking through the com link between them. Both of them wore headphones so that they could communicate. "I've taken the liberty to book us rooms at the Palmer House."

"Christ, you *do* take liberties, Dr. Stroud."

"Please, call me Abe. I have a feeling we're going to be a while at this, and we might as well be friends as not."

"All right, Abe."

"And may I call you Anna?"

She looked across at him. "Why not, since you're . . . taking liberties."

"If Kerac's on foot, as the Indiana State Patrol says, then he couldn't have gotten to Chicago yet."

"Unless he got another vehicle."

"All roads in were blocked."

"Then he'd go for another way in."

They looked at one another, and Abe said, "Port Authority." Abe instantly made a call to a Chicago police dispatcher he knew. "Hannah! Abe Stroud."

"Abe, you ol' sonofagun, how are you?"

"I've got a favor to ask."

"Shoot."

He explained that he was with Chief More and that they'd come to the conclusion that the asylum escapee and murderer headed toward Chicago, the subject of a three-state manhunt, might have gotten through by using a boat of some sort. "Has Port Authority been alerted, and if so, how long've they been on the case?"

"Checking, Abe . . ."

The chopper careened onward, the smoke of Chicago coming over their horizon. The dispatcher came back on.

"Looks like they were alerted a few hours after us. No sweat, they're on the job and have been."

"Any updates?" he asked. "Any recent killings pan out as our boy's work?"

"Nothing . . . just speculation, Abe. You know how the guys like to place their bets."

"Thanks, Hannah."

"Will we see you at Precinct One while you're in town?"

"I'll make an effort to stop by. Out."

"Looks like traveling with you will have some rewards, after all," said Chief More.

Stroud only smiled, before moving the helicopter toward downtown Chicago and Meigs, calling for airspace and a landing pad.

It was Anna Laughing More who spoke next as they were descending. "You are well known here?"

"Only in police circles."

"Good, then we can make inroads quickly."

"That's my hope."

Her voice took on a curious tone next. "I was told that you solved several crimes through psychic means."

"That's not entirely accurate, but close enough, I suppose," he replied. He didn't care for the label of *psychic*.

"Then the CPD will be pleading for you to help them, I suppose? And the newspapers will want interviews."

"Not likely. Not if I can help it."

"They will if Kerac is not caught or killed soon. What do you take me for, a—"

Stroud's patience snapped. "Chief More, my only concern is that Kerac is stopped before he kills again; that is all!"

"Really? The same motives as mine?"

"I'm not here on a joyride or an ego trip," he went on, ignoring her. "I'd much rather be somewhere else, somewhere far away from all *this,* I assure you."

Stroud concentrated on setting the bird down, cutting the engine. Chicago was blanketed by a low, gray cloud cover and the wind rose up off the mighty lake beside Meigs Field, finagling its wet, icy way across the landing site and past the slowing rotor blades and into the cockpit, causing them to shiver. It awakened Stroud's senses and made his teeth chatter. He said, "Ahhhh, I'd forgotten . . . Chicago in springtime."

All around them stood the monolithic buildings of Chicago's skyline. He got the impression they didn't mean a thing to Anna Laughing More, but the Indian woman from Merimac stared at them in a stony reverie just the same as she might overhanging cliffs. Only the buzz of the typical, busy air traffic made her look away and into Stroud's eyes.

"The millions of windows . . . like a million lives," she said, "or a million victims for Kerac. I don't know how I know, but he's here," she added.

Stroud took a deep breath and agreed. "I know."

A code 10, followed by a code 13—officer down—interrupted the silence that had settled between them. Various responses to the call were now coming over the radio. Police from every sector were converging on an area that Stroud knew, one of the many Chicago ship canals along the Calumet River, slip number 4.

Some cop was saying, "Awful . . . torn to ribbons. Never seen anything like it."

"Come on," said Stroud. "This could be it."

—7—

Stroud had arranged for a car for them at the airport, and they were soon crawling through thick police traffic past a sign for the Chicago Port Authority. While Port Authority cops had their own problems, and their own bureaucracy, the P.A. was closer to Customs than to the CPD. Still, officers of the Authority were considered policemen. They carried .38s, and when one was shot or hurt in some other manner, other cops responded. The place was like a convention, but there was another reason why so many policemen came by. They'd been hearing about the possibility of an escaped lunatic making his way here, and from descriptions over the police band, the extent of the mutilation of the officer down, there was a good bet that the Michigan maniac had come through the back door, taking a water route.

Stroud and Chief More had listened to the reports as they raced here through traffic. Stroud knew his way around the city well, and they'd made the trip in twenty minutes, catching the Dan Ryan and the Chicago Skyway for the Calumet River exit. For Anna More, it was a dazzling feat. The sheer size and congestion of the city unnerved her, but she said nothing.

Stroud found a niche for the car, a beige Ford LTD, unmarked police car on lend-lease from the CPD. He got out and went into the thick of the crowd of sailors and merchant marines standing about, emerging on the other side into a police barricade, where he was greeted by some who knew him.

53

Phil McMasters, Stroud's former police captain, came directly to him. Stroud extended his hand, but McMasters didn't take it. More caught up to Stroud just in time to see the gesture and to feel the intensity in McMaster's eyes when he said, "I thought we'd seen the last of you, Stroud. What're you doing here? Guy with your bucks ought to be lying out on the sand in Aruba."

"Good to see you, too, Phil."

The captain looked squarely at Anna More, a look of admiration in his eyes. "Keeping nice company, at least."

"This is Chief More from Merimac," Stroud said, calmly turning to her and nodding. "She knew Kerac before he went off the deep end."

"Indian blood, I understand," said McMasters, interrupting Stroud. "Looks like you're—how do they say it?—both of the same camp?"

"Brothers of the same campfire," she said without skipping a beat.

"Then I guess you know what we're up against."

"She knows what Kerac looks like; she's brought photos," added Stroud.

"Aren't there any fax machines in Michigan?"

"We're not here to do battle with you, McMasters," said Anna More firmly. "We're here to help put an end to this before anyone else is killed by this man."

"You're a little late."

Stroud pushed past McMasters. They'd never gotten on. Phil McMasters' plans for his own future were heavily laden with Chicago politics, and in political circles you didn't draw attention to yourself, but with Abraham Stroud on his "team" it was inevitable. The brew had really spilled over in the course of the Donovan investigation in which Stroud had all but "conjured" up the killer's image during a trance induced by a seizure, in which Stroud remained completely unconscious. When he had awakened, he not only knew what the killer looked like, but he knew that he went by the nickname of Smitty, wore a navy pea coat, sported a goatee and a single earring and had a missing finger on his left hand. This information led to an arrest. McMasters never forgave him.

"Go ahead, Stroud," said McMasters loudly, drawing everyone's attention, including reporters, "have a look-see, tell us what we should do next. Give us the benefit of your magic."

"And I thought *I* was nasty to you," Chief More said in Abe's ear.

"He's really a fun guy when you get to know him."

"I'm sure."

Others backed away from a Port Authority vehicle, the interior of its windows splattered with an array of blood. Forensics and evidence technicians were at work, and the bodies inside the car had not been moved or disturbed except by sprays and dustings and sample-takings by these men. One of them, a Dr. Ira Howe, recognized Stroud from his days on the force. They exchanged a quiet greeting. Stroud asked More if she could handle this. She said nothing, going to the windshield and peering through the smeared red screen at the decapitated body of one man and the limbless torso of another. She gasped, turned her eyes away and said, "It's him all right. It's Kerac's doing."

Stroud put his head in through the door. The odor of blood and destroyed flesh was as heady as the stifling odor of death in a confined place could be. Body parts lay in all sections of the vehicle, the dash, the floorboards, the seats, the back and front. The rear windshield was smashed, the remnant portions dripping with blood. It was like looking at a child's toys that'd been completely destroyed, the corpses like broken dolls, the car itself like a shattered plaything.

He needed relief from the scene, to get out of here quickly, but his eye was caught by a crystal of light and blood where a jagged edge of glass hung on to a teardrop of blood. Something in the microscopic pieces trapped him. Stroud suddenly slid to his knees, feeling a well of blackness overcome him. He felt someone grab hold of him, trying to help him up, but at the same time he recognized the symptoms of a blackout. They'd been less frequent, and for a time, he thought that he'd been done with them altogether, but the *god* in his head—the steel plate—worked in mysterious ways. His apparent "faint" before the crowd of cops and reporters being held in check was met with a rumble, a stir and some snickering. McMasters looked on, shaking his head as Chief More held Stroud in her arms there on the dirty, wet Port Authority causeway in sight of fishing trawlers, merchant ships and a naval vessel.

"Help me get him to a hospital, please!" shouted Anna More at the men who stood around gawking.

"Give him a few minutes," said McMasters. "He'll come out of it, when he wants. Charlie, Joe! Move him to his goddamned car."

The uniformed officers McMasters called on moved with alacrity, and these men deposited Stroud in the backseat of the LTD. More remained with him, watching the grimaces that came over his disturbed face. He was a handsome man, broad-shouldered, almost too much for the two cops to carry. He had the look of a man who had once been tortured; certainly, he had faced death before. More raked his long strands of dark hair off his forehead, which was wrinkled in thought. Under the eyelids she saw a kinetic pulse beat as if he were watching a film. She did not understand what was happening to him, and why his former captain was taking this so lightly. Stroud ought to be in a hospital. She lifted his hand in hers and began to think of the hours and tiring work he had put in at the farmhouse, his relentless search for the truth both there and at the prison. He'd stressed himself out over a murder which he claimed called out to him in his sleep some three hundred miles away.

"Stroud." She spoke his name, and it took on new meaning for her. "I'm here with you, Abe." She squeezed his hand. But Abraham Stroud was not there.

Stroud was not Stroud; rather, he was seeing and feeling and smelling from the body of another. He smelled blood all around him, as if it clung to him. He smelled an animal musk that made him dizzy, but for some reason it was faintly satisfying and familiar. He felt the movement of water under him, under a platform that moved, gliding over water. He felt alert, every sense as sharp and pointed as an ice pick. He felt things crawling on his body, microscopic things—creatures living off him. He felt threatened and afraid with every noise, every creak of the ship he was . . . he was hiding on.

I am Kerac, he told himself.

Accepting this, Stroud calmed and found the odors and the fear bearable. In flashes of insight he saw a large dark-haired figure coming down a gangplank. Someone, a fisherman, was right behind him. He saw flashes of light and then dark. His next image was of large handcuffs around his wrists. They seemed enormous, and yet they held him prisoner and tore at the hair on his wrists. He saw lots of hair caught in the cuffs, and his head throbbed with pain. Then he felt a surge of energy and power that was undeniable and unbelievable at once. He snapped the cuffs and held someone's cranium in his hairy hands, ripping off the man's head as if it were a twig. He saw blood spewing forth, felt it hitting his face and felt himself lapping at it. The final image was of shattered glass—a million pieces—and in the shattering he saw reflections of himself and Kerac merged as one, and over them both the image of a wild animal that he could not place, but a wild animal with fangs that dripped blood . . . like the shattered pane had dripped blood.

Stroud awoke from the blackout with a shiver and with a fearful insight that he dare not believe.

More had been shaken by his blackout, and Stroud felt a certain embarrassment with her now, although he could not say why . . . machismo, he suspected. Other cops had turned green, some had vomited at the sight of the two Port Authority cops mutilated in their own locked car, but Abe Stroud had been the only one present to "faint." Although he knew that it hadn't been fainting, that it was an uncontrollable affliction triggered by forces he had no control over, linked to the steel in his skull, this did little to quell the sense of shame it brought on under the circumstances.

He instantly pushed Anna away and got to his feet. Wobbly, a little white, he went for McMasters, Anna More following, telling him to take it easy.

"The killer came in on the fishing trawler, that one," Abe said, pointing it out. "Stowed away. Someone saw him, alerted the Port Authority. With our bulletin out, they checked it out. One of them, dressed in the fisherman's coat and boots, hit the stowaway over the head before saying a word to him. They cuffed him and put him into the car."

"Sure, sure," said McMasters. "I'm getting all this."

"You'll find a pair of cuffs missing from one of the P.A. guys."

Dr. Howe, listening, said, "We'll see if that can be confirmed."

"The cuffs are still on the guy."

"You telling me that this madman killed two men with his hands cuffed?"

"He snapped the bracelets, but they're still attached. He killed them with his bare hands, and he . . . he came through the back window because he didn't know how else to escape a locked car."

McMasters stared at Stroud a moment before he burst out laughing. But Dr. Howe said to McMasters, "Phil, when we got here, the doors—all four of them—were locked, and the keys were in the ignition. That didn't go out over the wire. There was no way for Dr. Stroud to know this."

"There's something else," said Stroud.

"May as well go on," replied McMasters with an impatient wave of his hand.

"This guy . . . he . . . he thinks . . . he thinks he's an animal."

"Well, Christ, we know that much."

"No, you don't get it. I mean he really thinks he is some kind of . . . of prehistoric animal. Cage was right."

"Cage?" asked Dr. Howe. "But he's in southern Illinois on one of his digs."

"He's in Grand Rapids, Dr. Howe, looking over Kerac's earlier victims."

"So what do you mean, Cage is right?" asked McMasters.

"Kerac kills with his teeth and his hands, or what Kerac sees as his . . . his claws."

"This is pretty weird shit, Stroud," McMasters said. "Even if the guy thinks he's a tiger or a lion maybe, Christ . . . he couldn't rip a man's head off like that with just his hands and his goddamned teeth."

McMasters curled his finger at Chief More, asking her to join him in a little private conference. As he took Anna More off a few feet, McMasters stopped to shout orders at the uniforms surrounding them to keep people back. Stroud knew that McMasters wasn't ready to accept him on the case, much less his bizarre theory.

He turned to Howe instead and said, "Lou's reports from Grand Rapids will be faxed into his lab here, Dr. Howe. He said he would direct them to you."

"Yes, of course. I'm in charge when he's away."

"Will you please call me at Precinct One or the Palmer House?"

"Of course."

"Thanks, Dr. Howe."

"I have to tell you, this whole thing is pretty bizarre," said Howe. "We have already established that the men in that vehicle were attacked by something ferocious; we were guessing a mad dog. Certainly enough fang marks to indicate that the killer was . . . inhuman."

"Oh, and Doctor," said Stroud.

"Yes?"

"You're likely to find that the killer took with him one or more of his victim's body parts."

"You really know this guy, don't you, Stroud?"

"Believe me, it's an acquaintance I'm anxious to end."

Stroud found More again.

"McMasters wants me to take him and his men to Kerac's relatives now," she told him.

"And he thinks it's a good idea if you do so without me."

"You know him well."

"Well enough. Watch his hands, Chief."

She nodded. "What about you?"

"I think I'll see you back at the hotel."

"You're sure it's okay?"

"Not a problem."

But it was, and as she walked from sight with McMasters holding her elbow, he worried again for Chief Anna Laughing More, who seemed at this moment like Alice in Wonderland. Phil McMasters carried a lot of weight in the city, knew a lot of powerful people, and he knew how to manipulate people. She was tough in Merimac, but this was Chicago. He wondered about the wisdom of leaving her on her own with McMasters. But he knew he couldn't hold her hand through this, and if he refused to let her go with Phil, she'd only resent him for it.

Part of his mind retained her soft touch and voice as she had sat there beside him, saying, "I'm here with you, Abe."

He got into his car and drove back for downtown Chicago and Precinct One. He'd spend the day looking over other possible leads. Kerac was nowhere near the port where he had first entered the city of several billion arteries, back alleys and other concrete terrain. He could be anywhere now.

—8—

The thin leads coming into the central precinct of downtown Chicago were not the work of Kerac. He seemed to have vanished in the city, or else he was waiting for nightfall to strike again. Meanwhile, members of his family were being interviewed and their homes staked out. At the same time, policemen in plainclothes were interviewing and questioning anyone they could find on the ships and about the port when the P.A. men were murdered. So far, they'd come up with one itinerant fisherman, one wino, two dogs and a cat looking for fish heads to eat. Nothing concrete.

The only good news came late in the day. Lou Cage called from Grand Rapids, and he had finished his reports on the farmhouse killings, tying these to the evidence that placed Kerac at the scene of his initial killings, north of Grand Rapids.

Lou sounded exhausted when he said, "God save us from this evil, Abe."

Stroud knew Cage well. He wasn't a man to exaggerate. "Then it's true. He killed them with his hands and his teeth?"

"Something like that."

"Be straight with me, Lou. I've got to know."

"Faxing the stuff to you and Howe now. Howe's going to think I'm ready for the funny farm myself when he reads this stuff."

"In a nutshell, Lou."

"It all matches—what forensics took on the bodies up here and those of the old people in Merimac, down to the wounds and the blood and the hair samples. Crazy thing is . . . hair samples taken from Kerac when he was in custody don't—I repeat, don't—match hair samples taken from the killer at the goddamned scenes of the crimes, Abe."

"What? That doesn't make sense, Lou."

"Tell me about it! I ran it six ways to Sunday. A good defense lawyer could get Kerac off with what we supply him."

"We know it's the same killer from the wound type."

"Wound type, yes . . . hair type, no. And another strange thing, Abe."

"Go on."

"Hair found at the scene matches animal samples. It's not human hair, Abe."

"What kind of animal are we talking about?"

"Red to brown to gray matted hair, some ripped out during the struggle—"

"What kind of animal?"

"Closest match we're able to make is that of a wolf."

"Wolf?"

"You heard me correctly."

Stroud said nothing for a long time, recalling the description of the "animal" that the guards at Merimac had given him. Stories of an animal of some sort that sprang out on the roadway, causing a collision, had also been reported at the border in Indiana where two policemen were killed when they encountered Kerac. Abe knew the inner workings of a police precinct well enough to know that anyone calling in with a sighting of a wolf on the streets of Chicago would become locker room grist for the joke mill, and certainly would be cast in the always-full in-basket for crank calls and nut cases to be looked into by the janitor. Stroud knew he'd have to be the janitor on this one, that perhaps some clue lay buried in the waste.

"A wolf?" he repeated over the phone.

"How's it going there?"

Stroud told Lou about the two P.A. men, the scene in the car. He didn't mention his blackout or the images he had seen during it.

Lou cursed into the phone, relieving his grief. Then he said, "I'm doing no good here. I'll be back in the morning. If you see Howe, tell him to keep this between us, for now."

"Will do."

"I'm too close to pension for this."

"Don't worry, Lou. You called it right. We've got the same mystery here now as we had at the farmhouse."

"This . . . this guy . . . Kerac, he must have some kind of animal fur he carries around with him—you know Indians—and he must be one hell of a strong sonofabitch is all I can tell, Abe."

"See you soon. I'll call and send the jet up for you."

"Thanks for the ride, pal."

Stroud knew he meant more than the plane ride. Abe thought about what the infallible Dr. Cage had told him, and he wanted now to read the reports faxed to Howe. He went to find Howe in an adjoining building.

Dr. Howe, a thin, balding man with glasses and an austere face, rarely smiled, but he was smiling now as the report from Grand Rapids was coming over. What in the report amused him, Stroud could not possibly understand, unless he liked gore . . . or unless he intended using the report against Cage in some political intrigue only he was privy to. Howe was Cage's subordinate. Stroud saw now how far out on a limb Lou had gone for him on this matter.

"I just spoke to Dr. Cage," said Stroud. "He's faxed the report. I'd like to see it."

"Coming over now."

"You find it amusing?"

"It smacks of the supernatural, I must say. Man and wolf . . . lycanthropy, all that."

"Guy's an Indian," said Stroud. "Who knows, maybe he can turn into a wolf."

"One explanation for the locked-car murders. But suppose this man has convinced himself that he can shape-change? That he looks at his own hands, face, body, and sees a horrendous monster there, and then he goes on a rampage? Is it then mental, or is it physical? Is it only imagined, or is it somehow made real by the fact it is *believed*? This kind of question intrigues me."

"Psychiatry was never my strong suit," said Stroud, "but you're into the science?"

"An avocation . . . once took courses toward a degree, turned to medicine instead."

This eased Stroud's concern about Ira Howe. Howe's interest in the case was very high, and he was making some judgments of his own about their quarry, Kerac.

"Just imagine what kind of a mind this man must have to so reconstruct his own self-image as to become an animal, to kill and feed as an animal. It's mind-boggling."

"Can that possibly account for the marks left on the bodies?"

"The intensity of the attack, yes. As to the physical rents, tears, bites, to a degree, yes . . ."

"But?"

"However, and this must surely be bothering Dr. Cage, the teeth marks are not those of a human being, any more than the hair this man leaves is human . . . you see?"

"Then he is no longer human?"

"I don't know."

"What do you mean, then?"

"He has become what he has dreamed."

The thought of it frightened Stroud as he had never been frightened before, realizing how many times he had felt himself be taken apart piece by piece by a dream, a nightmare, losing his own self, losing his way back. He'd always attributed this to the steel plate in his head, as part of the symptoms of the tortures, blackouts and seizures it put him through. But here was a man telling him that there was a human being on the planet who could reconstruct himself in the image of a hideous beast through the awful power of his own mind and be trapped by that power into a life of horror.

"Are you all right, Dr. Stroud?"

"Yes, yes . . . May I see the report?"

"By all means. Use my office." Dr. Howe was very solicitous, asking if he'd like coffee as well.

"Yes, thank you. Oh, and Dr. Howe, Dr. Cage asked that we keep the reports to ourselves until he can be on hand."

Howe, going for the outer office, bobbed his head up and down at this, his bow tie coming a little loose. "Fascinating case, really," he said on leaving.

Stroud's hot black coffee turned cold as he read Cage's report. He felt himself go cold with the findings, too. Findings indicated that in all the victims attributed to John Kerac, they were not dealing with the usual slash-and-dice mutilation killer, that in fact the wounds were inflicted by some force that Cage was incapable of pinpointing. But the words "animal," "catlike" and "wolflike" came up in his report—as if Cage believed that Kerac somehow commanded some sort of creature, a bobcat or a cougar, to do his bidding for him. This seemed as mad as the lycanthropy possibility that Ira Howe had tried to hoist on Stroud. Stroud had seen some amazing peculiarities in his lifetime; he had been privy to the Andover vampire colony in southern Illinois, and there were reams of unexplained phenomena in the literature of archeology, such as the power and mystery of the origin of the crystal skulls from the Mayan city of Belize, and the *horned* human skulls once unearthed in northern Pennsylvania which had been carbon-dated to prehistory.

The cast made of the print found at the farmhouse pointed to a large "wolflike" creature, possibly a disfigured one at that. Cage could not say. The slash wounds, he was more specific about. The depth and breadth of the tearing instrument indicated sharp, long teeth like those of a lion or tiger. Other marks were the work of talons or claws. Furthermore, there was sure evidence that whatever killed the Maclins, Perotto and the hunting group that Kerac had guided into the woods of northern Michigan fed on the bodies, or parts of the bodies it ripped off—that Kerac had cannibalized those remains. All most peculiar. Little wonder that Cage worried about the report going public.

Stroud thought of the vision he'd had at the Port Authority, staring into the backseat of the bloody tomb Kerac had made of the car. He thought of his feelings. They'd been those of heightened sensitivities: touch, taste, smell, sight, hearing—like those of an animal. He recalled the depth of his fear while he was inside the mind of John Kerac. He recalled the hairy forearms and hands and the odor that threatened to overwhelm him. Stroud then thought back to his first nightmares, those that had driven him to Merimac. They had been filled with the emotions of a frightened animal.

But could John Kerac have such power over such a vicious killer beast? Could he have had an intelligent dog, a pit bull that followed his master's command to kill? This explanation appealed to Abe's sense of balance; it would be tidy and acceptable to others, far more so than tales of a "beast master" who controlled passing wolves, and certainly more presentable than shape-changing from a man into a wolf.

It was late, the clock ticking toward dusk. Somewhere in the brisk Chicago night, Kerac would kill again. Of this Stroud hadn't any doubt. Of Kerac's "animal cunning" he had no doubt. Kerac would elude capture and frustrate the usual police procedures, for they had no idea what they were dealing with. For that matter, neither did Abraham Stroud.

Was their quarry no longer human? Did he command a beast at his side? Or was he the beast?

Stroud heard others coming. Ira Howe was escorting McMasters and Anna More into the office. Stroud was tired and slow to respond when McMasters said, "Having fun, Abe? Got to tell you, Kerac's family doesn't seem to have a clue about why he would suddenly become a mass murderer . . . but then, no one ever does, do they? Got Cage's report, I hear. Let's have a look."

Stroud was looking at Chief More, who hadn't said a word. "Did you speak with Kerac's people?"

"Are you kidding?" said McMasters, taking the report from Stroud. "She spoke to them in native tongue . . . had to translate for me. She's smart, a real smart gal, the way she put them at ease . . . got them on her side . . . real pro."

"As I am aware," said Stroud, still looking for Anna More to reveal something behind her stony gaze when he saw something lunge behind the eyes. It had kicked in when McMasters said, *got them on her side.*

"They trust me because I was honest with them," she said. "Poor people . . . living like they are . . . hearing this about Kerac."

"You knew them from before?"

"Yes, of course. They moved to Chicago looking for work, trying to escape poverty . . . but they haven't come very far."

"Around-the-clock surveillance on the two apartments," said Kerac. "Luck for us that they're in adjoining buildings. If Kerac goes near them, we'll have him sure."

"In his present state of mind, if he does go near them," said Stroud, "he could kill them all. You know that, don't you?"

"Don't worry," said McMasters.

"Are the family members worried?"

"Very," she said, going to the window and staring out. "The old man, the grandfather, said that John must be bitten by the Wendigo."

"Native American horseshit," said McMasters, stopping in his scanning of Cage's report to look up at her. "Superstition, right, Chief More?"

"Wendigo is Ojibway for a creature of the night that steals children from their beds and eats them alive. It comes with the wind on the silent feet of a beast that strikes more quickly and surely than the panther, and it has a lust for human flesh."

"Jesus," said Phil McMasters, reading Cage's words further. "Sounds like Lou Cage has been in the fuck"—he stopped to correct himself in front of More—"damned woods too long. You read this, Stroud. What's he talking about here?"

"Far as I can tell, Lou's got a killer with fangs and claws; not your conventional knife-wielding psycho, Phil."

"Between the Indians and you, Stroud, and now Cage . . . I think the joke's gone far enough."

"No one expects you to believe," said More, "but there are dark and mysterious powers at work in Kerac."

"Bad blood, bad chemistry, a screwed-up mind and fucked genes, maybe, but he's no supernatural monster that's going to come into Chicago and wipe out whole populations, Chief."

There was something that had happened between McMasters and More which Stroud could not place, but the strain now between them was evident. It was sexual in nature, but exactly what, Stroud was unsure. Had McMasters propositioned her, and had she refused? Or had they mutually consented? Knowing McMasters, Stroud went out on a limb and guessed that he'd made a crack about how he'd always wondered how Indian women were in the sack, had pursued the question all day and had finally gotten soundly rejected. At least, this was how Stroud hoped it had gone.

McMasters tossed Cage's report back down on the desk, having only half read it. "Ira, when Cage gets back, maybe we'd best measure him for a straitjacket."

"Captain McMasters," said Ira Howe calmly, "you'd better make it two straitjackets."

"What?"

"I've examined the worst of the wounds to those P.A. guys. I've also come up with similar conclusions to those made by Dr. Cage. We are not dealing with any knowns here. If there is a weapon that simulates the bites and tears of an animal so closely, I do not know what this weapon is."

"You're all . . ." McMaster's eyes fell on More. "Crazy." He stormed out with the fanfare of a man who'd like to rip a door from its hinges, locate the nearest pub and drink himself to sleep.

"I don't think we're going to get much cooperation from McMasters after tonight," said More. "He really doesn't want to cooperate on police matters . . . and if he has anything to say about it, his unit will apprehend Kerac without any further assistance from me."

"I take it you two didn't get on very well."

"Like two rams in the same stall."

"That bad, huh?"

"Don't give me that. You knew the moment you saw us again."

"I had an inkling."

"Your inklings, as you call them, may be our only hope of putting an end to Kerac's newfound career. So, keep inkling, Abe Stroud." There was a weariness in her voice like the strained breath of a racer when it's over and she's trying to recover. "In the meantime, Mac—as he asked me to call him—will be getting nowhere. The man is insufferable."

"At last," said Abe.

"What?"

"We agree on something."

This made her laugh.

"Nice to see you smile," he said.

"You must admit, there hasn't been an awful lot to smile about. You should have seen those nieces and nephews of Kerac's, all skin and bone and big-eyed, staring at me like . . . like I was some kind of answer to their prayers."

"Maybe you are."

She laughed again and shook her head. "No, not likely . . . although I did slip a twenty to their mother. Kerac's brother, who brought them all here, is out of work, can't hold a job . . . lost, like most Indians in a city like this. Does day labor where he can find it. Oldest girl has begun a family of her own."

"Do you think that Kerac will go to them?"

"Who knows?" Her frustration returned to the surface like a surging wave. "Who can read this man's mind? Who can second-guess a madman?"

"Look this report over, Anna," he said to her, "and I'll make some arrangements for dinner, and we'll talk about who can read Kerac's mind."

She stared at him a moment, taking the report in her hands. Howe had had some items to see to in the lab, and he'd faded from the room just after McMasters took his leave.

"There must be something interesting here," she said, going to the desk seat he'd vacated, placing the report below the lamp and taking a deep breath before diving in.

"Yes, there is much of interest in Cage's findings. But McMasters is right. It's near impossible to make any sense of the report."

"Maybe Cage *has* been in Michigan too long."

Now he laughed. "Could be . . . could be. I'll be back in fifteen, twenty minutes."

He left her alone with Cage's bizarre findings. He meant to use them as a path into his own "bizarre" findings. He wanted to share his awful vision at the P.A. car with her. He had to share it with someone, and Cage wouldn't be back for another twenty-four hours.

— 9 —

The soft light and soothing music provided a relaxing atmosphere, and the food at the Palmer House was the best in the city. Anna More came down in an evening dress which Stroud had left in her room via the bellman. Stroud was a little surprised when he saw her moving across the room in the dress, half certain she'd called room service and was going to stay in. He pictured her tossing the evening gown over the bellman's head as he sent him packing. But here she was, her proud bearing drawing attention to her. She might be a model or a star in town for a shoot, or so people around them must think as she elegantly stepped up to Stroud's table. She certainly didn't look like a cop.

"You look very beautiful," he said to her.

She smiled and slid into the plush seat across from him. "And you have exquisite taste, but how did you know my size?"

"You forget, I was once a detective."

"I can keep no secrets from you, then?"

"Oh, don't be so sure . . ."

"What?"

"There are many, many things about you I would like to know, but I fear I may never know."

She blushed only slightly under his gaze, the lighting here giving a tinge of turquoise to his eyes. In this light, they shimmered with something undeniably dangerous. "I am famished," she said, trying to avert her eyes from his, and his attention from her, going for the menu.

"I've taken the liberty of ordering for you. I hope you don't mind."

"You always like to take charge, be in control, don't you, Abraham Stroud?"

"It's a flaw, I know."

"Perhaps not, if you ordered well."

"I did, I can assure you."

"So full of assurances, too, aren't you? But tell me, Abraham. What assurances are there at all that we . . . you and I . . . have any future whatsoever together?"

"None, I'm sure. But tonight, let's be friends and let's enjoy the peace, the bread, the wine."

She smiled at his response, and he returned the smile. "Tonight," she said, lifting her glass as soon as he filled it with a blush zinfandel. "To tonight, then. May it end as peacefully as it has begun."

He accepted the toast, but there was an uneasy pulse beat that ran along his arteries and showed clearly in his eyes. She saw it there and realized the unspoken truth: the night would end in horror for someone outside the huge window where the darkness was accentuated by a million points of light.

"So nice here, like this," she said. "Why can't our lives be forever filled with moments like this, Abe?"

"I couldn't agree with you more."

"But they can't be. It's always out there, isn't it?" she said, indicating the dark just the other side of the huge panes of glass that overlooked the gusty downtown section of Chicago where shadows roamed unchecked.

"Evil is as old as mankind."

"And more clever."

"Yes, I suppose so."

"And it is relentless."

He nodded. "Anna, at the Port Authority, when I . . . lost it—"

"Your blackout, yes?"

"Let's call it a trance. Sounds better."

"McMasters said you quit the force because of them."

"McMasters is full of shit. I quit to become what I am, an archeologist."

"He said the . . . trances . . . were getting in the way of the performance of your duty, and no one wanted to work with you."

"I really don't care to discuss McMasters or my years on the force here."

"Oh, I'm sorry," she replied. "I was . . . curious."

"I came out of Vietnam with a steel plate in my head, a band that keeps my skull intact. Ever since, I've had premonitions, nightmares and the occasional blackout. During those blackouts, I am given information . . ."

"Given information?" She was incredulous. "By whom?"

"I don't know." It was much easier to say this than to go into detail about telepathy or talking ghosts. "All I know, Anna, is that for a brief moment this morning, I . . . I was in Kerac's mind."

"What?"

"I connected with him. I felt him . . . felt as if I *were* him."

She said nothing, sat sipping at the wine, looking off, hoping the food would come, covering her left hand with her right, legs and feet adjusting. Her nervousness with him had begun. "You knew I had some psychic capabilities," he continued. "It could help us locate Kerac, if we can put some of the pieces together."

"The pieces?"

"Fragmented images that I got. Some make no sense whatsoever."

"McMasters told me what you'd told him at the scene."

"And I'm sure he presented it in the worst possible light."

"All right, tell me in your own words."

Their salads arrived, and Stroud waited for the waiter to disappear before he told her all that had gone through his mind. He then added, "And as the day has gone by, other images, bits and pieces, really, have somehow come clear as if rising to the surface after being weighted down, images I had seen but which had been blocked until now."

"Such as?"

"Dead horses . . . lots of dead horses, some sheep and cattle, all dead."

She stared at him. "Maybe you're just too clever for your own good, Stroud," she said grimly.

"Why? What do you mean?"

"Someone in Merimac told you; Miller probably. Damn him."

"Wait, whoa, Anna, no one told me a damned thing about dead horses."

She tried to get up from the table, but he reached across and took firm hold of her, their eyes meeting. "I swear, this just came to me . . . like a dream."

"Kerac raised horses for a time when he was a teenager . . . with his father."

"Something happened to the horses? A disease maybe?"

"Someone systematically destroyed them, killed them. Kerac's herd was small. The loss of a single horse meant a great deal."

"Was this aimed at Kerac? His father?"

"It was random and indiscriminant."

"Other small ranchers, too?"

"With cattle, sometimes goats, sheep."

"How long ago?"

"Two years."

"Then it stopped?"

"Just like that, but not before Kerac was wiped out, his father dead and—" She stopped herself.

He saw the flash of thought go through her mind and finished it for her, "And you left him."

"Yes, and I left him." She was stunned that she had finally made the small confession, and he was equally stunned.

"I see. Were you married or just living together?"

"We planned to marry, but everything started to unravel. He didn't take it too well when I began to earn more money as a deputy than he was ever likely to make. It destroyed us as surely as the carnage to his horses."

"Carnage?"

"Carnage, yes. They were cut open, gutted, the throats slashed. Kerac had had the horses insured, but he never saw a penny of the money."

"Why not?"

"Because someone started a rumor that he had said during a drunk that he ought to go out and destroy all of the rest of his horses; people put two and two together and decided he was just wild enough to kill his own animals."

"Was he?"

"He was desperate . . . went strange after his father died. At the point that I left him . . . I don't know, but now . . . with all that has happened, yes . . . yes, he must've destroyed those poor horses."

"Why didn't you confide this to me before?"

"Christ, that was years ago. Kerac disappeared from the home reserve, went off to Chicago with his brother and their family with big plans. Next thing I know he's in Grand Rapids working as a guide, and I'm happy for him, because I hear he's really making a go of it. Then he's in the prison, in the asylum ward for butchering the last group of men he'd taken up into the woods, and the details . . . the details remind me of the dead horses."

"None of that explains the cattle and sheep on other farms," said Stroud.

"Story goes that Kerac, to cover his tracks and to collect on the insurance to the horses, went about destroying other animals as well, to make it look good, like the work of wolves or other predators."

"You have wolves up there?"

"We have everything in those woods."

"Do you believe Kerac was clever enough to do what everyone says he did?"

"The Kerac I knew loved horses, but . . . but people change. The mind is so fragile, and when people get desperate . . . who knows?"

"Was he ever arrested for these animal mutilations?"

"There was an arrest, but he was let go for lack of evidence. There was only hearsay to hold him on."

"And you were one of the cops that had to haul him in?"

"That's the way it went."

"And yet his brother's family today treated you so well?"

"Everyone knew that Johnny was a little different, a little crazy. Crazy Indian . . . and everyone accepted it, up to a point. Now, with what's following Johnny wherever he goes, no one knowing him would hesitate to put a bullet through his eyes, including his brother's wife. She's ready for him, if he shows. She intends to protect her children. Yes, they were glad to see me. They think I can stop him. I should be with them now, instead of here."

"Funny . . ."

"What's that?"

"The dead horses I saw were strangely colored—dead but standing straight up, rigid and silent, eyes wide with fright."

"Strangely colored? Kerac's horses were grays and browns, one or two Appaloosas."

"Spots, right?"

"Across the rump, yes."

"No green ones, huh?"

"Maybe in a UFO." She laughed nervously, afraid she'd said something she shouldn't have. Coming from McMasters, it would have been insulting, but Stroud knew there was no venom in her words.

"Yeah, a UFO horse, maybe."

The steaming vegetables and sumptuous lobster tails arrived, delighting her. Stroud called for more wine. For a time they ate in silence. Halfway through the course, she said, "You certainly have extravagant taste."

"Only when I'm with beautiful women."

"Which is often, I'm sure."

"There is no one quite as lovely as you in my life, Anna."

"Really?"

"Finish your meal."

"Why? Do you have further *plans* for me?"

"There," he said, pointing toward the four-member band, piano and dance floor, where several couples weaved about in close embrace. "I'd very much enjoy your company on the dance floor."

"Ahhhhhh, a rain dance to perhaps bring forth fruit?"

"Anything you like."

"Why wait?"

Stroud stood and took her by the hand, escorting her onto the floor, where they embraced, first awkwardly and soon naturally. Stroud filled his nostrils with the smell of Anna Laughing More. He found himself tightening his hold on her.

"Please," she said, "no trance while we dance?"

"Somehow, Anna," he whispered in her ear, "I think a trance is unavoidable with you here in my arms in that dress, in this light—"

"After much fire water, sure."

He brought his eyes around to hers, and without hesitation their lips met. The kiss was magical, firm and moist and full. Stroud found her tongue probing his mouth. After they separated, she said, "Perhaps we should continue this elsewhere."

Stroud's heart raced and he felt giddy. Smiling, nodding, he said, "I'll get your things."

They left the dining room feeling as if no one else in the room existed, and yet the eyes of almost everyone in the room were on the tall, handsome couple.

Stroud looked down at her and he felt as if he might fall into her dark, bottomless eyes. He remembered as a boy, lying along the Spoon River in Andover, the shock of life that spirited through his body when he tasted sex for the first time, and although that taste was little more than a petting party, the thrill of those first tentative steps had forever after escaped him. Here, now, the electrifying thrill of first love had been revived in him by Anna Laughing More. She'd dropped the gown, stepped from it, worked off her slip, and with his trembling help removed the bra and panties. Looking at her was giving him the strange sensation that there were no dimensions in the room, no up or down, no back or forth, no sky or air to breathe, no firm ground. Like a mad Chagall painting, his heart and body soared, rising weightless to the ceiling and the stars. No now and no then—only present life on the ceiling, with her floating below him.

Stroud's breath caught in his throat, making words impossible. She placed a finger over his lips to keep him from attempting to speak. Anna's breasts were large and firm, shrouding a cavern of mystery between them. When her nipples darkened as they came erect at his touch, her bronzed skin seemed lighter by comparison. Stroud thought her skin was the texture of warm red wine. She was as tall as he, opulent and until now so forbidden; now her curves and ravines, made the more wondrous by the half-light of the single bedside lamp, were his to explore.

Again he felt the sweet shock of young love when her hands went to his thigh, searching. He relaxed at her touch, and now, kneeling astride him, she began to rub his body with an oil she had earlier taken from her bag. The oil was warm and smelled of sweet herbs and witch hazel. She rubbed it into his chest and belly, following a trail to his groin, enticing him with her touch. As she leaned forward, working the oil in, he was touched by her breath, her cheek, her breasts as they swayed over him.

She was lying flat across him now, bringing her essence to merge with his. Her essence was bathing him now in the warmth of her. Stroud felt all the boyhood dreams of satisfied lust welling up in him as she pleased him, and pleased him and pleased him.

Astonishingly, she now took a mouthful of the warm oil, bent over Stroud and took him into the folds of her lips, holding the liquid there, whorling him around in it against her tongue. He watched, helpless, as she rose and fell on the eddies of his blood as it pumped through him. And all the while, her eyes, large and bottomless and loving, never left him.

—10—

It was three A.M. when the phone roused them both, making Stroud grab the phone to keep it from awakening Anna. He knocked over the oil she'd used on him that had been left open beside the phone. It was staining the carpet as he spoke into the receiver.

"Yeah, Stroud here."

"Ira Howe, Stroud . . . We got another one."

"Oh, Christ."

"What is it?" asked Anna, getting up, dressing quickly, knowing what it was. "Where? God, don't let it be the Keracs."

"Unidentified male, young, maybe twenty, maybe younger . . ."

"Where?"

"Alleyway offa Kedzie near Washington."

Stroud told her it was far from the Kerac home. He then returned to Ira. "Same condition of the body?"

"Same M.O. down to the missing parts. Attack, rip and run with part of the kill, just like a freakin' leopard. Like he takes it to a den to feed in isolation and safety."

"No lack of prey for this guy, is there?"

"None."

"Who's on it?"

"McMasters and his strike force."

"Anything we can do?"

"Beyond getting your faces rubbed in it? No, not really. This guy is bad, Stroud . . . very, very nasty. Newspapers've got it— guess you know. Quoted you in the A.M. edition of the *Times*."

"Hell they did?"

"Said you were honing in on the damned killer with a psychic rapier, or some such shit."

"Shit is about it. I didn't say a word to the press."

"Some guy overheard at the P.A. Talked to some other guys on the scene, pieced it together. Looked up your old records, ran the microfiche back to the days when you were on the payroll. Guy named Perry Gwinn; in newspaper circles they call him the Peregrine—you know, like falcon."

"And he drops shit like a buzzard, right?"

"Exactly, so heads up. McMasters is already pissed that you *spoke* to the press."

"I'm sure he is."

"So, you've got reasons aplenty for not coming out on this one."

Stroud looked over at Anna, who had finished dressing. "You don't know the half of it, Howe."

"What?"

"Never mind."

"Well, just wanted you to know. McMasters tried to contact More, but couldn't locate."

"I'll talk to you soon, Ira."

"*Ciao*."

He hung up. Stroud went to Anna. "There's nothing we can do tonight," he told her, taking her into his arms, covering her mouth with his own. "You know what you said, about seeing a future together?"

"Not now, Abe," she said, pulling away from him.

"Anna . . ."

"I'm determined to find Kerac, end it, Stroud. Now, if he has struck, I want to be standing in his last known position."

Stroud was feeling selfish. He'd wanted her all to himself a little longer. "All right, but I go with you."

"I'll go next door, change."

"Meet you in what, ten minutes?"

But she was gone, leaving a trail of coolness behind. She'd returned to being Chief More the instant Ira's call awakened her. Stroud realized that as long as Kerac was alive she was right: he and Anna had no future whatsoever together. At the same time, he could not help thinking of how incredibly serene she had made him feel, to the point that he had, for a time, been transported out of the mind-set of Abraham Stroud and into the mind of the boy he once was.

On the ride over to the Northwest Side toward Kedzie, Stroud asked her to tell him more about the mythical beast she'd called Wendigo.

She laughed and said, "That was for Phil McMasters' benefit. I knew it would get rid of him."

"Then you don't believe in the Wendigo?"

"I believe my ancestors used a term for an animal they did not know another name for, and they gave it supernatural traits, like most primitive people do for the bear, the fox, and goddamned crows and turtles . . . why not? Your people did the same thing in Germany or Ireland, or wherever you're from, with the green little people, didn't they?"

"All right, just tell me about what these things were supposed to look and act like?"

"That changes, depending on whom you are talking to."

"Some idea, any idea."

"Wendigos have the characteristics and cunning of wolves."

"Wolves . . ."

"So, you want to draw any conclusions from that?"

"Cage's report . . . you read it."

"I think Dr. Cage is reading too much into his own findings, maybe."

He looked across at her, trying to read her expression, but it was too dark in the cabin of the LTD. "Tell me more about these Wendigos."

"Wind-swept howls . . . they move with the wind, covering their own howls with those of the north wind. They come with the frost and cold down from Canada to wreak seasonal havoc on the Indians."

"Kerac's animals and the livestock of others around Merimac . . . were the attacks seasonal in nature?"

"All of a single winter, but—"

"I see."

"Kerac planned it that way, knowing of the superstition."

"Could be."

"Don't be ridiculous."

"All possibilities must be considered."

She looked now across at him. "You don't believe for a moment that the Wendigo exists? That would be like saying Sasquatch exists."

"Bigfoot, you mean."

"Sasquatch is the Indian term."

"And the Indians were the first to describe bigfoot. Tell me, have there been a lot of bigfoot sightings in and around Merimac and Grand Rapids?"

"We've got our share, but so does every rural community in the nation! Kentucky, Indiana, Ohio, for Christ's sake."

"So stories of Sasquatch and Wendigos circulate freely among your people."

"Don't make our people out to be fools, Stroud. Don't go turning into a goddamned scientific investigator of the paranormal on me."

"What do the old people in your tribe say about the Wendigo?"

She was silent a moment. "You're going to pursue this?"

"Humor me, damn it."

"Wolflike . . . wolves, all right?"

"Wolflike?"

"Yes."

"Half man, half wolf?"

"Something like that," she said, clearly exasperated and apparently embarrassed by her people's folklore.

"Anna, I've learned one thing in archeology about folklore, myth and superstition—"

"And that is?"

"That in almost every superstition there is some truth, even if it is just a grain. Typically, science is light-years behind medicine men, for instance, in finding cures. Now, no one would argue with the fact there once were 'bear men.' "

"Cavemen, you mean?"

"Exactly, and they were huge and hairy and they wore animal skins."

"And you think these ancient ones are the root of the stories told about the race of Wendigos?"

"It's possible."

"And somehow Kerac has slipped a disc in his brain and has become one?"

"It may be more than mental. At least in my vision, I saw him as a beast of some sort, and I've always felt this from the outset."

"So, you're telepathically connected, and if he believes himself a beast, then of course you will perceive him as such. Don't you see?"

"Perhaps, but that doesn't explain his great power, or Cage's findings."

She sat in dull silence, the sodium vapor lamps of Chicago dyeing the windshield orange, spraying her first with light and then with dark as the car sped along. Stroud reached across for her hand and squeezed gently. She placed her hand in her lap, out of his reach. "Kerac is only a man, and he will die a man. He is no more a . . . a werewolf than you or I."

Stroud wanted to tell her about the vampire monsters who looked human that he had encountered in Andover; he wanted to shake her into realizing that there was more between heaven and earth than meets the eye, and that appearances alone could seldom be trusted.

"Some sort of venom," he said.

"What?"

"Venom. Suppose Kerac was bitten by . . . by something that filled his system with some sort of venom, like the bite of a rabid bat, or dog, and this altered him forever, sent him out of control of his own mind and body, sent his hormones into overdrive, created of him a hairy throwback to . . . to what we once all were. Carnivorous—"

"That's crazy, Stroud, crazy. There are no Wendigos!"

"But the bite of one," he said calmly. "I mean in your folklore, did the bite of one of these beasts turn a human into one of them?"

She did not really answer. She didn't need to. He knew that he was right.

"Tell me this, Anna," he said to break her silence, "where would a Wendigo hide in a city the size of Chicago?"

She remained in her envelope of silence.

"And how do we take him alive?" he asked.

"What? What? Alive? There is no taking him alive, Stroud, you must see that."

Her tone was not that of anger but desperation. Something in her voice told him that she had come to Chicago to ensure that Kerac die.

"Why not, Anna?"

"Why? He will kill you if you try! Even in captivity, he will escape and kill again! You've seen that he lives for death, and to feed on your flesh, Stroud!"

"But taken alive—"

"To serve what purpose!"

"To serve many purposes."

"One—name one goddamned purpose Kerac can serve in this life other than bloodlust?"

"He can answer some goddamned questions, Anna, and tests can be run on him, and—"

"Like at Merimac? Sure!"

"—and we can determine something about how his mind works. Maybe prevent such occurrences in the future."

"You do that, Doc," she said angrily, "but as for myself, I shoot to kill."

"And that's why you came here, to kill him."

"To put him out of his misery, yes."

The police band crackled into life: "All units, all units! Suspect Kerac, armed and dangerous, sighted at Humboldt Park pavilion. All units respond!"

Stroud turned the car sharply at Western Avenue, heading south toward Grand and the expansive, lush park. "Looks like you're going to get your wish. Every cop in the city's going to put a slug into him."

She held fast to her weapon, readying to jump from the car at the first opportunity. Stroud sensed her catlike attitude.

"When we get there, stick close, Anna, do you hear me?"

"*You'd* better stick close," she told him. "You aren't even carrying a gun!"

In the distance sirens and gunshots could be heard. Stroud sped to a stop, the car careening up onto the curb and onto the lawn of the park beside a bench. Directly before them were bushes and a sloping hill that wound down to a small lagoon where a gleaming white pavilion stood. There were a few boulders strewn about, a walk path, a bicycle path and a horse path snaking through the park. Stroud knew the territory well, but there were so many cops beating the bushes and in and out of the trees that he felt unsafe.

Anna jumped from her seat, was headed into the foray, shouting to a uniformed cop, "Where was he sighted? You see him?"

"I didn't see anything. Calvin saw something move down there. He fired two rounds, but nothing's moving."

Stroud came around with a flashlight, and he shouted for some of the police cars to shine their spotlights down into the clearing where Kerac was supposedly holed up. The lights were quickly brought forth, everyone agreeing they'd like to see better. Someone fired off a flare that provided a brilliant blue light. People began to congregate around the edges of the park, curious; others at their windows in homes all around stared down on the scene.

"There!" shouted someone, and this was followed by a volley of fire that echoed down the streets and off buildings.

Stroud saw the thing that was Kerac.

He gasped at the sight, and he felt the torment of the creature, its confusion, fear and outrage. He felt the encrusted blood on its body, smelled the animal musk.

It was crouched, its limbs powerful and long, apelike, and it ran with an animal grace. Stroud saw a man take aim, fire, and he saw the bullet hit Kerac, and yet Kerac merely flinched and kept running, finding new cover. In the strange light, it was impossible to tell much, and everyone who had seen the moving form was asking others what they had seen. Stroud stood with his mouth open, amazed at the sight of the man who would be a wolf. . . .

"Goddammit," said one man, "he's unarmed. We just go in and take him. Come on."

A few of the cops went forth. Anna wanted to go with them, but Stroud stopped her. "A bullet isn't going to stop Kerac. You saw what I saw."

"Get out of my way." She barreled past Stroud. Stroud pursued her.

"Anna, wait."

"He's hit, and he's dying!" she shouted, pulling away from Stroud with determination coloring her dark features. "One way or another, Stroud, we end it here, now."

The small band of brave—or stupid—cops had reached the stand of trees and bushes where they'd last seen Kerac. They were a few feet from the water and a stone bridge, below which was a causeway for a bike path that was dark and cavernous-looking where the light had been destroyed by children hurtling rocks, no doubt. Suddenly one of the cops ahead of Stroud and More screamed horribly and was silenced when something dropped from overhead onto him, slashing his throat instantly. His two partners lifted their weapons, but the body of their comrade was hurled into them with such force that they were knocked over, their own uniforms smeared with the blood of the first man.

Anna drew a bead on the dark form camouflaged against the black greenery and fired, striking a tree. The streak of shadow that followed raced down into the viaduct below the bridge as

Anna fired off a second and a third round.

"I hit him!" she shouted. "I know I hit him."

She raced after Kerac, who let out with a blood-chilling howl from below the bridge, stopping her and Stroud in their tracks.

"We need nets, a goddamned cage for this guy!" shouted Stroud. "A bullet won't bring him down!"

Anna could not be dissuaded, pulling away from Stroud, going for the dark interior below the bridge.

Stroud rushed to stay with her, bringing the light along, flashing it ahead of them. He searched the nooks and crannies of the bridge, including the ceiling, imagining that Kerac might somehow suction his huge body against the stones there, to drop down as he had from the trees earlier.

Another pair of cops came at the bridge from the other side with the same design in mind as Anna More. Their light combined with Stroud's to tell them all that the fleeing killer was not here.

"The water!" said Anna. "Flash on the water."

All lights went to the lagoon, all guns trained on it as well. A few shots were fired into the water at branches that broke the surface, but nothing substantial was picked up in the lights. For long moments, the lights scanned the water. Another flare was sent up over the lagoon. More shots were fired at shadows. Some of the men said that John Kerac had swum out to the pavilion and had circled it and was hanging on there. Men on the ground encircled the pavilion with lights, firing into it, sending shards of white-painted wood in all directions, littering the pond with the result, making the black lagoon look like a field on which cut flowers lay.

"Cease fire!" shouted Stroud, but still some guns were going off. Some of the men were having fun; some of them wanted to make amends for their dead comrade.

Finally, the firing stopped.

"If he's in there, he's dead of his wounds," said Anna, "and thank God for it."

"We'll have to get some divers out here, dredge for the body," said Phil McMasters, who'd rushed here from the murder scene in the alley off Kedzie.

Stroud brought his light around to the bricks and stones of the bridge. In the commotion he'd heard a strange, metallic noise, but he had heard no rustling or disturbance of water. He moved closer to the bridge wall, and at the base of it, directly in the center, he found a large old grate that looked down into a black hole where water reflected his light back at him. Signs that the grate had been disturbed were evident, a deep cut in the concrete floor, a dusting of rust from the grate itself as it had been pried loose. There was also a splotch of blood on the multicolored stones where Kerac had placed a hand. Aside from this, there was hair glued against the stone by the blood, and small wisps of animal-like hair about the mouth of the grating.

"He's made his escape through here," said Stroud from where he crouched.

McMasters and Anna came closer, McMasters saying, "Christ, he's in the sewers."

"They go on for miles in every direction," said one of the uniformed cops nearby.

McMasters bellowed like a bull at this cop and all the others standing about. "So, get on it! Every unit down the streets, following the sewer lines. Sonofabitch's got to come out somewhere. Nobody's going to stay down there if they don't have to. I want cars covering every goddamned manhole between here and Cubs Park, damn it!"

"Conventional methods won't work against this . . . this man," Stroud said to McMasters, who merely put a hand on Stroud's chest and said, "You, Doctor, just stay the hell out of the way."

Anna came to Stroud, looked into his eyes, and he saw her inwardly shiver, recalling what she'd just seen.

"You saw it suck up those bullets, Anna. It's not Kerac anymore. It's a wild beast."

"McMasters!" she called out after the captain. "I want in on this."

-11-

The Chicago Police Department's efforts went for nothing. The following day, Kerac was still at large. Special teams of tactical experts had been brought in and swat teams circulated still in the city's sewers in search of the elusive savage. Stroud knew now that ordinary methods would not contain Kerac, and that he was safely holed up in a den or warren like any sensible and cunning animal. Stroud knew that bullets, while inflicting pain, were useless against Kerac unless they penetrated a vital organ, such as the heart, lungs or brain. Even this was questionable from what Stroud had observed the night before.

Stroud had spent his morning with animals—in the Chicago Police Department of Animal Control, talking with Bob Arnold, a division chief who had shared a unit with Stroud when they were both much younger. The place was as noisy as a dog kennel, and there were animals of every size and stripe locked in holding pens, most of them waiting for a death sentence to be carried out. In one pen an agitated raccoon spat through the bars at a squalid house cat beside it. The cat huddled in a corner as far from the raccoon as it could get. A dog below these two was foaming at the mouth, rabid.

Arnold was a no-nonsense, hefty black man with a perpetual crooked smile which might be taken as a sneer if you didn't know him; his close-set, squinting eyes made of his features a large question mark where the eyebrows joined whenever he was confused. Stroud was confusing him now.

"Wait a minute, Abe. You want me to set up a trap for a man? Same as I would a mad dog?"

"That's about the size of it."

"Ankle snare, cage?"

"Net, cage—you're the expert."

"Hell, you going to read the guy his rights while he's looking out from the bars?"

"You have any idea, Bob, how bloody dangerous this man is? Have you seen the results of his fun?"

"All right, all right, Abe. I haven't said no to the idea."

"He's a lunatic, Bob."

"So I heard. A lunatic with a bad attitude and a lot of hair, according to some. Rumor has it that forensics has him sprinkling wolf hairs wherever he goes. Bizarre, pal . . . but then, you always were in the thick of the nut cases, as I recall."

"Just tell me, Bob. Hypothetically, if there was, say, a wolf roaming Chicago, how would you go about catching him?"

"Come on, I'll show you my contraptions."

Arnold led him into an inner room filled with various mechanical devices for snaring animals of all sizes and wits. He demonstrated for Abe the usual traps used by hunters that acted on the spring-coil principle and might take an animal's foot halfway off, latching on to the bone and anchoring there. He showed Abe other devices which could take an animal's head off, or send it flying into the branches of a tree, tethered on a line. His showroom was something of a macabre museum of deadly objects. The walls were lined with explanatory information on various traps, along with pictures of the results.

"This one's only good if you know his exact whereabouts and can count on his stepping down a path where you plant it, Abe. Camouflage, all that."

"He'll smell it before he sets foot in it," said Abe. "He's got a heightened sense of smell."

"Hmmmmmm. All right, then what about the neck snare, if you want to kill the SOB outright?"

"No, I don't want him decapitated. I want him caught, alive."

"Why didn't you say so?"

"I thought I had."

"Not to me you didn't. Come on."

"This guy's too smart for anything buried below a few leaves or strung across a causeway. He'd see the snare. He's got . . . excellent vision."

"Sounds like goddamned Superman."

"Close."

"You still have to know where he is to throw a net over him, or trick him into a door that's the entryway for a cage. You have any idea where this guy's holed up?"

"Not yet, but could you have a team at the ready should I call? With these?" Stroud pointed to a huge steel-mesh net that hung on the wall like a fisherman's net.

"Best choice . . . Sure, we could be on alert. Don't know how it'll be viewed from above, or how the press'll deal with us, but if you think this is the only way to get this mother, then I'm your man, Abe. My guys and me know every hole and back alley and gutter in the city where an animal can hide. Problem is, there're just too damned many of them."

"Exactly."

"Causeways, undersides of porches, below cellars, bottoms of steps, and I hear this guy's in the sewers."

Stroud went to a map of the city that Arnold had pinned against one wall. He found Humboldt Park on it and pointed. "He went in here, and inside ten minutes had eluded police in all directions, and they haven't figured out how."

"River's not too far from there," said Bob Arnold thoughtfully.

"River?"

"Tributary of the Chicago River, runs here, curls along here, goes up past Western and north. Used to be the centerpiece of the old amusement park, Riverview, remember?"

"So, you think he could've gotten to the river, swam out and away from the sewer system while McMasters and the rest of his crew were concentrating on the system?"

"Phil's probably figured it out by now."

Stroud stared at the map. "In which case McMasters would have sent his search teams south and north along the river."

"If they didn't give up."

"No, they're still out . . . new shifts coming on."

Stroud studied the map and the area along the river where Kerac might have eluded them. If he followed it northerly, he was going in the general direction of the residence where the Kerac family was still being kept under watch. Perhaps he was trying to make his way back to his brother and his brother's family. Perhaps in his calmer periods, Kerac still held out some hope that these people could help him . . . perhaps.

"We have stun guns, too. Very effective in rendering an animal helpless."

"Drugs?"

"Electricity, disables them long enough so we can get firm hold without getting torn to ribbons. That's how we got that pit bull out there."

"Good idea. Thanks, Bob. I'll get back to you when I have some idea where Kerac is."

"Look forward to it."

"And Bob—"

"Yeah?"

"Not a word to anyone about the operation, or that we had this conversation."

"Hey, man, since you left I've got rank! I call the shots from here."

"Great . . . knew I could count on you, Bobby."

"I have to talk to my men about the objective, however. Got to be sure they know what they're up against and how we plan to operate."

"Sure, understood, but—"

"My guys are the best, and they're loyal to me, Stroud. Not to worry."

Stroud thanked his friend again and left, going through the den of noise past the animal cages that lined both sides of the hallway. Animal Control needed more space.

Almost out the door, Stroud felt a shudder ripple through his body, a shudder of pain, fear and cold. He felt Kerac, as if the man's eyes were on him. He turned and saw the angry, snarling pit bull Bob had mentioned, staring into his gaze, his fangs bared. The dog butted its head viciously against the cage. It wanted nothing more than to tear out Stroud's throat.

Stroud's mind flashed on the standing, multicolored dead horses again.

His eyes were locked on the dog's eyes and he saw clearly what the meaning of the dead horses was.

He rushed back into Bob Arnold's "armory" room and went back to the map, Arnold astonished at the look on his face.

"Assemble your team, Bob. I know where the bastard is."

"Where?"

Stroud pointed to the map, his finger covering the area of Western Avenue at Addison.

Arnold knew what he meant in an instant. "Yeah, if I was right, and yeah, if he followed the river north."

"Horses, Bob."

"Horses?"

"He's in a place with a lot of stiff horses."

"Stiff horses?"

"A merry-go-round. It was a merry-go-round all along."

"Riverview Park?"

"How long will it take to get set up?"

"Place like that . . . to come in unnoticed . . . we'll need time to prepare."

"And about that stun gun, Bob. Bring 'em along, sure, but this guy is fast. You may need a dart gun with a dosage that won't kill a man, but is strong enough to bring down a . . . a wolf."

Bob Arnold looked squarely at him. "You think this guy's got a wolf with him for a pet?"

"It's no pet like you've seen before, Bob."

Just then they were interrupted by one of Arnold's staff who had escorted an aged man back to them. Stroud instantly recognized the old man's features and eyes as that of an Indian.

"I am here to talk to Stroud. Laughing More sent me."

"I'm Stroud." He extended his hand, but the old man did not take it, lifting his palm instead in the traditional gesture of greeting. Stroud returned this.

"I am Sam Warren. My tribal name means nothing to you. My little girl married Billy Kerac, and now my family is in danger."

"Oh, yes, Chief More told me about your situation, but I assure you the police are watching your house very carefully."

"This does not trouble me," said the stern old man, whose skin resembled dried leaf.

"Then what can I do for you?"

"She—Laughing More—thinks I am an old fool. She told me I should talk to another fool."

Stroud half smiled and said, "Meaning me?"

"Yes. Can we talk freely here?"

Stroud introduced Arnold and said that Arnold could be trusted. The old man began a tale about Wendigos, and, as an excuse to leave, Bob Arnold asked if anyone besides himself wanted coffee. After he was gone, the old man continued.

"Kerac was not a bad man, and now he is a wild animal. It is the work of the men who are wolves, the Wendigos."

"Then you believe they exist?"

"It is something that is hard for many to believe, but I saw such creatures once with my own eyes and have never forgotten. I saw many of them, in a bunch."

"How large a . . . a bunch, Mr. Warren?"

"Fifty, like buffalo, on the move."

Stroud wondered at the old man's story. He seemed a gentle man, but he also seemed out of his head.

"I knew you would not believe me, so I have brought you my pouch."

"Your pouch?"

"Strong medicine." He opened a leather bag and poured out its contents. "After I watched them all move off, I was curious about their hiding place, and I went into a cave there. I know it was foolish, but I was a boy then. I found a dead one there, but it was far too heavy to carry off, so I took these things from it."

Stroud was staring at a fang, and a thick dead finger with a huge claw attached. It was definitely an apelike or manlike finger, and the claw was far more than a long nail. It was like that of a bear. "Laughing More said you doctors study the hair of the beast and cannot determine what kind of hair it is. Take this to your doctors. Let them examine it, if you do not believe me."

"Are you sure you want to part with this?"

"For the good of my people, and yours, I must."

"And Laughing More sent you to me?"

"Yes, and now I will return home."

Stroud asked if he would like a ride. The old man was in baggy cotton trousers and a plaid shirt with a ripped, brown leather coat over this. He wore his hair braided beneath an old-timer's hat. "No, I must walk . . . good for the heart. Stroud, there've always been Wendigos . . . but now their numbers are growing, and they're coming down from the woods . . . Killed all of Kerac's animals and others' . . . and now people."

He left, and something of the old man remained behind, filling the room and filling Stroud's mind.

Cur . . . no, Ker . . . Ker-something . . . Kerac.

Kerac could not remember how he had gotten into the city; he could not recall how he had gotten the bloody wounds in his limbs that stung like so many bees, the pain spreading to his muscles, immobilizing him for most of the night and day. He was feeding on a bone, all that was left of the fleshy meat he had torn from a forgotten source. He feared the light in this environment and knew he must wait until nightfall to go on . . .

but to where? Where had he been going? There had been a need, an urgency to get somewhere, but now he didn't know what that need or that place could be.

Those hunting him had gone by in a boat along the river, doing a cursory search of the delapidated old area. None of them from the night before had come onto the concrete shore. He'd shivered, wet and cold, most of the night, hiding deep within the broken-down walls of a strange, dark structure. Across from him, directly in his line of vision, were the staring red and peeling eyes of an army of horses, all hard and cold to the touch. Something about the hard, lifeless animal touched a faint but resounding chord in his brain, something to do with a *Kerac.*

On another side of him were dirty, old and empty trash pails, stacks and stacks of delapidated posters and doorways . . . hundreds of multicolored doors standing on end, ripped from somewhere and dumped here. There was a wide, dark avenue just beyond, a valley lined with booth after booth to hide in just like the one he lay in now. Overhead, on wires, scraps of paper-thin, odorless flesh, batlike in appearance, flapped in the wind, suspended against the faint light that came from a noisy street not far away.

He heard the gentle lap of the water nearby. His lair was a good one. It had grown dark out. It was time to hunt and to feed.

He crawled out from below the cover of the weather-worn carnival booth when he heard a loud, crashing noise. He guessed from which direction it came and started away from it. He heard a similar noise, and another and another. It was a rattling, clanging, frightening noise and it grew louder and louder, and nearer and nearer, now coming from all sides.

He crouched and made his way to another booth, hiding there, staring out in all directions when he saw movement. They had found him. They were circling and closing in. His heart began to race, and fighting back the pain of earlier wounds, he raced to yet another booth along the fairway. They were closer still, the noise now deafening.

"Kerac . . . Keeeerrrraaaaac!" he heard a voice call out as if it were inside him. It so frightened him that he leaped from his hiding place and saw the gray and black figures with their lights encircling on all sides. He raced at one who screamed, shoving him down and continuing on, faster and faster. But the voice in his head he could not escape as it said, "Keeeeerrrraaaaac! Keeerrrraaaac!"

The chant sent him loping over a high fence.

"Fire! Fire!" he heard one of them shouting. He felt a ping graze his calf and something lodged into the fence beside him, and he was over the side, racing for the lights.

Car tires screeched in response, horns blowing as he raced for the darkness of an alleyway. Under the sodium vapor lights, Kerac's hairy body took on an alien glow. Cars collided around him. Men were coming over the fence in pursuit of him, swearing at one another.

"Fire!" he heard another shout, and suddenly he felt something sharp and painful strike his back. He tore at it with his claws, ripping it from him and throwing it down, where it shattered.

He saw a dark hole and crawled into it, knocking garbage pails over himself as he did so, his mind reeling in unfeeling circles when something like a heavy blanket clanged over the top of him and the metal cans.

"We've got him! We've got the bastard!" shouted Abe Stroud, waving the others on. Bob Arnold stood at his side with the dart gun that had fired the projectile that had struck Kerac between his shoulders.

"Yeah, but what the hell is it?" asked Arnold.

"A werewolf," said Stroud. "Or at least a man who thinks he's a werewolf."

The lights revealed an enormous, hairy humanoid below on the concrete steps where a drunken woman opened her door on the scene and screamed at the thing at her feet.

"Do you have a cell at Animal Control that will hold him?"

Arnold said, "Yeah, sure we do. We've got one we've never used . . . for a bear."

"I want him secured there. How long before the drug wears off?"

"Fifteen minutes tops, but we can use the stun on him now."

"Stun him enough, we'll kill him."

"Christ, Stroud . . . this thing . . . this ain't no man."

"What in hell is it?" asked one of Arnold's guys.

"Treat it as you do a dangerous pit bull that'd like nothing better than to rip off your arm and eat it before your eyes," said Stroud. "It's already killed twelve known."

"Maybe we ought to just put this thing down, then," said Bob Arnold, a look of disgust coming over his features as he stared at the writhing, intoxicated form of the wolfman. Its body hair covered most of its features, but the white palms, the eyes above the protruding snout, the erect way in which it had run, were humanlike.

Stroud said, "No, we can't chance it. If there are more like him, like the old man said, we have to know about their existence; we have to know how many there are. We may have to kill him in the end, but not before we are sure."

"This is too damned big for Animal Control, Stroud."

"If we turn it over to McMasters and regular channels, Bob, we'll never learn the truth."

"You're asking me to write this up as a dog-catching operation? I don't know if I can do that."

The Animal Control van was backed into the area,

"Please, Bob . . . just until we know the extent to which these . . . things exist. A couple of months ago Kerac here was a man, like you and me. Now look at him."

A plaintive howl escaped Kerac where he lay. Arnold sounded bitter and annoyed, but he shouted, "Careful with this one, guys; let's load him up. Keep your stunners at hand, but remember two blows at once could kill the . . . the thing. And we don't want that."

With that the men began hefting Kerac's half-conscious body as Kerac's wails brought people to their windows. Kerac was quickly got from sight and both Stroud and Arnold shouted to the lookers-on that they'd had a run-in with an escaped gorilla that didn't like the Shriners' company. People shouted remarks back, but soon disappeared.

"You really think you can get this past McMasters, Stroud?"

"Maybe not, but if we move fast, who knows." Stroud knew that McMasters was up all night and most of the day with the sewer dredging. If he acted quickly, he could conceivably return Kerac to the scene of the original crime, to the very spot where Kerac had first become a werewolf. In doing so, he could possibly locate the pack—if there was one.

He'd just have to be absolutely certain he didn't lose Kerac. And he'd need lots of help. Help from Anna More and Lou Cage, who'd gotten back today.

—12—

Abe Stroud held a light on Kerac there in the unlit cinder-block basement room at Animal Control, amazed at what they had captured. He'd read of rare sightings of creatures like Kerac, mythical man-beasts that recurrently appeared in rural places in France. In 1929, headlines had read, "Lionlike Creatures Fired on by Police, Leaving Hyenalike Tracks, Unharmed by Mere Bullets." He had heard of the Mineola ape, a creature that was seen by a dozen policemen in Mineola, Long Island, fired on but unharmed in 1931. The creature was described as walking upright, like a man, about four or five feet tall with a brown chest—like Kerac's—covered with coarse, bearlike hair. Like Kerac, the so-called Mineola ape was said to have a long, wolfish, gray face. Some ten people within a three-day period saw the mysterious animal. Police officials thought the "ape" was a baboon or gorilla that'd made an escape from a menagerie or traveling circus, but there had been no such carnivals in the area. It escaped into the forests and was never seen again.

Kerac's snoutlike mouth was a gray muzzle, his elongated teeth behind the curled lip were inhuman in size and shape. The dimensions of his snout showed a preponderance on the mouth, and his horribly deformed hands and feet displayed the tough talons of a beast ready to tear Stroud apart if he dared come too close.

It was truly a remarkable discovery. Kerac's condition was no longer that of a lycanthrope, for he no longer enjoyed even a brief moment as a man any longer. The beast within had taken over wholly and completely. It was a phenomenon that destroyed all known laws of physics, and without Kerac as Stroud's physical evidence, no one—not even those looking at Kerac as Stroud now stared across at the beast—would be willing to believe it possible.

The enormous claws, which had already done so much deadly harm, shot out toward Stroud, and Kerac bellowed in a roar that shook the room.

"McMasters and the others get a hold of you and you're dead, Kerac! Is there any part of you left that understands me?"

The beast bellowed, a sad final note from the complaining brain before it sat in a ball in the corner of its cell. It looked for all the world like a bored ape in a zoo, but the coloration, the gray snout, and the wirelike brown and gray body-hair was that of a grizzled dog or wolf.

Stroud had read up on the history of man's superstitions regarding wolves, the greatest of all being that the bite of a wolf could turn a man into a wolfman. Most of the stories settled for medicine men who dressed in the skins of the dead animals, covering their faces with the dead snouts, frightening a primitive people into subjugation. But why, then, was the idea of lycanthropy and the wolfman so doggedly persistent in the human psyche? Suppose that the old Indian was right and had actually seen a band of roving wolf-people? Had one of them bitten Kerac during his journey into the forests with his charges? Had these creatures and not Kerac killed the hunting party, Kerac somehow surviving, only to become one of the wolf party himself?

Stroud had called Cage telling him to come secretly to Animal Control. Stroud knew that he could not long keep the fact of Kerac's capture from the authorities, but he knew men like McMasters wouldn't hesitate to place a bullet through Kerac's skull, since he was the worst kind of vermin in police circles—a cop killer. As soon as the P.A. policemen were murdered, 30,000 cops had but one aim in mind for Kerac.

Lou Cage came into the darkned room now. "Abe? You in here?" Cage found a light and turned it on. Kerac let out a bloodcurdling scream as the fluorescents caused great pain to his pupils. The creature covered its eyes in a mad scramble, forcing its muzzle nose into its fur, hiding within itself like a terrified dog.

"Jesus, Mother of God!" said Lou, staring at Kerac.

"Cut the lights, Lou!"

Cage did so, fumbling. "Why didn't you tell me?"

"Not over an open line."

"What, is there some secret here?"

"Lou, he's no good to us dead. I want to fly him down to the mansion and—"

"Andover? You're going to take him to Andover? Stroud, you know the scene in *Frankenstein* where all the townsfolk come after the doctor's head?"

"Lou, I have good reason. I suspect there are *others* of his kind."

Lou Cage said nothing in the semidarkness; from up above, the two men could hear the wailing and noise of caged animals. Kerac was curiously quiet. "Strange," said Lou.

"What's that?"

"Kept denying it myself."

"Denying what, Lou?"

"The marks on the victims in that hunting party in Grand Rapids. All the work of the same monster, yes, but it didn't all add up. Like, some tears and rips were small by comparison to others—all clawlike, sure, but some were small, and so were some of the teeth marks, and I kept saying to myself, it doesn't add up."

"Then there's evidence that Kerac was not alone in his attack on the hunters?"

"Stroud . . . I wasn't looking for it, but some of the wounds seemed to be made by smaller animals. I chalked it up to passing raccoons maybe, or a badger, you know? Sniffing at the bodies. They lay out there for several days . . . but now . . . I don't know."

"If there are others, and if they propagate, there would be young ones in the . . . the pack."

"McMasters learns you're keeping this from him, Abe, and you could be jailed for obstruction; hell, both of us—for conspiracy to . . . to . . . what is it we're doing?"

"I've already arranged to take him out. Once we're established at the manse, you can send us some word on the blood samples you're going to take."

"Blood samples? Mind telling me what I'm looking for?"

"Anything unusual. What makes him a beast? What's become of the man inside? What precisely are we dealing with here? I want you to take some venom from—"

"Venom! That's it. There was a toxin in the old people which I couldn't identify, like a snake's venom—paralyzes prey."

"And when the creature doesn't feed on its prey, the paralysis wears off, but the venom remains in the system, turning a

normal man into a madman and killer and what you see before
you now."

"A werewolf . . ."

"You see the importance of keeping him alive, don't you,
Lou?"

Cage considered this a moment. "If there are others . . . yes,
we must track them down."

"And destroy them. They're not benign creatures, and if their
population is on the rise, accounting for the many bigfoot sightings
all over that area . . . well, you see the danger Kerac placed this
entire city in."

"But you found him. How did you do it, Abe?"

"The curse again . . ."

"Not a curse this time. Thank God for your *gift*, Abe; no telling
how many lives you've saved. McMasters can choke on that."

The door burst open and Stroud thought he'd find the affable
Bob Arnold, but when he turned, his light illuminated the faces
of Anna More, McMasters and several uniformed policemen, the
blue-suits with their guns pulled and pointed at Stroud, Cage and,
in the backdrop, the wild man, Kerac.

"Now we got your ass, Stroud," said McMasters nastily. "We
got your whole damned scam on tape. Room was bugged, pal!"

"Are you crazy, McMasters!" shouted Cage. "You should be
thanking this man. He's stopped Kerac from killing again where
you failed."

Behind the crowd strode a huge man with white hair in a
three-piece suit. Stroud recognized Police Commissioner Aaron
Burns. Burns had worked on a case in close connection with
Stroud in the past, and Stroud was glad to see him.

"Where is this thing?" said Burns, ignoring the others and
stepping close to the cage. "Put a light on it." Burns was always
gruff, always anxious to cut to the core of things.

"Careful," said Stroud. "You get too close, and he'll take an
arm off or bite a hole in your face."

Burns was paralyzed, however, as the light played over the
thing in the corner of the cell. A big man, Burns blocked the
view of the others. Anna More went to the far side of the cage.
She, too, seemed mesmerized by the monster.

"Do you really expect anyone to believe that this thing was
once a man?"

"Commissioner Burns," said Stroud, "Kerac is *it*. *It* is Kerac,
and there *it* stands."

He turned, shaken; he looked deeply into Stroud's eyes. "This man changed into an animal?"

"Yes, Aaron, from all we can deduce—"

"And you suspect there are others?"

"That is a possibility."

"And you want to study him, and eventually release him?"

"That's madness!" shouted McMasters.

"Quiet, Mac!" said Burns. He took Stroud aside. Stroud's attention was half on Anna Laughing More, however, as she was still frozen in place, staring at what remained of Kerac. Kerac made a plaintive cry, heart-wrenching, like an animal caught in a trap. Stroud wanted to go to Anna, put an arm around her, steady her, but Burns was in his face.

"You're sure . . . absolutely sure?"

"My instincts tell me so, and the evidence supports it."

"What evidence?"

Lou Cage piped in. "Forensics, sir, points to the strong possibility there are others of them."

"Where?"

"Wooded areas north of Grand Rapids would be our target area," said Stroud.

"Do you have any idea how this would read in an official report, Stroud? What the papers would do with it?"

"Yes, sir . . . I think so."

McMasters pushed forth. "I say we gas the damned thing the way we would a rabid dog. Now."

"McMasters!" shouted Burns. "Consider it *out* of your hands."

"What?" He was incredulous. Stroud himself was a little surprised that Burns was taking his side. "But, sir!"

"Wait outside," he told McMasters firmly, and the other man grumbled but left. Burns called out after him, "And not a word of this to anyone."

Burns then took Stroud further from the others, Stroud glancing back at Anna, who still stared into the cage. Burns said in his ear, "There's been another report out of a small town north of Grand Rapids, report of some sort of mutilation in triplicate. A farmhouse attacked. Everyone destroyed in the same manner as Kerac's victims. Yet Kerac is here in custody . . ."

"I see."

"Just got it fresh an hour ago. McMasters knows nothing about it; he's been up all night searching for what you have aptly brought under control, Abe." His tone changed in the darkened room. "I think your plan is the best chance we have. Take Lou Cage, and whoever else you need, and whatever assistance the CPD can give. You just contact me, understood?"

Cage, leaning in to hear, said, "Thanks for asking, Commissioner."

Burns shook Stroud's hand, grasping with both his own in the gesture of a man running for office, but in Burns' case, the gesture was genuine. "We're all counting on you, Dr. Stroud."

"Wish I had as much confidence in myself."

"You're the man for this job. Keep me posted, and contact me for anything you may need."

"Will do."

"All right!" Burns shouted to the uniformed cops around the room. "Everyone out. Let Dr. Stroud get to work." He stopped at the door and turned and said to Anna More, "And very nice to have met you, Chief More."

She said nothing; she just stared down at the hairy creature balled up in its cage, wooden-looking toenail-claws extended like an angry cat. Burns disappeared, leaving Cage and Stroud to deal with Anna Laughing More.

Anna pulled away from Stroud's touch. "We should kill him here and now, like McMasters says!" she shouted. "Put him from his misery! Are you forgetting that there is a human being in there?" She backed up, lifted her gun and aimed and fired just as Stroud grabbed her wrists, diverting the shot aimed at Kerac's head.

The gunshot ricocheted off the cinder-block wall with a deafening scream and spat to a halt somewhere the other side of the room where Cage cursed, "Sonofabitch!"

Stroud wrenched the weapon from her and she slapped him. "That's enough, Anna!"

"This is wrong," she cried, "inhuman!"

"He's our only link to the others."

She began to cry, going for the door. He pursued her and turned her around. In the dark, their eyes met. "I understand how you feel—"

"Do you?" she asked. "If that were someone you once cared for?"

"We need Kerac alive for now."

"And should he escape you?"

"Cage is going to put a transmitter on him. When we release him, we'll know his every move."

"You've got it all worked out, then. Every detail. He's just a specimen to you now."

"It's not like that, Anna."

"I wish I could believe you."

"Burns didn't tell you about the new attack?"

"What new attack?"

"I suppose he figured your people contacted you from Merimac, but there's been a fresh kill, another family . . . north of Grand Rapids."

"Coincidence," she said lamely, her eyes filled with doubt.

"Maybe . . . but then, perhaps the old Indian man was right. Maybe there are others like Kerac—a whole army of them. It would account for the slaughtered livestock, Anna."

She said nothing, shaking her head, not wanting to believe.

"That's why we need him alive. If it's any comfort, I don't think there's anything left of Kerac inside this thing. I get no sensations or feelings from him than those of a purely instinctive beast."

"Creature comfort," Cage said a bit glibly. "No moral compunction, no ethical problems to solve, just feed."

"Any chance Kerac has is in Cage's hands," said Stroud.

"Me?" asked Cage.

"If we can extract the venom, perhaps some sort of antidote could be found."

"Whoa, Stroud. Isolating the venom, finding a cure, could take forever."

"Don't you think he's suffered enough?" she asked.

Stroud squeezed her hands in his. "No, not yet, I'm afraid."

"Your plan could take a long time. I won't be a party to it. I . . . I will be returning to Merimac."

"I see."

"There I will tell them that Kerac was captured and killed."

"You . . ." Stroud hesitated. He didn't want her to leave this way. "Are you sure?"

"Yes. It's time I got back . . . and removed myself from this. When . . . if . . . you return to Michigan with your werewolf hunting party, call me. I will want to be there."

"Anna," he said, holding firm to her hand, "I will miss you."

She said nothing, dropping her eyes and rushing out.

–13–

Several days and nights passed with Kerac firmly in place in Abraham Stroud's mansion, in Andover, Illinois. Cage had extracted blood and venom samples from the creature before leaving Chicago, and now the results were in and Cage sat in the huge drawing room, explaining the results as best he might to Stroud. Below them, in a room that was once a torture chamber of sorts, at the heart of the old manse, Kerac enjoyed the accommodations less than he had the police pound where they first met. Whenever the eyes inside the creature's head fell on Stroud, they filled with murderous rage.

Stroud's mansion in Andover, Illinois, had been left to him along with a fortune in family funds by his grandfather, who had spent his life as a shrewd businessman by day, a vampire killer by night. The dark, old stone mansion with its wrought-iron gates and bars across the windows had survived the Civil War, and more recently a war with vampires. Evidence of destruction was being obliterated by the army of repairmen Stroud continued to employ.

Andover was providing a quiet, out-of-the-way place to keep Kerac in captivity and out of sight. Meanwhile, the tests went ahead. Kerac's cell was monitored twenty-four hours a day via remote cameras. The film was sifted for any changes in him, particularly any changes back to his former self. There had been none.

"He's been totally taken over by the beast," Stroud told Cage. "Not once has he reverted."

"So much for the myth," said Cage. "Lon Chaney, he isn't."

"And your findings?"

Stroud and Cage shared a plate filled with meats and breads and cheeses as well as their wine. "Afraid I'm going to destroy a few other illusions we have about werewolves, Abe."

"Destroy away."

"Well, the blood is thick with animal red corpuscles, quite similar to a dog's, coyote's, or wolf's, and genetically that thing you have downstairs is a wolfman. Human genes disfigured by those of a wolf. Massive changes at the cellular level . . . accounts for the shape-changing. Quite Jekyll-and-Hyde-like at first, but then Hyde won over completely, as you say."

"Then he . . . it's no longer human?"

"Not in a biological sense."

"What sense, then?"

"He may retain some human characteristics, cognitive skills—"

"He still thinks human thoughts?"

"I would hazard a guess, yes."

"What kind of human thoughts are we talking about? Home, family, kids?"

"Survival."

"Just glad Anna isn't here to hear this."

Cage nodded. "I second the motion. She'd start shooting again." Cage filled his mouth with food.

"What about the venom? You said you had isolated the paralytic properties."

"Form of curare—"

"But that's a plant toxin."

"Tubocurarine chloride, Abe. He somehow manufactures it in that primitive brain. It renders a man helpless, paralyzed; unfortunately, the victim is quite aware of his surroundings, just unable to move."

"For how long?"

"Depends on the dosage. Enough and it'd kill a man."

Stroud shook his head, went to a large window and stared out through the bars there. "Strange, you'd think it'd kill him if it was in his system."

"Only way to determine how he gets it from the brain to his teeth, or fangs, rather, is a dissection."

"Out of the question. We need him, Lou, alive. What about an antitoxin?"

"You're asking the impossible, but that stuff we gave him to keep him calm may hold some promise. Seems to short-circuit the venom. If we can boost it, maybe."

Cage was speaking of the antipsychotic drug thiothixene, which had had the desired effect of keeping Kerac in a peaceful state of acceptance. Cage had said that if the authorities at the Merimac facility had seen to it that Kerac got such a drug, the venom in his system might not have taken control in the first place and the oddity of a werewolf would not have surfaced.

Cage began talking as if to himself now. "Fascinating creature, we have here, Stroud. Somehow cytogenic. It can—"

"Cyto? Genic?"

"It has the ability to create living cells, new cells we've never seen before. Those tissue samples I took . . . amazing. Yes, cytogenic, like the ovaries or testicles, capable of regeneration of living cells—"

"And child-bearing by extension."

"Exactly, but what I was getting at is the fact . . . It would appear that one of his organs, the thyroid or the parathyroid, acting at the behest of the thalmus—"

Stroud knew this was the more primitive part of the brain.

"For Christ's sake, I don't know. Pure speculation, but something up in his head directed a gene change, remolded his goddamned chromosomes with some kind of hormone we may never discover, Abe."

"Man-made monster . . . brainchild of mankind? Manufactured in a primitive part of his own brain," said Stroud. "Just needed a boost. Waiting in the dark interior all the time—just for a boost? Strange . . ."

"I suppose it could be released in any man, Abe . . . any one of us."

"The beasts within . . ."

"Exactly . . . The shape of things to come? Or the shape of things long gone?"

"We've got to create an antidote. Failing this, we must have an effective weapon against the likes of Kerac," Abe said after some silence.

"Dr. Stroud! Come quickly!" It was Ashyer, Stroud's manservant, who had been taking a turn at monitoring the camera focused on the creature several flights below in its cell. "He's . . . he's changing!"

Stroud, followed by Cage, rushed to the display screen. There they saw some features fading from Kerac's face. The coloration from brown to gray to lighter tones and back again. The snout was receding. Kerac was screaming in pain and terror. "We'll have it on film," said Stroud. "He's metamorphosing. Lycanthropy, filmed for the first time."

"Hold on," said Cage. "He's regressing."

It was true. The flickering images of the man beneath the beast died away quickly, recaptured by the features of the monster. The snout raised to the camera, and it wailed out in a mournful, even sad cry, wishing desperately to be released.

Stroud was disappointed for reasons other than the film that would have made history. He was disappointed for Kerac, who, apparently, had given in wholly to the disease that had claimed his mind, so powerful that it had made of him a thing of inhuman proportions, a throwback to man's ancestral ape.

When they ran the tape back, searching for signs of the minimal change that'd taken place, it lasted but forty-nine seconds, and the focus was not good. A disappointed Stroud said, "Kerac was a weak man. Maybe he could have fought this thing if he wasn't weak."

"He was taken over by a very toxic drug, Stroud."

"Nevertheless, he was inherently weak and that's what ultimately sealed his fate. Well, feeding time for him, Ashyer, and be certain to take all the usual precautions. Nowhere within ten feet of the damned thing."

"Not to worry on that score, sir."

Stroud and Cage sauntered back down the long corridor to their waiting lunch. As they did so, they talked quietly. "I'm beginning to feel like a friggin' zookeeper here, Lou. And every day we hold him here is a day closer to his being discovered."

"Yeah, I know . . . saw a few reporters in Andover, you said?"

"Definitely Chicago written all over these guys. One in particular is stalking us."

"Your sources as usual are good."

"One persistent reporter followed you from Chicago, the man known as the Peregrine—Perry Gwinn. He's been hanging about the Holiday Inn, asking a hundred questions, certain he's onto the scent of a big story. McMasters probably spilled it to him."

"So, I may have to go with an alternate plan now the transmitter's been implanted under Kerac's skin. Can't wait for an antivenin much longer."

"You've had the implant done?"

"Last night."

"Someone you can trust, I hope."

"Had him flown in for the operation. He was shaken up a bit, but Dr. Orin Grammersy did a fine job. Placed it below the skin of the forearm after sedating Kerac."

"Grammersy? University of Chicago? Christ, no wonder the word's leaked. He's got a big mouth."

"I've sworn him to secrecy."

"And you're just naive enough to believe that means a god-damned thing to a man like Grammersy? Oh, Stroud, you have a lot to learn, and as for those archeologists at the U. of C., if they get wind of this—"

"You really think that Kerac is a walking *missing link* of some sort?"

"Undeniably, and it proves the old theory put forth by Leaky and Robert Ardrey, that man evolved not from a benevolent ape, but a murderous, ravenous beast." They sat in silence a moment.

"Come on, Lou," said Abe. "I want to show you a weapon I have in development."

"Here?"

"I have a team of scientists living in the east wing, and they've been given everything they need. As we've received reports from you, we've worked on combating agents. They began with some acids."

"Acids?"

"Yes."

"Do you have any idea how sensitive Kerac's olfactory organs are? Not to mention his eyes and ears. You'll not get within feeding distance, and if you should, he'll choose you over an acid anytime, Abe. He likes red meat."

"We're working on an odorless version."

"To you and me it may have no odor, but to Kerac it will always have odor. He'll detect it."

"If they're hungry enough, they'll overcome distaste and distrust to bite, Lou. We just have to bait them."

Lou shook his head, saying, "Sounds too much like fishing to me. Damn it, you'll need the real thing once you're up there in Michigan."

"I know that, but as you say, it's getting warm around here."

Cage's mouth dropped open when Stroud pushed the doors to the east ballroom open. The expansive room was filled with laboratory equipment and men in white coats. "All at your disposal, Lou."

"What do you want me to begin with, Abe? Silver-bullet fashioning maybe?"

"You might tell me what properties in silver might weaken or destroy a thing like Kerac, see if the old tale has any validity."

"Silver . . . yes . . . as a counteragent to the unknown hormone that creates such growth in the bones and muscles . . ." Lou was already anxious and curious. "Perhaps silver nitrate as a poison."

"Can we get it in a form that can be used on the tips of our bullets?"

Lou laughed lightly. "Yes, I see your point. I'm off to work again."

On the monitoring screen, Ashyer stared as never before at the creature he had been feeding. He had had no idea that below the hair was a man. He knew that Dr. Stroud was a good man, and that all he did was for everyone's good . . . but he had been shaken by the man's eyes deep within the furrows of the creature's brow and mane. It was as if he had seen a drowning man inside the creature, and Ashyer wanted to extend a hand and pull him out of death's maw.

Yet, Stroud had interviewed Kerac every day, trying desperately to reach out to the man who was drowning, to no avail. Perhaps it was too late. Perhaps he had drowned. Perhaps he knew no more than a caged animal, after all, thought Ashyer. At any rate, Ashyer owed his life to Stroud, and he would not betray the man who had freed Andover of its vampire curse. Still, the sight of the man within the monster continued to haunt Ashyer long after he was relieved, and long after he lay his head down on his pillow next to his wife, who, thank God, had been kept apart from the creature.

Perry Daniel Gwinn had been the first to cultivate his own nickname, Peregrine, first in college, where he was the editor for the Northwestern University *Norther,* and later with Lerner News in Chicago, and finally with the great and famous Field Enterprises newspaper the *Chicago Tribune.* As an investigative reporter, Gwinn had toppled crooked aldermen, brought randy judges to their knees and helped put an end to unsafe practices in geriatric care in and around the city. But he had done his best work on the crime beat, and when he got the scent of a big police story, nothing could stand in his way, not even distance. He had flown in a private jet to the little-known town of Andover, Illinois, where Abraham Hale Stroud kept an aged mansion encircled by huge, black wrought-iron gates.

Gwinn had been standing in the crowd of reporters at the Port Authority, and he had seen the mutilated bodies of the two P.A. officers; he had seen how Stroud entered the scene with such odd dispatch and diffidence, a strange ability to distance himself from the gore, and then his sudden and theatrical fainting spell. It all smacked of some sort of strange collusion on the part of the police and this outsider who was, according to Gwinn's sources, a former insider—one of the cops. Gwinn had reviewed Stroud's record, which was impressive but puzzling. Stroud had been called Chicago's "psychic cop." But Gwinn was beginning to wonder seriously if the man should not have earned the title of "psycho cop" instead. He was what Gwinn's northern New York relatives would call a very odd duck.

Why had Stroud suddenly shown up again there in the city, ostensibly trailing a maniacal killer that had mysteriously broken free of a maximum security prison in Merimac, Michigan? How much did he really know about this man the police were after, this John Kerac? Had Stroud somehow been involved in Kerac's release up in Merimac? Odd stories about Stroud that circulated about the Chicago Police Department characterized him as a fringe lunatic himself, and the records of Hinze V.A. Hospital showed that he was the recipient of a steel plate in his head after his tour of duty in Vietnam.

Gwinn had done his homework, but it was not enough to explain the dire consequences of the horrific killing spree of a former Grand Rapids trail guide through the streets of Chicago, and then the sudden end of the spree and the coincidental announcement from the police that Kerac had been killed by the police and his body cremated at the cost of the city along with the disappearance of Stroud and company. Gwinn wasn't sure he bought it; Gwinn wasn't sure that Stroud, with all his inherited millions, was not involved in a complicated and bizarre experiment involving the use of asylum inmates, especially murderous ones like Kerac.

Who knew, who could guess the limits of power such a fortune as Stroud's could reach; who had any idea how much the man could buy into? Stroud had left Chicago to take up his grandfather's wealth when the old man died, but he had also by then become a genuine, certified archeologist with a degree from the U. of C. Gwinn wondered at the combination, thinking it an odd mix: criminological studies to archeological studies. Was Stroud into crime through the ages? Certainly had a massive canvas, if it were so. But what about crimes being committed by Stroud himself now?

Gwinn imagined Stroud in the little village of Merimac, *buying* the use of the criminally insane for some experiment which Gwinn had as yet to determine. Gwinn imagined Stroud taking this character Kerac—for whom there existed not a single photograph—under his tutelage and care. He could even imagine Stroud buying the man's freedom for visits to some secret laboratory, all very much against human decency and law. Gwinn imagined Kerac being given electric shocks and concoctions of drugs and mixed elixirs of all sorts, trying to make some determinations about the "archeology" of the criminal mind. To make head or tail of a man like Kerac who had diabolically eaten his victims!

What had led Stroud to the slip on the Calumet River to view the bloody work of a maniac gone free to rampage a city? Had Stroud known that Kerac was posited on one of the incoming ships? Hidden in a box deep in a cargo bay by Stroud's army of gofers? Had Stroud been shipping the sonofabitch through Chicago to his place in Andover for further and exhaustive studies?

By God, Perry Gwinn was going to find out.

When Stroud disappeared from Chicago, Gwinn had kept Stroud's old friend, Dr. Lou Cage, the coroner, under constant surveillance. Now he had followed Cage to Andover and to the site of the infamous Stroud Manse just outside the small, rural city. Here—if sources could be believed—the eccentric millionaire held court, and he sometimes condemned people to chains in an old dungeon somewhere below the enormous pre–Civil War collection of stone the house represented. Much of what was said about Stroud had the ring of nonsense and lunacy, and yet Gwinn had learned that even from the worst source something could be culled, and it was in the culling that Gwinn felt a quickening of his pulse and a high like nothing sex or food had ever proffered his way. Gwinn had seen much on his Chicago beat, and the kind of lunacy he often reported in the daily pages in his adopted city had opened his mind up for anything—*anything*.

He found it intriguing that Stroud was something of a psychic and that people like Commissioner Aaron Burns regarded Stroud with something akin to awe, or political hand-holding, or whatever the fuck it was. He also thought it of great interest to the people of Chicago, Gwinn's reason for being, his public. They had a right to know more about Abraham H. Stroud's presence and the fact the CPD was being led by the nose by a rich citizen who happened to have once been a detective. Moreover, Stroud had been seen at the Port Authority slaying looking like a man who had lost a boa constrictor and was anxious to get it back. If his Chicago contacts in Animal Control back home could be believed, the rich man had gotten his snake back under lock and key, and the thing that had killed those people in Michigan and then in Chicago was here somewhere.

Gwinn determined to find out—to get snapshots and the full story.

Lights in the mansion were going out all over. Gwinn moved in with the rats.

He skirted about the perimeter of the old house, finding no guards, encouraged. He went about the grounds, peeking in ground-floor windows through the odd black bars. He noticed the bars formed black crosses, finding the pattern bizarre. He made his way around back and was almost seen when he turned a corner. He ducked back. Two young fellows in white smocks catching a smoke, looking out at the meandering Spoon River in the distance, one pointing and the other shoving him and laughing. They'd apparently exited a doorway that now stood open.

Gwinn tried to think clearly. In a moment, he lifted a stone and flung it into the distance. This caused a stir between the two smokers, and together, they went to investigate the source of the noise. Gwinn slipped past them and through the hallway door they'd exited. He was on the inside.

Ashyer could not sleep, try as he may. He could not rid himself of John Kerac's shimmying features and eyes within the horrifying form of the creature. He had an idea, perhaps a useless one, yet one which he could not hold in check. He would go to Kerac and sit with him, trying to coax him back. He would tell him how Stroud's grandfather had once coaxed Ashyer and his wife back from death when they were languishing victims of the vampire bite. And if this did not work, he would talk to Stroud about two possibilities: either torture Kerac, to bring him to *feel* the man within, or put the poor bastard out of his misery. Stroud's grandfather would do no less.

He'd try sitting and talking to the beast as one man to another first. Ashyer felt it useless, but he must try.

He was on his way toward the door and stairwell that would take him to Kerac when someone grabbed him from behind, placing a choke hold on him.

"Do as I say, and you'll come to no harm."

"Who are you?"

"Never mind that. I've seen on your monitor what you men are holding in the cell. Now take me to the cell. I want to see this man you're holding hostage."

"But he's extremely—"

"Shut up! Do as you're told!" Perry Gwinn tightened the hold on Ashyer. "I have a gun and will not hesitate using it, if necessary. Lead the way, and no tricks."

"It's not a man."

"Shut up! I saw him on the monitor."

Ashyer wondered if he dare believe that Kerac had changed again. At the end of the hall he could see that the man who had been at the monitor had been knocked out by the intruder.

Ashyer hesitated at the door. No one was to know of the secret chamber below, the circular room that was the focal point and the psychic energy of the mansion. A cold, hard gun barrel changed Ashyer's mind. "Yes, sir."

They made their way down the spiral stone steps leading to the dungeon room where Kerac was being kept in a man-sized cage.

Ashyer was pushed through the final door by the intruder, falling to his face in his pajamas, scraping a knee, within a few inches of the cage, certain the monster would have his head in the next instant. But he looked up to see a naked man with a nasty, filth-ridden appearance staring down at him from inside the cell. It was Kerac.

"Whhhhooooo arrrrrrr yuuuuuuu'?" Kerac asked them. "Wheeeeerrrr am I?"

Ashyer, getting to his feet, saw the terrible, dirty gash on the man's penis just before Gwinn's gun struck him in the temple, knocking him senseless.

Gwinn searched the room for the key and found a large jailer's key on a peg in the wall. He went for the cage, about to open it, when Kerac's hands came through and grasped his, holding firm.

"Let go, you fool! I'm getting you out! I'm a reporter. You tell me what this creep Stroud's done to you, and we'll see he's put away for life!"

But Kerac's grip on Gwinn only increased. So painful was the hold on his wrists that Gwinn thought his bones would pop, and then he heard the bones cracking, and he saw Kerac's features changing before him, saw the screaming snout erupt from the dirty, bruised face, saw the hair covering all, felt the claws dig into him as they grew out of Kerac's hands. Gwinn screamed again and again, feeding the raw desire in Kerac, fueling his change.

Gwinn's eyes bulged as the pain of the twisting of his left arm from its socket made him go limp, while the creature was gleeful at tearing his arm completely off, throwing it across the cell. Gwinn's screams died in his throat, lost there when Kerac's claws severed his jugular, spewing forth blood that exploded to the walls, the ceiling, and across Ashyer's prone form.

Gwinn's heart gave out long before his blood.

–14–

Stroud stood at the monitor, helping the man who had been knocked senseless there to his feet, when his ear was alerted to Gwinn's screams coming through the monitor. This was followed by Kerac's familiar bellow. Stroud stared in horror at the scene played out before him as the cameras rolled. Kerac's snout came to Gwinn's face in an obscene kiss, and snuggling through the bars, he tore off Gwinn's left side, chewing on the tissue before Gwinn's glazed other eye. The moment he was bitten, Gwinn's screams subsided and he went slack, unable to kick or fight, but quite aware of what mad thing was happening to him.

Stroud had no idea who the poor bastard was. Then Stroud saw Ashyer lying in a heap near the back of the cage. Lou and some of the others found Stroud as he shouted, "Jesus! Ashyer!" Stroud ran for the stairs, praying he could get to Ashyer in time, praying the monster would continue to feed on its first kill before going for his servant.

Stroud took the stone stairwell two and three at a time, shouting Ashyer's name out, trying desperately to rouse the unconscious figure.

Something like a hand pushing at him in his sleep had roused Stroud, and he sensed now that it had been the ghost of his grandfather. He fell coming down the stairs, got to his feet and pushed through the half-opened door. Kerac's eyes looked up at him with the venom clearly sparking fire there. He was watching

Stroud's every twitch, every gesture, and Stroud sensed that if he tried for Ashyer without a diversion, Kerac would surely tear into him, just to spite Stroud. For the moment, Kerac still held the limp, blood-gushing body of his first victim. The animal's snout was red with Gwinn's insides. Parts of Gwinn had been ripped off and pulled through the bars.

Stroud made a show of trying to help the intruder, but below his feet lay the key, so Stroud made for this, coming dangerously close to being grabbed by Kerac, whose claws cut a swath in Stroud's nightshirt. All the while, Stroud was shouting for Ashyer to get up and get out of harm's way. Cage trundled in at the same instant. Stroud shouted for him to get hold of Ashyer and pull him off as Stroud tempted the monster with himself now as bait. Gwinn's lifeless torso was hurled angrily at Stroud.

Cage pulled Ashyer by the feet away from the monster's reach.

"Get back, Abe!" shouted Cage. "I've got Ashyer!"

Stroud stood his ground, bloodied from the carcass that had been cast at him. He stood eye-to-eye with Kerac, just out of reach of its grasp as the creature tore at him. He could feel the powerful claws as they swiped by his eyes.

"You bastard thing," Stroud said to it. "You're going back to the Hell from which you came. I'll see to that."

Stroud stepped off to the wail of frustration and hatred coming from the creature behind him. "Who is he, which of the men is this fool?"

Some of the white-coated scientists had to give way to Mrs. Ashyer, who pushed through, frantic about her husband. She found him and held his head in her lap, assured by Cage that he was all right. She saw the remains strewn about the concrete floor and walls, but she had seen so much over the years in this manse that she did not scream.

Cage flashed a light onto what was left of the Peregrine. "That's Perry Gwinn, of the *Trib* in Chicago . . . I think."

"Christ, that cuts it. What'll we do with him? Send him home in a box to the city editor?"

Inside the cage Kerac was feeding on one of Gwinn's arms.

"Sedate the damned thing again!" ordered Stroud. "I'm sick of this, Cage. Sick to death."

"I think you'd best call Commissioner Burns," replied Cage. "Let him handle this one."

"Maybe Anna More was right, Lou. Maybe we ought to destroy Kerac while we have him—now, tonight."

"Everybody out," said Lou to the others gaping at the carnage. "Get the dart gun, Harris. See to it the creature is put under so we can get this mess cleaned up."

"If we'd gassed him in Chicago like McMasters said, another man would be alive today," Stroud said, staring back at Gwinn's brutalized remains, half a face and one eye staring back at him.

"This is not your fault, Abe! Gwinn was a fool to come in here and go near that cage! What could have been in the fool's mind? Taking the key, going within reach of that beast?"

Ashyer had come around and he now groaned and said, "Kerac was a man again . . ."

Stroud knelt down beside Ashyer. "What're you saying, Mr. Ashyer?"

"I saw him . . . fully returned . . . as a man, and so did this other fellow, the one that hit me, sir. He thought we were holding a man against his will, torturing him, from the look of it. Kerac was filthy, wounds clearly visible, blood-clotted."

"That's the remarkable property about the animal-like blood," said Cage. "Much more effective clotting agents, high concentration of platelets."

"Then Kerac is still alive," said Stroud. "Alive and trapped inside *that*." Stroud pointed at the snarling monster.

Harris, one of Cage's assistants, had returned with the dart gun. He aimed and fired, the dart striking Kerac in the rump. The creature grabbed at the dart, yanking it out before becoming woozy. In a moment he stumbled, got up and weakly slid along the bars, falling facedown, his bloodied snout poking through the bars.

"It's time we make our move, Lou."

"But we haven't perfected a killing agent, Stroud."

"We go with what we have, the poison—"

"Won't work."

"The silver nitrate."

"You have to give me more time."

"You have until nightfall tomorrow. I'll have assembled a strike force and we'll be on our way to Michigan with Kerac in tow."

"What kind of strike force, Abe?"

"Mercenaries."

"Men you know?"

"I know their leader. We served together in Vietnam."

"I see, and he hasn't quit playing soldier yet?"

Stroud dropped his gaze at this. "Lou, I know of no one I wish to endanger further with this madness, but these men are ready, willing and capable to fight any enemy so long as they are paid well."

"Well, when they see Kerac, they're likely to want double. What about me? You don't intend to leave me behind, do you?"

"No, I'm afraid your services may be needed."

"And Chief More?"

"She's out of it, and I'd like it to stay that way."

"She telephones here daily, asking when, Abe. She's no fool. She'll know, and she has a vested interest."

"I don't want her in harm's way."

"I understand that, but—"

"No more said about it, Lou."

"Well, we have work to do in the lab, Harris," he said to his assistant, "get whatever help you need, clean up here and return to the lab." Cage then poked Abe Stroud with a stern finger and said, "No one could have anticipated this ridiculous reporter's actions. You have no right to blame yourself, Abe."

"Then why do I feel so lousy?" Stroud pushed past him and went up the winding stairs looking like a man defeated.

Sedated, Kerac was being moved by helicopter the following night. Aside from Abraham Stroud's chopper, two combat-ready police helicopters had been flown down from Chicago thanks to Commissioner Burns, but Stroud had handpicked the men he wanted to go in with. He had contacted Earl Saylor. Saylor was a combat veteran with Stroud in Southeast Asia. Together, they had seen a great deal of time in the mud and mire that was the life of a U.S. grunt. Saylor had been on alert status for Stroud even before he left Chicago with Kerac, but Saylor had only an inkling of what he had gotten himself and his men in for. They had only been told that there would be a hunt in Michigan deep woods, and that the enemy could be sizable and very deadly.

Saylor was overseeing the loading of the helicopters now with provisions, supplies, guns and ammo. Stroud had flown Saylor and his men in earlier in the day. Now, for the first time, they were seeing what the enemy looked like.

There were five in the mercenary group and they were familiar with one another. One was a woman who looked as tough as any of the grunts. The others called her "Nails," but her true name was Yolanna Nells. She was of mixed Nicaraguan-Caucasian blood and had survived on her wits and weapons knowledge through the fighting there. She'd tired of the command decisions and drifted north, and had somehow gotten into the States through "military" contacts.

Joe Blue was a "dyed-in-the-blue" soldier of fortune like the others. Blue had a stiletto smile and the eyes of a killer; Stroud thought he looked like some of the murderers he had himself put away for life while he was a police detective in Chicago. One glance at the way Blue hugged a weapon, and it was obvious he loved using it.

Warren Priest was a silent, brooding member of Saylor's little team. He wore wire-rim glasses, looked as if he'd stepped from the campus at Stanford, except for the fact his face was scarred where he'd been tortured as a POW. His wounds went deep.

Wil Tulley was the largest of the mercenaries, looking like a bear, his arms like giant pistons. He was the picture of the big, dumb soldier with the Neanderthal forehead and deep-set eyes below a bushy, black mane, and yet he was sharp, quick-witted and in tune with Saylor's every whim. Saylor and he had fought now in seven guerrilla actions in places as diverse as the Congo and Colombia, sometimes hiring out to drug lords. They didn't care where the money came from, just so long as they could fight and be paid for the pleasure.

Saylor himself balked at the size and appearance of the quarry, however, when he looked at the prone figure of the sedated wolfman. Kerac was strapped to a stretcher, a syringe at the ready should he suddenly overcome the drug that had silenced him. The mood of the mercenaries was one of awe, wonder and fear, yet they hid their fear well.

"This is what we'll be hunting?" asked Saylor.

Stroud nodded, adding, "As I indicated, we fear there are more. Just how many more is, at this time, anybody's guess. We have a single report that places them at fifty, but it's not a reliable count by any means."

"Fifty?" said Blue. "You hear that, Nails? Maybe we can catch one, send it to Nicaragua, put it on a soapbox and run it for President."

Some of the others laughed. Nails said, "Make sure the one we bring back for my country is a woman, then."

"Damned thing is big," commented Warren Priest, taking down his glasses, squinting at Kerac as the monster was being boarded.

"Bigger'n Tulley!" said Blue.

"Tough as Nails," said Tulley, joining in Blue's fun.

"You better hope that bastard doesn't come to during flight," said Saylor. "Could be havoc in the air!"

"He's havoc wherever he is when fully conscious," said Stroud. "But we've taken precautions." He showed him the hypodermic needle.

Once inside the craft, Stroud showed his friend Saylor the tracking device they would use on Kerac. He explained about the implant.

"Looks good. It's a go, then?"

"We're waiting on something that Dr. Lou Cage is working on—silver nitrate solution. According to Lou, if we douse all our ammo in the nitrate, enough of the poison will solidify around the metal projectile to give us a kind of poison dart for these things. Bullets alone will not bring them down, Earl."

Earl Saylor looked incredulous, but then his eyes went back to the thing in the cargo bay, and he said, "All right, whatever you say, Abe . . . or should I call you Doc these days?"

"It's always been Abe with you, Earl."

"Looks like you've done all right since I last saw you, Abe." He indicated the grounds and the house with a nod of his head, the thick, red-to-brown curls falling over his large forehead. "Nice place."

"And you?" asked Abe.

"About same, Abe. You know what drives a man like me . . ."

"Yeah, I do."

Saylor laughed. "That's why you called me and mine, and we're here to do our usual good work."

They had already worked out the details of payment and how the money would go into an account. Saylor had made it clear that he would not show anywhere until the transaction between their banks had been made.

"I'll see how Lou's coming."

Stroud got out and Kerac let out a deep, guttural moan that froze the various mercenaries in place, causing a couple of gun safeties to be clicked off. "It's all right," said Stroud. "He's under and will be for a few hours."

"I told my people all about what happened to that reporter," said Saylor. "Nothing like that's going to happen with us, Abe. So, sedation or not, you be quick. If this thing rouses—"

"It'll be all right. Just finish provisioning the helicopters."

Saylor turned to his men, seeing the uneasiness in their eyes flit by like a shadow as they tried to conceal it. "Just like any other goddamned bad guys, people!" Saylor shouted, his words sounding rote, but his commanding voice boomed about the little circle of soldiers. "Store those AKs, Nails! Blue, we got more ammo to load! Priest, get off your thumbs!"

Tulley took up the military tone. "You heard the man! Move it! Move it!"

"Just glad we brought all our firepower," said Blue as he went back to work.

"Sure those lightweight bazookas'll bring a sucker like that down, are you?" asked Nails.

"Just watch me!" he replied.

Earl Saylor turned and stared at the restless, moaning creature in the cage that Stroud's people had carried out. It had taken four men to carry it. Saylor saw a fang in the curled snarl where Kerac's head lay perfectly still for a moment before jerking, causing Saylor to gasp and look around to see if any of the others had noticed his reaction. No one had. Saylor then studied the enormous claws and toenails. He had never seen anything like this beast before.

Joe Tulley came alongside him and said, "Whataya think, Earl? Bigfoot?"

"Damned if I know, Joe. But the newspapers get wind of this and they'll call it animal cruelty; Stroud and the rest of us'll be put away if . . ."

"If we're not killed by the damned thing first, you mean?"

"Imagine an army of these things, Joe . . . imagine it."

Stroud had returned within an hour, guiding a pair of encumbered white-coated men, followed by Dr. Louis Cage, who was shouting, "Careful . . . very careful with that stuff. You'll need every ounce of it."

The men were carrying a large vat, about as heavy as a ten-gallon fish tank filled with water. Saylor and his men watched, some scratching their heads.

The vat of sloshing, silvery liquid was hoisted into another of the choppers. Saylor asked Stroud what was going on.

"Silver nitrate. We know that ordinary bullets do not slow this creature down, that it somehow absorbs and closes over bullets. But we have reason to believe that silver nitrate, poisonous as it is, will slow it down, or even kill it."

"Then you were serious? You want us to silver-plate every one of our goddamned bullets?"

"As many as possible, as we proceed, yes."

"Sounds crazy, Abe . . . but you're the boss man."

"Humor me."

"Consider it done."

"One final thing, Earl, before we leave."

"Yeah?"

"I want you and your men to see a film."

"Film?"

"Of Kerac here."

"I don't get it. We see what we've got here, this Kerac thing as you call it."

"Earl, your men deserve to know exactly what they're fighting . . . and what they'll be fighting for. It's imperative."

"Very well." He then shouted to his men to assemble, telling them that a movie was on schedule just for them in the mansion.

After a moment's rustling, Blue joked, "There any popcorn?"

" 'Fraid this movie'll just put you off your popcorn, Mr. Blue," said Stroud.

They made their way back to the large old structure of Stroud Manse by the light of the half-moon. In a viewing room, they watched the details of Perry Gwinn's death in stark silence and horror. When the lights came on, there wasn't a face in the room that did not bear the mark of terror. The film had caught Kerac in his human form, had shown his lycanthropic nature and his gruesome feeding habits.

Stroud spoke up. "I thought it only fair that you know what this enemy is capable of, that it is cannibalistic, and that it is a shape-changer. I've studied the film very carefully, and I've come to the conclusion that Kerac—or what Kerac has become—is very cunning, and that while once he could not control his shape-changing, now he does. I believe he changed into the human form in order to lure Gwinn close enough that he could get hold of him. Gwinn would have gone nowhere near the creature if he were in his present form."

"That seems to be giving this creature more intelligence than may be due him, Abe," said Saylor.

"My manservant had been trying for hours to get Kerac to come out of the beast form. He'd talked and sat with him to this end. I don't think it was purely coincidental that he should change when he did. I think the creature planned his moves."

The others murmured among themselves. Blue said shakily, "I can't believe you didn't blow the cocksucker's head off after . . . after seeing what he did."

"We need him, to track," said Stroud, "to lead us to the others."

Just then the door creaked open and Anna More stood there saying, "Ironic, isn't it? Kerac was a guide. Now you use him to guide you to the others. You were planning on leaving without me, weren't you, Stroud?"

"Anna, how . . . when did you arrive?"

"Never mind that. I want in."

Stroud looked from her to Lou Cage, who shrugged and said, "I told you she would know."

"Anna, I really don't think you ought—"

"You needn't worry about sparing my feelings, Stroud. I am here to see that Johnny is killed. You would put a mad dog from its misery, but—"

"I need *this* mad dog alive. Is there anyone here who understands that?"

"Yes, I understand . . . your *greater* responsibility."

"Who is this bitch?" asked Nails.

"Show her the film," said Priest quietly.

"Anna, we have to wipe out the disease. Kerac is only an offshoot, a symptom."

"You want to exterminate his kind! But you don't know that there are more. Meanwhile—"

"We have to make sure."

Blue seconded Priest's suggestion. "Roll the film again. I want to see this again myself."

"Roll it," agreed Tulley. "If she still wants in, let her in."

After the film was shown a second time, Saylor was the first to speak. "I say we go find this thing's brothers and sisters and make 'em extinct. Now, Stroud."

"Kick ass," agreed Blue loudly.

Nails screamed, "Let's do it!"

With this the soldiers of fortune rushed out toward the helicopters. Cage straggled behind, sensing that Stroud and Anna needed to be alone.

"Our plan is to release Kerac into the area where he was first bitten. And—"

She was crying.

"—and, using the sensor device implanted under his skin, we expect to be led directly to the others."

"If you're right . . . if there are others like Kerac . . . it will be dangerous."

"We haven't kept Kerac alive for nothing. Cage and his scientific team have uncovered some weaknesses."

"An antivenom?"

"No, no breakthroughs there, but he's learned that there is something in the component parts of silver nitrate that works its way into the creature's system. A milligram of it has subdued Kerac to his present state. It's even more effective than a narcotic."

He held up a silver-tipped bullet to her eyes. She stared at it. "Then he is a werewolf," she said, "and there is some truth in the old legends."

"Cage has found that Kerac's immune system is highly advanced, terrifically efficient. Blood clotting, closing over wounds—even bullet wounds—at an accelerated pace. A bullet wound to it is like a sliver to you or me."

"These people you're bringing with you," she said. "You can trust them?"

"I've paid heavily for their services."

She nodded. "And you want no assistance from the police?"

"If we flood the woods with hundreds of law-enforcement officials who have no idea what they're hunting, we could lose a lot of lives, but we could also lose the herd."

"The old Indians who grew up listening to campfire tales, they still speak of the creatures that lived and survived in the wilderness like wolves," she said thoughtfully. "According to them, many unsolved crimes—missing persons—dating back to the eighteenth century . . . well, when I grew up, educated in the white man's school, I put aside all such beliefs. Perhaps I was wrong . . ."

"No one is blaming you."

"There is something I must tell you."

"Yes?"

"The old man . . . Kerac's father-in-law, who came and spoke with you when you were in Chicago."

"Yes."

"He died."

"I'm sorry to hear that."

"His daughter sent me some papers he had. He apparently believed in the Wendigo all of his life. He kept a record of strange events, missing people, mutilated cattle."

"You brought these with you?"

"No, but I studied them closely, Abe, and if they can be believed, your . . . your werewolf colony is much larger than the fifty he originally told you about. The incidence of crimes the old man attributed to these creatures—including those Johnny Kerac took blame for—has risen to much greater numbers. Also the alleged sightings of what you whites call bigfoot and what we call Sasquatch have risen. The old man's estimation of the growth in numbers, based on the number of sightings and kills, places them between two hundred and two hundred fifty, Abe."

"My God . . . that's a great deal more than I'd counted on."

"You need more help, Abe. You need more time to prepare."

Stroud thought about her words, took her hands in his and said, "No, no . . . no more time can be lost. We're ready, Kerac is prepped . . . it's a go."

"All right. Then I'm with you."

–15–

Everyone aboard the three choppers was equipped with earphones, and as they rose up over the Illinois plains and thundered toward Grand Rapids, Michigan, Abraham Stroud from chopper one informed them all of the possibility they may be facing as many as 250 of the enemy. The soldiers took the increase in stride with such comments as Blue's "The more the bloodier."

Stroud gave instructions for all the ammo loaded on number two helicopter to be "sugar-coated" while en route. Aboard number one chopper, Kerac's groaning and pitiful wail could not be heard over the rotors.

"Those metal-cased vials brought on board each chopper are filled with a gaseous form of silver nitrate," he told the others. "One of these can cover a city block in a gas cloud. The creatures inhale this stuff, it won't be like one of your bullets. It will take time to work through their systems, slowing them down and eventually killing them, we think."

"We think," repeated Tulley. "Sounds like the friggin' high command in Nam, doesn't it, Earl?"

"At any rate, not even your silver-nitrate-bathed bullets will bring one of them down if it doesn't strike a vital organ, such as the heart, lungs, brain. The silver nitrate to the other parts of the body will take time to be absorbed and carried by the blood."

"So, we nuke the herd from the air," said Saylor, "and then we go in for the kill?"

"That's dangerous, Earl, because the nitrate can kill us, too. We have masks and air tanks to wear, but that won't help visibility in a gas cloud. So, we'll have to go cautiously there."

"Might be more prudent," said Cage, "to nuke them and give it time to weaken them before rushing in."

"Prudent ain't a word I can use with my people, Dr. Cage," said Earl. "They don't know from prudent."

"We'll want to fire as much from the air, bring down as many from overhead, as possible," said Stroud. "Once we're on the ground with them, we're in their element, and they are most deadly in their element. Problem is, it's very difficult, even with the best high-powered rifle and sight, to bring down a moving target if you have to hit it exactly right."

"My men are up for it, Doc."

"Not a man living, Earl, is a match for one of these things on the ground."

"If you must ground-search," said Dr. Cage, "then you'll wear the remote cameras we've stowed in the choppers."

"What's that, Abe?" asked Earl, confused.

"Every man going it afoot will wear a remote camera, fitted over his shoulder so we have a complete picture of what's occurring from chopper one. Each remote is hooked into your vital signs, and there's a man on board who will help you into the apparatus."

"No one said anything about—"

"Earl, it's vital we have a command post, and that command post sees what you see. We must assure every man's safety, not to mention our need to document this show."

"I got my insurance!" said Nails. Stroud watched the woman hefting her 9mm Parabellum 92S for the men to admire.

"Get that ammo dipped," said Stroud.

Saylor gave his men the order. Rocking in the cargo bay, the soldiers went about the business of dipping and retrieving the ammunition with the help of one of Cage's people who wore metal gloves that were soon shining with the silver that clung to them.

"*Soooooo,*" said Nails in her thick accent, hefting one of the bulky shoulder cameras, staring at it. "Even in war now, your American big brother is watching?"

"Trust me," said Saylor. "Stroud is nobody's puppet, and he's nobody's big brother."

"Shit," agreed Blue, "whata we need this for, and all this silver concentrated shit, Earl? We got high-powered weapons, we got grenades and bazookas. We can just blow the freakin' things into little pieces."

"We try it Stroud's way, people. Then—and only then—we fall back on our own methods. The man's calling the shots right now."

"But not for long," said Tulley.

The three chopper pilots were also hired by Stroud, each man being combat-prepared.

In the cargo bay of chopper one, Stroud, Anna More and Cage were now standing around the metal cell that held the weakened, confused animal that Kerac had become. The smell of blood and animal musk filled the bay. Cage said quietly, "I've never shot anything except skeets, Stroud."

At the same moment in time that Stroud's army is making its way toward Michigan a campfire in the forests fifty miles northwest of Grand Rapids is warm and it creates a circle of light around which the campers huddle, laugh and talk. The darkness of the Michigan forests has come in around them like a blanket encircling an Indian. Trees which were clearly visible fifteen minutes before have now become an amalgam of dense gray-blackness, as if a child has spilled her paint over the landscape. The earth beneath the campers where they sit has taken on a cold quality. The birds and forest animals of daylight have given way to the far-away howl of a bobcat that sounds for all the world like a woman in distress, or a banshee tolling death.

Here, too, the irritating hoot of a persistent owl wishing for attention, and something vaguely like the baying of a wolf, infiltrate the night.

The temperature has dropped, and the campers, two couples on holiday, huddle together, sweatshirts and jackets around their shoulders. The fire both attracts and repels passing animals. The sound of human voices does the same.

The eerie half-moon and the clouds moving past it at what seems an accelerated rate cause one of the campers to talk about ghost stories. The second man in the group begins telling a "true to life" local horror story about a party of hunters who'd come to these very woods with what seemed like a friendly Indian guide at the time . . .

"I read about that," says one of the women. "It was in *USA Today*."

"But the guy's in jail now," the other woman assures her.

"Was," corrects one of the men.

"Ex-scaped," says the other, "about a month ago."

"Jesus, Tom! Did you know this? And still, you brought us out here?"

"Sugar, Frank's full of shit. Take it easy. He's just trying to scare you."

"Why do guys think that by scaring a girl it'll get her in the mood?"

They laugh nervously after this. One says, "Frank's doing a good job . . . Scaring me, I mean."

Frank, feeling encouraged, goes on. "I mean these guys were armed with high-powered rifles, but they were literally torn apart by this guy—their guide. Wiped out by a fiendish madman. From what I hear—"

"Enough, Frank!"

"Tom, make him stop."

"The cops caught the guy someplace in Chicago," says Tom.

"Yeah, caught him chewing on some guy's—"

"Frank!"

"Stupid fucks over at Merimac let him ex-scape."

Tom takes his girl and goes for their tent. "Come on, we'll let Frank and Bridgette be alone."

"Don't leave me alone with this creep!" Bridgette's protest goes unanswered, except by Frank.

"Hey, hon! I was just funnin', that's all."

"Call that fun?"

"Keepin' you safe and warm in my lovin' arms, babe? Sure."

"Not if I'm scared shitless, it won't be, Frank. I don't make out when I'm scared. I'm too busy shaking."

Frank nuzzles her ear. "Just do all the shakin' you want, babe . . . just so long as it's under me."

From Tom's tent some laughter wafts out to them. They look into one another's eyes and kiss. "Time to turn in?"

"Yeah, let's."

Aboard chopper one, Abraham Stroud had fallen asleep where he had for a moment lain down on a stretcher. He had gone without sleep for a long time, catching rest here and there. The incident with Gwinn had made him feel guilty that while he slept another man was being viciously killed. But fatigue now had overcome him and it had forced him down. More and Cage intermittently looked back over their shoulders at the prone, sleeping figure,

More averting her eyes from Kerac.

It was difficult to tell which sleeping figure was the more restless.

Stroud was locked on a dream that seemed idyllic, lovers on a camp outing in the woods; his mind drifted to Anna More, and the faceless people of his dream took on her features and his. They were locked in embrace, their lust unquenchable. Somewhere nearby there were others in the dream, lots of others . . . seemingly watching, prowling, coming ever closer. These dark figures crawled like crabs over the lovely dream.

Stroud's dream was turning into a nightmare . . .

Watching from just outside the circle of fire, standing all around the camp, are the dark forms and red eyes of a pack of some thirty werewolves. Inside the two tents, the young lovers are warming themselves with the magical touch of their bodies. Scuttling noises outside are ignored at first, but the women, alarmed by Frank's earlier story, are already on edge. Something snaps—a twig. Footfalls, distinct and animal-like, very near. The sound of many footfalls and the sensation that something awful is breathing along the spine.

Frank is pushed off Bridgette, who shouts, "What's out there, Frank? Something's in the camp."

"Probably Tom trying to scare us. Come on, forget it."

He continues kissing her, caressing, trying to recapture the moment.

"Damn it, Frank!" She pushes him hard away.

"Tom!" Frank shouts. "Get the hell outa here, will you? Messin' up my night, boy!"

There is no answer from Tom, but a large shadow floats across the exterior of the blue, shining nylon tent, followed by another and another, reflected from the last embers of the campfire.

"My God, Frank, what was that?"

"Don't worry, honey." Frank pulls forth a long-barreled Remington .45. As he does so, they both hear the screams of pain and horror coming from the second tent.

"Ohgod, ohgod, ohgod!" she shouts, pointing to the formidable shadow now standing over the tent.

Frank fires the six shots from the Remington, the revolver cranking around in rapid fashion, the explosions dissipating in the vast night. The shadow over the tent is still there. Tom's screams can still be heard.

Frank tears past Bridgette, leaving her lying naked as he crawls out the back of the tent. Behind him he hears her screams and sees the enormous claw that cut a swath in the back of the tent in an effort to grab him. The hole cut by the claw reveals the hideous sight of wolf-snouted, hairy beasts fighting over Bridgette, ripping parts of her off and gorging themselves with her flesh. Frank trembles, falls, scrapes his way away and races for the camper.

He no longer hears Tom's anguished screams, but he now hears Bridgette's as she is being devoured alive.

Frank reaches the camper door, tears it open with all his energy when something reaches him round the neck from overhead, lifting him to the top. He is bitten once sharply, the fangs like two needles going quickly in and out. He is then lifted toylike over the head of the enormous, satanic thing that has him in its grasp. Kicking and screaming, Frank is hurled down into a circle of others awaiting the prize captured for them by their leader.

The flight and fall of Frank's body, some forty yards, mercifully knocks him into a daze, but it also paralyzes him. Frank can't feel a thing, and yet he knows that they've lifted him again and are passing him hand over hand along a line of them, each ripping at him and all of them howling like mad dogs. His eyes register the fact that they are dancing, cavorting with their prizes—all of them, the pieces of Frank's friends—all dead and beyond knowing or feeling. Frank wishes for a swift end, but it does not appear he will get it.

Frank sees the wolfmen, women and children as each fights for a piece of Bridgette's flesh. For some reason he is being held, not given over to the frenzied feeding. Then the largest one, the one that had captured Frank by the neck and thrown him to the others, bays at the half-moon, and the others stop what they're doing, and they, too, bay up at the moon.

When the leader stops, he turns his burning, red devil's eye on Frank, and with saliva dripping, he sinks a fang into Frank's throat, choking off his screams.

Abraham Stroud's body twisted in anguish, his hands covering his own throat as he felt the Kerac-like things taking bite after bite of his flesh. His body tumbled and he lay next to the cell holding Kerac, careening into it with a clash that alerted Anna, who alerted Cage. A sickening, air-escaping noise came from Stroud. He seemed in a fit, as if attacked by an invisible enemy. Kerac had been disturbed by Stroud and was crawling toward him now, about to grab through the bars at him, his eyes wild, the claws extended.

Anna More rushed to Stroud, trying to pull him to safety. Cage fought with his seat belt, and the pilot looked over his shoulder, sending the craft to a sharp left, causing Cage to fall, the stun gun skidding from his grasp.

"Stroud, Stroud!" Anna was shouting.

Kerac's firm hold on Stroud's arm dragged him closer to the cell.

Anna pulled her gun and forced it into Kerac's eyes, slowing the creature, but Kerac wanted Stroud badly. He tore at the arm, bringing Stroud out of his sleep with a scream.

Cage fired the stun gun; Kerac instantly stared at the source of his pain, and from the hypo his eyes lifted to Cage. All the while, he never let go of Stroud. He tried desperately to get his snout and fangs through the bars to bite Stroud, but Anna, with Stroud's help now, kept him from doing so. Stroud thought his arm would be pulled from its socket when suddenly Kerac loosed his grip, stumbled and went to his knees. Kerac's watery, pitiable eyes met Stroud's just before the creature fell again into a deep, forced sleep.

"Christ!" shouted Abe. "What happened?"

"You rolled into the cell, and Kerac took advantage," Anna told Stroud.

Stroud's arm was bleeding where the creature's claws had ripped into it.

"Better put something on that immediately," said Cage, coming around to them. He began ministering to Abe's upper arm where the muscle was lacerated and bloodied. "Nasty wound. Must ward off any infection. No telling what could happen if this thing festered."

"You had a bad dream," said Anna, holding Stroud's head in her lap.

"It was more than a bad dream," he said quietly.

Cage applied a sodium-based cleansing solution after ripping away the tattered shirt sleeve. "This isn't going to be enough," he was saying when he took a small vial from his pocket. Inside the vial was a mercurylike substance. "Silver," he told Stroud, who was staring at the vial. "Who knows . . . can't hurt in the dosage I'm going to apply, and it might do some good."

As Cage worked a minuscule amount of the silver nitrate into the sodium cleanser, and went about the business of applying this, he and More listened to Stroud's description of a camping party that had just been mutilated and consumed by a large band of werewolves in the area of the woods they themselves were speeding toward.

"But it was just a nightmare," said Anna.

"It was no dream, Anna."

She shook her head. "Will he be all right?" she asked Lou Cage.

"No," said Stroud. "None of us is all right . . . none of us is safe, Anna."

She looked to Cage for an answer. He said, "I've learned one thing about this bugger, Stroud. I never question his visions."

Stroud said, "Where we are going, we will find more dead."

—16—

At dawn the helicopters had arrived at the appointed area. Aboard chopper one, the aerial maps and the view were near identical. Stroud called for the geodesic map that would show any unusual rock formations and depths, rivers and streams. The geodesic map was almost fifteen years old.

"Something down there!" shouted the pilot. "Catching some reflection. Looks like metal."

"Bring us closer," said Stroud as he strained to see the over-turned camper. As they drew nearer, the sight of torn, flapping tents—two of them—came into view amid the thickly forested area. The campers had come off the road about twenty-five yards in from a dust-track ribbon that led to a bridge and another dirt road which they had found off a country road that hadn't been repaved in a very long time. There was a stream nearby that threaded its lazy way back to the bridge and beyond in zigzag fashion. A canoe lay on the earth beside it, its paddles missing or beneath it. At the center of the scene was a large circle of stones—almost too large—where a fire had been.

"Can you find a safe place to set us down?"

"Wide bend in the road back a piece."

"Do it."

With the others remaining aloft, hovering and circling, Stroud, Anna More and Cage went in to investigate. Stroud had shared his premonition with Saylor's people as well now, and from the look of it, the awful foresight had been true. The chopper pilot in number one wasn't pleased with the idea of remaining alone with Kerac, despite the fact the creature appeared sedated still. Lou left the pilot the stun gun. Stroud told him under no conditions was he to go within ten feet of the cell.

Now they entered the camp site, the odor of carnage striking their nostrils even before they did so. The large stone pile over the fire was partially a bone pile where burned flesh and bones still lay. All about the dirt, amid the leaves and wild grass, there were scattered body parts, most shorn of flesh down to a few tendons and stringy matter.

The three living people stood in stark silence for a time, in horror and rage and reverence at what they saw. The camp was strewn with the remains of the werewolf meal.

Then Stroud noticed a silence overhead. The other two choppers were gone. "Damn them," he said aloud.

"This is awful—unbelievable and awful," said Anna.

Lou found a place to vomit, but as he did so, he heard the approach of living things all around them there in the woods. He rushed to Stroud's side, with Anna coming to them as well. They all heard the movement inward toward them. Stroud readied his weapon, one of the AK-47s from Saylor's store, the bullets having been silver-doused before leaving Illinois. He rammed home the speed loader and was prepared to fire. Anna More steadied her weapon, as did Cage.

Cage said, "Sounds like they're all around us."

"Hold your fire!" It was Saylor's voice. "We're coming in."

Stroud breathed a sigh of relief, but he shouted, "You were told to stay airborne."

Saylor and the others stepped into the clearing. Priest, Blue, Nails, Tulley—all of them at equidistant points around the circle, all pointing their deadly weapons.

"God!"

"What a slaughter."

"Ain't seen nothin' like this since the Chicago stockyards closed down."

Stroud shouted, "Saylor! What the hell're you doing here? I told you to—"

"We're paid to fight, Abe, not piss out a helicopter. Besides, we want to see what's happened here as well as you."

Anna frowned, looked at Abe, and then said to Saylor, "Look around . . . have a good time. I'm going back to the chopper."

"No one goes alone," said Stroud.

"I've seen enough," said Lou. "I'll see she gets back safely."

Saylor shouted to Blue and Nails to escort the two of them back to the road. The soldiers complained about it, but did as they were told.

Saylor then turned to Stroud and said, "You're crazy to come into an unsecured area like this, Abe. What're you paying us for? My men are here to ensure the success of this mission, and you endanger yourself this way, without buttoning up the perimeter—"

"Earl, I knew there were none of *them* around. That they were long gone."

"Oh, I get it . . . you *sensed* it?"

"Something like that. A place of death usually speaks very loud to me. Remember those three days I lay out in a death field in Vietnam with a hole blown in my head? That kind of thing . . . it sticks with you."

"So, if you were so sure, why were you about to blow my friggin' brains out with that?" He touched the barrel of his weapon against Stroud's.

"Instinctive reaction. You were told to stay aloft. I wasn't expecting you. And when I give an order, I expect it to be obeyed."

"So long as the order makes sense, Abe . . . so long as it makes sense, I won't second-guess you. But my people have a right to see this."

"Okay, we start here . . . from this point, with Kerac," said Stroud, not wishing to argue with Saylor, knowing he could not win—especially in front of his men.

"We let him loose here," said Saylor, nodding. "He picks up the scent of his kind . . . follows their trail . . . sure. Good move."

"Your men aren't above carrying a heavy load, I hope?"

"Just so long as the mother's out . . . and I mean cold."

"He's still smarting from his last dose."

"And what about you, Stroud? How's that arm?"

Cage had bandaged the wound and it had oozed a stain of rust.

"I'm fine."

"Good . . . good. Let's do it. Tulley, we're pulling the freak in the cage; settin' it down here and lettin' it go on its way. See to it."

Tulley and the others made their way back. Stroud and Saylor stayed put, surveying the terror that lay before them.

Meanwhile, Lou Cage and Anna More made their way back to the relative safety of the helicopters. Lou had to test the effectiveness of the remote cameras and the monitors that signaled the vital signs of each of the soldiers on the ground. Anna More had become silent and withdrawn; Lou understood her fears and concerns.

Kerac was kept under sedation there in the clearing until what was left of the four bodies of the campers had been given benefit of burial. Stroud took charge of whatever wallets and other identification could be found, to be turned over to the authorities when they got back to civilization. Stroud thought of the families who would be searching uselessly for the four campers. He stacked a series of flat rocks atop one another, creating a steepling cairn. The heap of stones served as a marker and a crude headstone.

The soldiers had become unusually quiet during the burial detail, as if each man and woman was alone with, and fearful of, his own thoughts.

With the burial detail completed, Stroud said a handful of words over the young strangers, and then the group went quickly to work, grateful to be busy, grateful to walk away from death.

They now deployed the metal cage and its unconscious cargo atop a slight grade, so that the cell door, when Stroud removed the lock, swung open on its hinges. In front of the cage, Stroud spread out a meal of raw meat for the creature.

Within half an hour the cage holding John Kerac was jiggling, Kerac coming around. Stroud and his mercenaries had long since moved off cautiously, looking back from time to time, their shoulder cameras documenting their actions.

Back at chopper one, high overhead and out of Kerac's visual range, Anna More and Lou Cage watched the monitor. Cage hurried those on the ground out of the area, saying, "If Kerac picks up on your scent, he'll follow you, Stroud, instead of going in the direction you want, in pursuit of his pack."

"Copy that, Lou," Stroud replied. "Vacating as fast as we can."

The party of mercenaries followed Stroud back toward the other two waiting helicopters. With Kerac still woozy, Lou Cage told Stroud that the electronic bug in Kerac's forearm was sending a clear signal. "You can break off visual contact now. Get clear of there, Abe!"

"We copy you, Lou, and we're coming up!"

"Roger that," replied Lou, "and thank God."

The additional machines went aloft.

Lou kept the channel between them open, saying, "Signal is working perfectly, Abe. Should be a piece of cake, following Kerac."

"I expect that'll be the easy part, Lou."

"He's on the move, Abe."

"Say again?"

"Kerac—he's moved from the cage."

"How far?"

"Just a matter of a few yards, but he's up and moving, clearly out of the cell."

Stroud pictured the blood dripping from Kerac's fangs as he tore into the present of raw meat left him. "Now, people, we pray."

Kerac awoke to find himself alone in the forest with the confining cell door swinging open. He might have ripped the cell apart, bent its bars to his bidding, if they had not chemically controlled him. He still felt woozy and weakened. But they left him with a lion's share of red meat, which he now feasted on. As he ate, his eyes were alert to the scattered leavings all around him. His nose was alert to the odor of humans, and to the odor of his own kind. After feeding and prowling about the camp, Kerac made his way northeasterly, following the scent of those who were like him.

This is where I belong . . .

He moved off at a slow pace, feeling heavy and lethargic but quite hopeful. An annoying itch troubled him. It was not a bodily itch, but an itch of the mind. Something he must do . . . something to combat and beat this human the others called Stroud. Something he had put away in his mind but could not yet recall. The drugs and weakening agents they had used on him had shorted out the powers of his mind and his cunning.

But slowly . . . surely, those powers would return. Like the cunning of having used his shape-changing to lure the one fool into his grasp. He knew such an attack would send Stroud racing to him. He wanted nothing more than to die with Stroud at the end of his fangs.

The hatred for Stroud had kept him alive. His hatred for this one man transcended every other consideration. He did not know why—not completely. He did not know how Stroud had managed to track him. He did not know the full significance of the dark-eyed, dark-haired woman who stared into his eyes whenever she came near, and who hung on Stroud. But he knew she was Stroud's weakness; that if he could get to her . . . then he could get to him.

Kerac made his way deeper and deeper into the forests, feeling gay at the freedom that was his. He made his way down from the hill and up along ridges, following the path of a secret and hidden stream where the only scents were those of animals.

From above the cloud cover, the whirlybirds waited as Cage monitored Kerac's movements from the air. Chopper one, with the others following a close second, kept Kerac within the range of the transmitter. Cage's words were like a chant as they filled everyone's earphones: "He's moving, moving, moving fast . . . almost a straight line . . . moving, like he knows where he wants to go. Moving on."

The beep of the transmitter was impossible to hear with all the noise of the helicopter, but the light was unmistakable. They stealthily followed on Kerac's trail.

"Signal's getting weaker," announced Cage. "Some interference."

"Bring us down, Dave," Stroud told the pilot, who responded immediately, dropping their altitude. Below and ahead of them they saw a large valley into which Kerac had gone.

"We're going to lose him in there," came Saylor's voice over the radio from the helicopter behind them.

"Anywhere to set down, Dave?"

"Just to the left . . . looks like a bald ridge."

"Do it."

"Signal is really now interfered with, Abe," said Cage.

"What's the cause? Can density of trees do that?"

"Perhaps some, but this is irregular fluttering."

"Damn it," said Saylor as his chopper was settling down beside Stroud's, "we're going to lose him, aren't we?"

"No way."

"Something's wrong with the transmitter, Abe," said Cage.

"But you implanted it yourself, Lou."

"I know that, but look at these fluctuations."

"I say we stop fooling around and just track the bastard," said Saylor, speaking for his men. The third helicopter's rotors now came to a spinning halt on the knoll that overlooked the darkness into which Kerac had disappeared. The soldiers hopped from the machines at the ready, spreading out on Saylor's orders, told to stand at watch.

Saylor had pulled away his headphones and was now standing at the cargo bay door, where Stroud waved him over. "Something's going haywire with the transmitter, but I'm not so sure we ought to go down in there, Earl. This isn't going to be like fighting other men, and if you and your men rush into their territory . . ."

"Abe, you're paying us to do it for you. So, we'll follow your orders. But I don't see how we're going to keep Kerac in our sights. If the bug's not doing it for us, then we have to use the eyes in our heads."

Stroud understood the logic, but he feared sending anyone down into the big gully where the wash seemed to go on forever below a canopy of jack pine and other fir trees.

"They start getting the scent of all that raw meat you brought with us, your band of wolfmen are going to be coming to us," said Anna More. "And maybe that's how Mr. Saylor would like it?"

"Not a bad idea, ma'am," said Saylor. "But how's this for an even better one?"

"Go on," said Stroud, hearing that Cage inside was still having difficulty with the transmitter equipment. Much static was blazing from it now.

"Take the choppers over toward the other side, upwind. Drop the meat in a clearing, guide us by radio contact to that clearing, and we'll open fire on the damned beasts when they come to feed on it," Saylor said.

Tulley had joined the conference, and now he added, "Guide us toward the static. We'll still pick up Kerac by the static, on foot, if you lead us in from the air. Hell, it may not be working cleanly, but it's still working and it's surgically implanted, so we ought to be able to track the sucker."

"Good idea," said Stroud. "All right, let's do it, but for God's sake, Saylor, all of you, take great care with these beasts, and at the first sign of darkness, get to a designated rendezvous point for pick up. We don't stand a chance in there in the dark against them. Cage tells me they have night vision."

"You ought to hold back here, Dr. Stroud, with the choppers," suggested Saylor.

Stroud shook his head vehemently. "No, no way. This is my show, Earl."

"You're sure?"

"I'm going in, too," said More, tossing down several of the gas masks they'd be carrying, and hefting one of the TV remotes she'd have to carry on her shoulder.

"Anna, you're staying with Cage. He'll need your assistance."

"Not this Indian," she said firmly.

Stroud saw there was no use arguing with her, and Cage was shouting from inside that the transmitter was nearly faint.

"Indicates he's still moving," said Abe.

"No time to waste," said Saylor. "Let's be at it!"

Provisions and the silver bullets were unloaded along with the AK-47s. Everyone also had to heft a canister filled with the gas that was lethal to Kerac's kind. They took very little of the raw meat that had been impregnated with the toxic poison, not wishing to become Kerac's target. As the provisions were being downloaded, Lou Cage voiced his objections to anyone going in after Kerac on foot.

"I thought this was going to be done strictly from the air, Abe! This is madness, to go in there afoot without knowing how many of these things you face!"

"I'm not about to send men in there to risk their lives when I'm not willing to do it myself, Lou."

"But we need you in the air, in control."

"That will be left to you now, Lou."

Abe turned his back on his old friend and began preparing for the descent into the valley that gaped below them. As the soldiers, Anna More and Abe assembled their bulky gear, behind them the helicopters lifted off; this made them all turn and stare after the choppers. With the helicopters went any semblance of safety, along with the large stores of poisoned meat that would be dumped at an agreed-upon site.

As they moved into the woods, Blue said to Nails, "These devils get a whiff of you, Nails, and we could all wind up like those happy campers we saw this morning."

"Give your mouth a rest, Joe."

Meanwhile, Stroud and Saylor checked their communications line with the helicopters as they all moved along.

Anna More drifted toward the other female in the group, curious about her, and also feeling some connection with her. As they walked, More asked Nails, "Why do you do this?"

"What?"

"It couldn't be for the money."

"Why not for the money?" asked Nails a bit scornfully.

Anna said simply, "If you and the others did this for money, and money alone—but maybe it's none of my business."

"You got that right, Chief!" said Nails sarcastically.

They continued on in silence a moment, but then Nails cleared her throat and said, "Me and Blue have a thing going, you know. We love to hate one another, but we love it more than we hate it . . . I don't know."

Anna half smiled at this, nodding. "Think I know what you mean."

"I noticed something between you and the doc," said Nails.

"Is it that obvious?"

"Obvious? It's all over the two of you anytime you're within sight of one another. He's a handsome guy, and from what Saylor's told us, one brave sonofa—well, he's okay."

After another pause, Anna asked again, "Why are you here, Miss Nells?"

The other woman laughed and mimicked this. "Miss? Nobody's called me Miss in years." She hefted the AK-47 to Anna's eyes. "Where else am I going to get to play with toys like this, huh? That answer your question? Think about it."

There was some static between Stroud and Cage, but when this cleared, Cage's voice came over, making everyone relax. It was good to know they had contact with someone on the outside of this world without rules.

"Take every precaution. From the air, we've seen nothing of what you'd call a herd movement, Abe. They seem to be invisible. Probably everywhere around you."

"Thanks, Lou . . . that's comforting to know."

"Abe, you should get out now."

"Lou, you yourself just told me that Kerac can't be tracked by air."

"But Abe, you're risking everyone's life—not just your own."

"We allow these things to spread, Lou, and who will be safe?"

"Damn it," replied Lou. "Just, all of you, be extremely careful."

"Will do, my friend."

All of the soldiers had stopped in their tracks to listen to the dire exchange. Cage was sounding more and more unhinged, and he was safely away. The soldiers of fortune looked about at one another and Priest said, "What good's the money, Saylor, if we don't live to use it?"

"Can that crap, Priest. We're better equipped to handle these . . .

these things, and we've got more brains than they do. So, can the bull."

Blue cleared his throat to say something, and Saylor shouted, "You, too, Joe!"

"Will do," replied Blue, who took Nails aside for a private word.

The soldiers were anxious to get in. "Let's find this herd!" Tulley shouted, his gaunt frame like that of Clint Eastwood.

"The moment we locate the main colony, the strike will again become an air raid, do you understand, Tulley, Saylor?"

"Roger," said Saylor.

"Ditto," replied Tulley without enthusiasm.

Stroud spoke by remote to Cage overhead. "Keep us within your monitor range, Lou."

"Absolutely, Abe. Pilots are scouting ahead for good sites to dump the meat, and for rendezvous with your unit."

"Roger that, and thanks."

"Take every precaution, Abe."

"Understood and out."

They began making their way through the brush, Nails and Blue at the point.

–17–

Abe Stroud stared down at the hand-held monitor that was picking up the weak signal coming from the transmitter in Kerac's forearm. He recalled how they had sedated Kerac and how Lou Cage had surgically implanted the device, closed it over with stitches, and until now it had worked perfectly. He wondered what could have gone wrong with it. From overhead, Cage, too, was continuing to get poor, unpronounced readings, and it was touch and go as to exactly where Kerac was.

"Anything?" asked Anna More, coming alongside Stroud now.

Just as she spoke, Stroud began to get a stronger reading. "It's getting stronger, indication is southeast." He pointed. "That way."

"I see your reading is stronger," said Cage from far above, monitoring through Stroud's shoulder remote camera. "Also, we have located a clearing for pickup about seven hundred yards from your present location, bearing—what is it, Dave?—twenty degrees northeast."

"That's a long way off," said Stroud. "And we're going away from it. Can you find anything closer to our location?"

"Nothing quite so safe," said the pilot, "but we'll have another look-see."

The signal was very strong now. "He's close," said Stroud. "We must keep silent. He has extremely good hearing."

They moved in the direction of the signal. In fifteen minutes they were atop it. Stroud indicated it was right before them, but there was no sign of Kerac. The party moved in cautiously, guns at the ready. Stroud was frustrated by the cat-and-mouse, disappointed that things were going so badly. Should Kerac suddenly leap from one of the trees and be shot to death with the lethal silver-tipped bullets, the hunt would end here and the others of his kind would never be found.

Yet, there was no sign of Kerac. Only the beeping signal disturbed the pristine silence of this place until Nails suddenly shouted, "Oh, Jesus! Over here! Over here, now!"

Blue was the first to reach Nails' location, and he stared down to the leaf-strewn earth, pointing and saying, "There's your damned monster-findcr, Stroud! Christ! We've been following a useless signal all along!"

Tulley, Saylor and Priest joined the other two, all the men standing in a circle, staring down at what remained of Kerac's left hand and forearm where Kerac had literally broken the bone and ripped or chewed through his own limb to free himself of Stroud and the others. Stroud and Anna now stared at the hairy forearm, matted with blood where ants and flies picked at it.

"Sonofabitch."

"Damn."

"Unbelievable."

Stroud stood shaking his head. He tried to recall what, if anything, had ever been said within Kerac's earshot about the signal implant. Stroud and the others had been too cavalier about how much Kerac understood, and just how cunning he could be. "We can't ever underestimate him again," Stroud said now.

"Got to hand it to your little pet, Stroud," said Saylor. "He'd make one hell of a soldier."

"Think you could do that if you had to, Blue?" asked Nails.

"If I had to, yeah," lied Blue, making the other soldiers laugh.

"Well, now he's suckered us in deep," said Tulley. "What do you suppose his next move'll be?"

Priest did a 360 turnabout, staring up at the trees. "Bet he's looking right at us, right now. Having a good laugh . . . or growl."

The others began to search the forests for signs of the creature. Every tree and bush was in spring growth and some of the underbrush was so thick they'd have to walk around it or spend hours cutting through. Saylor said, "Stand down, relax. If he was within a mile, we'd smell him. Take five."

They all went for their water canteens, some pulled out smokes. Saylor, Tulley, Stroud and Anna More came together to parley over the situation as Stroud informed the helicopter crews and Cage about the turn of events.

"So we gathered from the remote pictures you're sending back," said Cage. "Should have considered it . . . should have implanted it in an unreachable area, say the small of his back, but—"

"Who knew he'd do such a thing? Who knew he was even cognizant of what we were doing?" countered Stroud.

"Oh, he's cognizant, all right. First Perry Gwinn, suckering him in the way he did . . . and now this."

"Give us again the location of the drop," said Stroud.

Cage did so. It was about a mile in the opposite direction. "That'll put us within good distance to the proposed pickup site," said Stroud.

"That was the general idea, Abe."

"Roger that, Lou. We're on our way."

Tully and Saylor agreed that the raw-meat drop was their next best move. If it drew Kerac, theoretically the bait would draw the others as well. It had been shown that Kerac could little resist such temptation, even if he knew the odds were high.

"Move out!" Saylor told his men, and once more they stalked their prey.

The search party was halfway to the drop when they heard a resounding, blood-chilling roar. At the same time, Lou Cage came over the radio from above. "Sighted Kerac and others, Abe! We've glimpsed them amid some rocks and trees—"

"Read you, but where in relation to our position?"

"You're dead on, Abe. Straight ahead of you."

"How far?"

"Two, maybe three hundred yards."

"Can you get in for a closer look?"

"Not without alerting them."

"Hold on that."

Stroud called Saylor and Tulley.

"I say we go in for a closer look," said Tulley. "Get a head count."

Saylor agreed. "We're downwind from them, and my people are the best, Stroud. Let us begin to earn our keep."

Anna More stared at Stroud, who considered this. He contacted Lou, who argued against getting too close, wanting to dust the trees with the gas first.

"We need a look first, Lou. But be ready with those gas bombs."

Stroud had to shut down the radio on Lou's protests. The party moved forward at a clip now, silent and steady and of one mind, like a single animal. Ahead of them, they heard more howls, bayings, cries of pain and torment.

"Christ," shouted Blue, "it's another attack on some poor slobs out camping!" Blue went charging far ahead.

In ten minutes, they were on their bellies amid an outcropping of stones that littered the otherwise lush landscape of the deep woods. They looked down on another gully that seemed a duplicate of the wash basin they'd first encountered so far behind them now. Stroud felt a sense of déjà vu about the place, except that here they saw flashes of the hairy beasts that they'd come to exterminate. All of the men and women looked down into the rocks and trees lining their vision, trying desperately to make out the silver and black shapes and movements of the living animals they were now trying to draw beads on. Their movie cameras sent back pictures to the men in the air as they scanned for the noisy but near-impossible-to-see creatures.

"There," said Priest, pointing, but then it was gone.

The roars came again. "Keep quiet," said Stroud. "They can hear at incredible range. Go to radio contact only."

All of them placed headphones from their necks to their heads and ears. Now they could communicate privately without fear of alerting the enemy to their presence.

"Careful of your footing, careful of this pack of shit we've got to carry on our backs, men," Saylor cautioned his people.

Tulley said, "We've got to get in closer. Can't see shit from here."

"Roger that," agreed Blue, who started over and down, remaining on his belly. He was followed by Nails. In each person's ears, even through the headphones, the roaring was becoming deafening. The werewolves were feasting on something, but this was not the drop location.

There were no human screams and for that Stroud and the others were thankful.

They moved in closer, following Joe Blue's lead. Priest tumbled down like a silent rock to a new position. Tulley and Saylor fanned out, widening the circle of fire they would open up on the enemy. Stroud and Anna remained close together, Stroud not wanting to lose sight of Anna.

"Are you okay?" he asked her.

"Let's just get it over with."

Stroud thought of the slaughter of buffalo by hunters in America in the late 1800s. He wanted this slaughter over with quickly.

But as they gained their new positions, Stroud realized no one was opening fire, and that all the seasoned soldiers were staring in awe instead. Below them were hundreds of hairy humanoids, all roaring and stomping and jumping at the sight of two of their number locked in combat. It appeared a combat to the death. Dirt, dust, hair and blood commingled and flew all about the combatants. Stroud pulled forth his binoculars and magnified, zeroing in on the dueling pair. Amid the furor, he saw that one of the fighters had only one claw: *it was Kerac.*

The fighting between the two beasts was furious, and it held Saylor's people, Stroud and Anna in rapt attention. All round the dueling werewolves, others waved their arms and leapt up and down on the rocks and amid the trees. Stroud tried desperately to make an estimate of their numbers.

Flesh and hair were torn from Kerac by the other man-wolf, who was huge and powerfully built but older and silver-streaked over a third of his body where his hair was gray. It soon became apparent that the older one was the leader of the pack and that Kerac's sudden appearance among them had called his authority into question, resulting in the mauling Kerac was now taking. But suddenly, Kerac lifted a huge rock with his one good arm and pounded it into his opponent's head, bashing in the other's skull, sending the silver-backed one into a paroxysm of nervous twitching, and left him on his back as Kerac pounded first the air and then his chest with his only hand. The roar and din and screech from the males, females and children in the enormous pack sent up a shrill noise from the basin floor.

Suddenly, gunshots rang out and some of the creatures fell in response, dead of their wounds from Blue's and Nails' AK-47s. The instant Blue opened fire, the rest followed suit. Stroud had heard no order given to fire, but now there was little else to do. But no sooner had the first few of the creatures fallen to bullets than the others had simply disappeared.

"Where are they?" shouted Tulley through the com link.

"Everyone up!" ordered Saylor. "Full pursuit! Now!"

The soldiers tore over the ridge and careened down into the basin, their weapons at the ready.

Stroud shouted for caution, and he ordered them to place their gas masks on. As soon as everyone had the opportunity to cover their eyes, mouths and noses, Stroud ordered Lou to come in with the gas bombs. Each helicopter came in low and dropped a casing of the gas that would work its way into the nervous systems of the creatures.

With the cloud of gas masking their view, creeping over the entire scene before them, they came into the area where the monsters had frolicked at having seen their leader killed by Kerac. Except for the old man of the group, still alive and twitching, and those few brought down by Blue and Nails—all of whom were dead—there was not so much as a sign of the others. They had simply vanished.

Priest suddenly fired, tearing a tree trunk to ribbons, making the others laugh, until he hit one of the brown werewolves. It'd been camouflaged against the tree.

"How did you see it?" asked Tulley of Priest.

"I didn't."

Others suddenly appeared all around them, stepping from the brown background of trees and rocks, scurrying off, seeing they could be harmed by these strange intruders. Nails and Anna More opened fire, bringing down several more of the creatures.

Tulley and Saylor brought down several more who lifted straight off the earth, having blended in with the pine needle forest floor fifty yards distant. Stroud saw some unusual movement at the periphery of his vision overhead, and firing into the trees, two more of the werewolves fell dead to the earth.

"Wasting too damned much ammo!" shouted Saylor. "Hit what you shoot at, and no more scatter-gunning!"

"Silver's working," said Stroud.

Priest hadn't brought down a single creature. He'd fired several rounds, and he had hit several of the fleeing creatures, but they merely rushed on. Stroud went to him and said, "You didn't get your ammunition doused, did you?"

"No . . . I didn't."

"Didn't think it'd make any difference, did you?"

"Hell, bullets are bullets."

"Not anymore they aren't."

Something dropped from nowhere, atop Nails, slashing her across back and throat, her gun going off where she held it, sending Blue to the ground. A second creature jumped Blue. Saylor fired point-blank, hitting the creature on Nails' back between the eyes, killing it instantly. The gas floating down over Blue made Stroud hesitate while Tulley fired two shots into the thing on Blue, who tore away, screaming.

Anna More was the first to get to Nails, whose throat was spurting blood. Anna tore out a plastic bag holding some beef jerky, emptied it and pressed it firmly into the wound at Nails' throat. Nails was trying to breathe and talk at once, but nothing was coming out. Anna held her, feeling her life ebbing beneath her, shouting, "Get something to make a tourniquet, quickly! Quickly!"

Stroud rushed to Anna with a first-aid kit, tearing out the bandaging. Anna held firm to the plastic bag, stopping the blood flow as Nails was battling to stay conscious, her eyes bulging. Stroud looped the bandaging around and around Nails' neck, Anna regaining the pressure hold with each pass. She'd sunk the plastic in tightly against the wound, and now only time would tell. Nails' back was scarred terribly, too.

All the while, Lou Cage and the others skyborne were shouting over the communications link, pleading for information as to what had happened. They were aware that Nails' vital signs had fallen off with the loss of blood and shock.

Blue, bleeding also, but on his feet, had been saved by the camera on his back. The creature had ripped it to smithereens instead of Blue's helmeted head. Blue stood blubbering over Nails, pleading for her to pull through.

"Come on, Nails! Come on!"

"Jesus, Abe! I told you fools not to go in there!" Lou was shouting.

Nails was rasping, trying desperately for air, the sound making them all ill.

Tulley told Blue to regain his senses and keep his eyes open. Tulley and Saylor were watching for the next attack wave, but no one could see anything now that the gas fog had blanketed the entire area.

One of the werewolves stepped from the gas fog, lurching at Saylor, who fired several rounds into the thing's stomach before it fell over Saylor, who shoved it off and got up trembling. Priest had thrown down his weapon and grabbed Nails' and now he scanned the gray emptiness of the fog.

"They rip your mask off, you're dead that way," Tulley assured everyone.

"What do we do now?" begged Blue. "Goddammit, what do we do now? What, Saylor? Tulley? We just wait for the damned things to come get us?"

"Shut up, Joe! Just shut up!" shouted Saylor.

"We've got to backpedal," pleaded Priest. "Earl, we got no choice!"

"Just shut up! We don't move a muscle until we can see! Going back the way we came is crazy."

"This gas," said Tulley. "Thought it was supposed to slow the mothers down!"

"It doesn't work instantly," Stroud reminded them, "but it will."

"Meanwhile, we're fuckin' blind, man!" shouted Blue.

"That's enough, Blue!" said Saylor, rushing to Blue and shoving him hard. "Get hold of it, grunt!"

Tulley fired, causing everyone to jump. He'd just killed again the silver-haired one Kerac had defeated where he lay twitching on the ground.

"Goddammit, Warren! Waste no more of that ammo!" Saylor screamed.

"Hey, man! He was alive. Seen a lot of dead gooks get up and kill guys!"

"Let the gas do its work," Stroud tried to reason with Priest and Blue. "Before you got trigger-happy, I was trying to estimate their numbers."

"So, what's your guess, Doc?" asked Saylor.

"I think we've certainly got upwards of two hundred and fifty, maybe more."

"This damned gas better work, then."

"Give it time."

Blue rushed at Stroud, "And what about Nails, huh? How much time can she lie here like . . ."

Blue and everyone stared, somehow knowing what Anna More had known for some time now. Anna said sadly, "She's dead."

Blue went to his knees over his fallen comrade. The others fell silent. There was a quiet over the area that added to the eerie feel of the gas fog, making it seem a cemetery before dawn.

"Awwww, no, no!" Blue wailed.

Saylor indicated to Stroud they should talk, and the two stepped a little away from the others. "We go for the location Cage gave us, for the bait. We take out as many as we can there."

"You hold on to it, Blue," Tulley was advising the other man when they rejoined them.

"Appears they've cleared out," said Saylor. "Their noses should take them to where we want them to be. Cage and the others can drop on them anytime at that location—"

"Nails is dead, sir," Blue told his commanding officer like a small boy in shock.

"And we're going to avenge her, Joe."

Blue got to his feet, nodding, "Yes, sir . . . but we can't just leave her here like this."

"You want to pack her, Joe?"

"Yes, sir."

Tulley started to object, but Saylor put up a firm hand to his second-in-command. "You go right ahead, Joe. Maybe lighten her up a bit. Just keep the gun belt and the canteen. All right, Joe? Priest, you take her weapon."

"We leave her here . . . they'll come back . . . feed on her," Joe Blue said. "I ain't going to let that happen to Nails, sir?"

"Course not, Joe. Your choice, Joe."

Joe went to her and removed the heavier objects from Nails' dead body. He hefted her, his eyes meeting Anna More's. "Thank you, ma'am, for what you tried to do," he said. "She was . . . was one hell of a soldier."

Anna More, shaken to the core, lifted her hand to Blue, who took it. She squeezed Blue's hand and said, "You were good friends. I'm sorry."

"Let's move," said Saylor quietly.

Stroud uselessly informed Cage above that Nails was dead. Cage said, "Yeah, I watched her vital signs go."

"We did all we could, Lou."

"Don't be fools, Abe. Make for the rendezvous point now. Forget trying to combat these things on their own ground. It can't work."

"We've got to try, Lou. We've got to try."

"Until you're all dead?"

Around him, Stroud heard the standard commando hoopla designed to get soldiers to go into a place that meant almost certain death. It was a chorus of encouraging machismo.

"We've got the weapons! We've got the guts."

"And we got the power!"

"Let's waste 'em, Blue!"

"For Nails!"

"Let's do it for Nails!"

—18—

From where Louis Cage sat, everything was visible and everything was invisible. The fog created by the gas bombs dropped by the helicopters was clearly visible, yet it masked everything beneath it. There was no way to be sure in which direction the werewolf colony had migrated from Stroud and Saylor. Cage had only to look at his partitioned screens to see what was occurring at ground level. One of those screens had suddenly gone dead—Nells. The others now only recorded a dense soup of fog through which the company of soldiers, Stroud and Anna More traveled. Like the people on the ground, all that Cage could see was the few feet in front of them. When Blue and Nells were attacked, he'd lived vicariously and died vicariously with them; when Saylor was attacked, he'd been staring right at the fog and the thing that had come out of it seemed to materialize from nowhere.

The shock had taken years off Lou's life, he reasoned, and a great deal more off Saylor's. It amazed Lou that the man had had the presence of mind to fire when the creature came at him as it did.

Now all that Cage saw on each monitor frame was the cloud they'd created, an occasional lock in on a dead beast that had succumbed to the bullets. Cage asked now that some of the beasts be examined, to determine if any had been killed by the gas.

Saylor told his men to see to it, but to be careful. Several werewolf bodies without bloody wounds were found, and it was assumed that the gas did indeed have a deadly effect upon them.

"Good, good!" said Lou. "Now we can fight them from the air, Abe. Now you people can be pulled back without any further casualties."

"No way," said Saylor. "We're playing this out, Stroud, whether you like it or not."

"That's right," agreed Tulley.

All of them stopped in their march toward the drop site. Blue, coming up the rear with Nails over his brawny shoulder, agreed. "We're not wimping out."

Priest frowned, said nothing, only hefting the AK-47 that had been Nails' and made a gesture of agreement.

"You two go to the rendezvous point, Stroud. Get the woman out," suggested Saylor, his steely gray eyes not leaving Anna's.

"Now, just a minute," said Anna More. "Stroud doesn't talk for me. I'm here to see this thing through."

"Cage," said Stroud through the com link below his gas mask, "looks like we're going to stay."

"But Abe!"

"We put it to a vote, Lou."

"Move out," said Saylor.

"You're all crazy!" shouted Lou from above. "You know that?" In the chopper, Lou could see the expressions of each man's face as Anna More looked from one of them to the next, settling on Stroud. In a partition shot, Lou saw More's face behind her gas mask. The two of them, Stroud and More, seemed at first in a test of wills, but Anna's camera panned down to her hands and Lou saw that Stroud held her hands in his.

"They know the lay of the land," she told Stroud. "They know every hiding place, every crevice."

"Cage, see if you guys up there can advise us on location of our prey."

Cage was angry. "Damn it, Stroud, I'm telling you they vanished. Just vanished."

"They chameleon themselves against the land," Stroud told him. "At night, you'll have to go to infrared."

"You fools aren't planning to spend the night down there!"

"If we have to, Lou, we will."

"Crazy . . . all of you are crazy."

"Watch the drop site. Let us know when they arrive."

Stroud said to Anna, "I only hope they take the poisoned meat. Kerac'll try to dissuade them. He knows it's poisoned, just like he knew about the transmitter."

"He's beaten down their leader. They'll listen to him," she said.

"Afraid so."

"Perhaps bringing him back here alive wasn't such a good idea, after all, Doctor?"

More started away, Stroud's eyes and his camera watching her go. Cage realized the depth of Stroud's feelings for More for the first time as he watched the scene unfold.

Then all of the brave, foolish people disappeared in the dense, sulfuric cloud that hung all around them. The cloud offered cover, of a kind. It also offered a kind of sanctuary, now the creatures understood its deadly effect on their kind. Still, it was eerie and terrifying to walk in the valley of it, not knowing what moment might be one's last.

Kerac, his painful forearm throbbing, surrounded by his followers, looked down on the valley of death where others of his kind lay facedown in the pine needles. He'd tried desperately to herd them all away from the deadly spray of gas that rained down on them, but some—many—failed to heed his bray of warning. He saw some of them stumble now from the periphery of the fatal mist, coughing, retching and keeling over, their bodies twitching as the gas made its way through their systems and finally to the heart. It was a gas concocted by this man named Stroud.

The others were following Kerac now, fully cognizant of his wisdom. Showing was better than telling. He led them blindly to find shelter among the thickets and toward the other side of the bowl of earth they had climbed from. Kerac was hearing rumblings from the others now, and a large portion had moved off in another direction, and Kerac feared the worst when he scented the sweet odor of blood in the air. It was Stroud's meat, dropped from the machine they had brought Kerac here in.

Kerac rushed toward the front of the herd wildly, trying to warn the others, but he was being ignored.

He came to a clearing where some sixty or seventy others had already gathered, feasting and fighting over the gift left by Stroud.

Kerac bellowed in rage and anger, racing in, tearing at some of the other males, ripping meat from their mouths and pointing to others of their kind that lay on the earth, groveling and writhing in wicked pain, as if their insides had been skewered with sharp hooks. Again, Stroud's silver poisoning.

Kerac lifted one huge chunk of red meat after another and hurled it far into the air. Some of the others raced after it, as if it were a game. Kerac then threw himself at others who continued to feast. Some simply could not comprehend the situation until one and another and a third of the writhing ones stopped writhing. This was followed by others, two, four, six, eight, ten. Now all who had taken the least bite of the tainted meat began falling, knees buckling. Some rolled their large eyes up at Kerac, who stood on the carcass heap dropped by Stroud's devils. All around Kerac, his followers were dying, all but those who were just now arriving.

Overhead, a helicopter soared across the field and Kerac lifted a clenched claw up at it and bellowed his frustration.

A second helicopter flew by. This one dropped something from its cargo hold, and Kerac's bellow of frustration turned into a roar of warning. He raced as fast and as furiously as he could from the meat, and behind him, he could hear the deadly weapons open fire on his kind.

Kerac climbed and clawed his way over the bodies of his dead brethren, knocking aside others in his way to get free, knowing that just one of Stroud's silver-doused bullets meant his death. Suddenly, one of the deadly bullets struck him in the leg.

Kerac collapsed on a second heap of meat. He bent full over and clamped his teeth down hard on the bullet's entry wound, tearing out his own flesh and the bullet lodged there, spitting it out in rage. He then got up and leapt a full ten yards onto the earth, away from where the bullet had come from. The dirt beside and around him exploded in short, powerful little bursts, and a tree he passed was cut in two. Someone among the killers was aiming directly for him. Stroud, no doubt.

He fell instinctively to the earth, pretending he'd been hit again and killed. From this vantage, with the deadly rain of toxic gas coming ever closer, Kerac's eyes met those of the Indian woman again, the same one who had stood outside his cell aiming a gun at his eyes. She fired again, but her gun jammed. When she looked up, Kerac was gone, replaced by hundreds of others like him. She fired into the mass, instead, watching them fall.

Warren Priest opened fire with the others in a mad attempt to strike every howling beast before them, including those already poisoned by the meat. Ringing in his ears was a deafening mix of automatic gunfire, the roaring of wounded and affronted monsters, and Stroud's powerful voice shouting a warning about the need to return to their masks. Priest looked up and saw the cloud of gas descending rapidly over them, realizing it could kill him quicker than it could the beasts for which it was intended. He stopped firing long enough to strap on again the full face mask and turn on his oxygen supply. As he did so, he realized that Tulley, ahead of him every step of the way, had already covered himself in this regard and was continuing the fight.

Priest again lifted his own weapon when suddenly he felt an enormously powerful grip take hold of him from behind. He tried to bring his gun around to fire on the thing that had hold of him. He screamed for Tulley, but his voice was drowned out by the roaring and gunfire all around. He realized that the werewolf that had hold of him had appeared from what seemed a hole in the side of the earthen hill, hidden by the dense foliage. The beast lifted him off his feet, and suddenly Priest registered the awful, gut-wrenching feeling of its enormous fangs as they lodged into the flesh and bone at the nape of his neck. It was the last sensation he felt, and his hands opened in nervous reaction, the unlucky AK-47 that had been Nails' dropping to the earth in front of him. He saw it as if it were happening in slow motion. He felt himself dragged into the darkness as if it were a dream.

Priest realized that he was drugged and stiff and unable to use any of his limbs or muscles. He could not speak, and his hearing had become desensitized. It was a condition that would drive him mad. He could not even feel the force tearing him along now through what seemed a crevice in the earth known only to the beasts.

Priest's heart felt as if it would burst with fear, and yet, it would not burst. Even this horrendous fear was controlled by the deadening venom coursing through his body. He was worse than dead, he told himself. He was trapped alive by the werewolves.

He felt himself lifted and turned as if on a spit to come face-to-face with the maimed Kerac, who was crouched and bleeding and angry. Something dire and wicked crossed the features of the cunning bastard, and Priest knew that his fate would not be so easy as Nails' had been.

Priest watched Kerac wrestle a long polelike stick from another of his kind. Priest's eyes seemed the only thing working over his entire body. He saw Kerac circle him with the dirty stick, and he felt the nudging and force as Kerac worked at his back, roaring and shoving the others from Priest. Then Priest felt himself go suddenly horizontal and he was suspended in a macabre fashion somehow, staring down at the earth, his feet off the ground. He felt his own dead weight being jostled and bumped along as his body was being moved now through the cave. And when Warren Priest saw his own dripping blood discoloring the earthen floor, the soldier of fortune mentally retched, as his bodily need to do so was quite out of his control. Priest realized what Kerac had done with the pole; realized they'd attached him to the dirty stick, ramming it through him like a pig sticker.

"Masks! On with your masks, again! Now!" shouted Stroud. They had circled the clearing to almost better than halfway when Kerac leapt in, tore away at the others, trying to frighten them off. They saw Kerac climb atop the tainted meat, fending the others off in a macabre version of King of the Mountain. Then the choppers came in, dropping their deadly balms, and then Anna More fired, hitting Kerac.

To the amazement of the humans, Kerac tore out a large portion of his leg to combat the poison to his system, as he had with the implant. Now, bleeding, he appeared for a moment shot again where he fell, and then somehow he eluded them.

With the first volley from Anna More came a full-scale fire barrage from the others, racing to kill as many as possible before the gas closed in around them, blotting out their targets. Stroud and Saylor had told Cage to hold back with the cloud this time until they could destroy as many as they could with the bullets, but Cage either misunderstood or had simply disobeyed Stroud, fearing for their lives.

Many of the beasts came straight at them, launching a counter-attack. Blue relentlessly mowed them down, as did the others. Tulley and Saylor feared some of the beasts were getting around them, preparing to cut them off from one another, and they were right. Several came at the soldiers from behind.

Stroud fired a volley that brought down some of these. Others slinked off and blended in with their surroundings so well, Stroud may as well be trying to fire on a gnat. Stroud kept Anna plainly in view, covering her back as well, turning, when suddenly gunfire exploded near him and a huge beast fell into him, dead. Anna had just killed one that was about to take Stroud's head off. The weight of the creature knocked Stroud dizzy, and he dropped his weapon. Anna rushed to him, to drag him from the helpless position of being half under the huge werewolf, when another leapt from a tree. Stroud grabbed for his weapon, but it was inches from his fingers. Blue, screaming and firing, rushed in, tearing the creature in two with a rain of bullets.

Saylor raced to Blue, yanking his gun from his control and slapping him from side to side. "One bullet per customer, damn you, Blue!"

Anna knelt over Stroud, and with some assistance from Tulley, pulled him free. Together, the humans formed a circle and Tulley said, "Where's Priest?"

No one had any answers.

Stroud tried to hail Cage, to ask after Priest. The others began shouting for him.

"Warren!"

"Yo! Priest!"

No answer came, and Cage was out of range. "He must be hurt, unable to answer," said Anna.

"Where'd you last see him, Tulley? He was with you, wasn't he?"

"He was beside me when the firefight started, but after that . . . hell, I guess I didn't see him."

"Scout around, eyes peeled. Careful of the trees," said Saylor.

"Priest! Priest! Where the hell are you, man?" shouted Blue to no avail.

"He chickened," said Tulley. "That's it. He chickened, doubled back."

"How do you know that?" asked Saylor.

"Was talking funny, Earl. I told him to drop it, but he was talking funny there for a while."

"What kind of funny?"

"Like maybe the guy in the helicopter was right; like maybe we ought to just nuke them from the air; like this is crazy, what we are trying to do."

"And so, you think he split?"

"If he did," said Stroud, "alone, out here, he's dead meat."

"What the hell're we going to do now?" asked Blue.

"We carry on with our mission," said Saylor just as Tulley screamed.

A tree beside Tulley had reached out and grabbed him by the throat, choking him, except that the tree had become one of *them*. "Shoot! Shoot it!" shouted Blue.

But there was no way to shoot it without killing Tulley in the bargain. Saylor knocked Blue's weapon from him as Tulley grabbed his bayonet and began stabbing at the powerful hands about his throat. The grip loosened, and the thing that had Tulley went to its knees and crumbled like a dying flower, a victim of the gas.

"Jesus," said Tulley, gasping for breath, "these things are everywhere."

"Damn that Priest," said Saylor. "I never would've taken him for a deserter."

"Maybe he didn't desert," said Stroud.

Anna More agreed. "Maybe they've got him."

This thought silenced the professional soldiers.

"If that's so, then we'd find his weapon," Saylor finally said. "Take me to the last position you two took up, Tulley—exactly."

They followed Tulley to the spot, and there lay the AK-47 that Priest had commandeered from Nails.

Tulley hefted Priest's weapon, inspecting it carefully. "It's hot, but the magazine's near full."

"No sign of blood," said Stroud, "either on the gun or the ground."

"They've taken him alive," said Saylor, a bit shaken at the thought.

"No sign of his mask, or any of his other equipment," commented Anna More.

Stroud had to agree. "It does look like abduction, and if that's the case, it's the work of Kerac."

"Abduction for what purpose?" asked Tulley.

"Anybody's guess," replied Stroud, not wishing to state the obvious.

Saylor didn't mind stating it, however. "Took him to bait us, didn't they, Doc? Didn't they?"

"Possibly."

"Christ!" shouted Tulley. "He was right beside me the whole time. First Nails, then . . . now Tulley. Who's next? Huh, who?"

"Wil, get hold of yourself!" shouted Saylor to Tulley, whose eyes went from Saylor to Anna More before he nodded and apologized.

"Tulley's goddamned right, Earl," said Blue. "Time we got out of this gig, man!"

"We're in it till it's over, you men got that?" shouted Saylor.

"Oh, Christ," Blue suddenly said, looking pale and stricken.

"What is it, Joe? Joe?"

"I . . . I had to leave Nails' body to cover yous . . . and, oh, God, if they got Tulley—" He was racing away with his last words toward the trees where he had left Nails' corpse.

The others pursued Blue, but when they caught up to him he was pounding his fist into a tree, and where the grass had been matted by Nails' remains there was nothing but empty space. "They've got her, too! Damn them! They've got her, Earl!"

"At least, Joe, she won't feel another thing," said Saylor.

"Can't say as much for Warren," added Tulley. "With Priest it'll be a different story."

"We've got to find him," said Anna More. "Find him and do what we can for him."

"That'd likely be to put him from his misery, ma'am," said Saylor.

"I would hope that you men would have the guts to do it for me," she said. "We're wasting time here, Abe."

Stroud shouldered his weapon and hailed the helicopters circling over. He'd have the sad duty to report the terrible turn of events to the men aloft.

"Cage, Cage! Come in, Lou!" Stroud tried to locate Cage once more. "We've lost Priest. Do you have any indications from there where he is? Are you showing any vital signs for the man?"

After some static, Cage came on. "He's alive, Stroud."

A cheer went up among them, but it was soon silenced by Stroud, who was having difficulty hearing Cage.

"He's alive, but he's in shock. They have him, Abe."

Stroud moaned in response, shaking his head, looking at the others. "Can you give us any idea on his location?"

"To your left, perhaps a mile off. These things travel fast. His only hope is if we can get to him by air," said Lou. "My only fear is that his mask might've been ripped away."

"We didn't see a thing from here, and we didn't hear a scream," Saylor told Cage.

"Why do you suppose he is still alive?" asked Anna More. "Why didn't they kill him?"

"Only one reason," said Tulley, wiping his brow where the mask was irritating it. "To bait us."

"We're going to see if we can assist with the birds," Cage told the others.

"Lou," said Stroud, "take every precaution."

"I think if I were in Priest's shoes, I'd rather die by the gas, wouldn't you, Abe?"

"Yeah . . . yeah . . . do it. We're on our way."

"Move out," Saylor ordered what was left of his men. Stroud and Anna More brought up the rear.

The march was over difficult terrain: swamp ooze, high grass, rock cliffs, and fallen trees slick with the green paint of wood-boring microbes and moss.

Cage came back on communications. "Abe, they've got him, all right. His camera's come back on. He's regained consciousness and he's watching one of those things chew off his goddamned arm, Abe! But Kerac's there, too, and he's fighting off the others, keeping Priest alive."

"Kerac?"

"Yes!"

"Kerac's behind the abduction, then. He's using Priest to bait us! Just as we suspected."

"Precisely."

"Could you see Priest?"

"Negative."

"Have you located where they're holding him?"

"Yes, and we're going in with the gas. Even if Priest is alive, Abe, he's been subjected to the venom. For all intents and purposes, he is one of them now—or soon will be."

"I'm sure Kerac would like to convert us all," Stroud said flatly. "All right, carry it out. We'll get there as soon as we can."

"And Abe—"

"Yeah?"

"We're running low on the gas canisters. This may be our last air strike."

"Roger that. Go for it, Lou."

"And what do we do?" shouted Tulley. "Just forget about Priest? Write him off?"

"Stow it, Tulley!" shouted Saylor. "We'll maintain discipline, for one thing."

"I say we make for higher ground. Someplace where the helicopters can pick us up," said Stroud. "We can't do any more here without further casualties, and I'm afraid Dr. Cage is right about Priest. There's nothing we can do for him, either. We've got no

•

antidote to the venom that's pumping through his body now. If we could get him free, it would be like regaining Kerac. He'd have to be killed by one of us, as surely as we must kill Kerac and the others."

They made their way for the rock ledge ahead, which announced a ridge far above. According to every indication, it was the rendezvous point where the whirlybirds were to meet them. It was growing dark now, and even Saylor and Tulley agreed, it was time for a pull-out, that they wouldn't survive a night attack by the werewolves.

"We've got to make for the top of that ridge," said Stroud. "Looks like an hour's climb."

Saylor agreed with the assessment. "There's nothing more we can do for Priest or Nails now."

"And we go with our tails between our legs?" shouted Tulley. "We've got to salvage something from this, Earl, some shred of . . . of . . . something."

"We'll be back at first light," said Stroud. "I haven't given up on the idea we must exterminate these monsters."

Tulley and Blue held out a moment, looking at one another for support, before Tulley said, "All right . . . all right . . . we pull back."

Anna More was staring through her binoculars, scanning the upper reaches of the ridge, when she saw some movement in the underbrush. She shouted to Stroud to look. Stroud and the others took up their own field glasses and scanned. There was movement around the rendezvous point.

"Unfriendlies," grunted Tulley. "Looks like they're smarter than we give 'em credit for. But how did they know where we'd be moving to?"

"They've probably been watching us all along," said Saylor. "Bastards. They're good."

Stroud suddenly realized that it was all part of Kerac's plan. "Kerac's got Priest, holding him for the helicopters to come in while his followers circle the clearing where they'll land to pick us up. We've got to warn Cage and the others!"

"They're out of range," said Saylor.

"Damn it, then we've got to get up, cover that hill!"

"Break out our supply of the gas," said Saylor.

"And the bazooka," agreed Blue.

"Looks like you're going to get your wish, Tulley," Stroud told the other hard-bitten man.

"Yeah, some wish, huh?"

"Double time. Meanwhile try to get Cage or one of the others!" Saylor shouted to Stroud.

Anna trotted alongside Abe. "Do you really think Kerac planned all this?"

"I hope I'm wrong, but it does seem to be shaping up that way. If his friends get to the helicopters, we're all stranded here."

They picked up the pace.

—19—

Dr. Louis Cage had been monitoring what Priest's camera was picking up. He'd gone out of range of the others, and so he now concentrated on poor Priest, whose sufferings he could hear as well as see. Kerac hadn't been able to fend off the others of his kind for long. They had at it with Priest like ravenous vultures in the end, ripping off parts of him and gorging themselves before the man's eyes until he fell away in a dead faint. Kerac was furious with his brothers and sisters there on the outcrop of granite where they'd assembled, clearly daring the helicopters in, having tied Priest to the top of a tree that reached this point. He dangled there like meat on a hook, and when the occasional beast would get past Kerac to rip a piece of Priest away, Priest and the top of the tree would sway in and out from the ledge.

The three choppers swooped in. Priest's camera equipment was now torn away, as was his mask. Cage felt he was saving the man any further pain when he dropped the final cask of deadly poison over the granite ledge. As he did so, the were-wolves, now fully cognizant of the threat the giant birds brought with them, scurried down below the level of the cloud as it rose, almost useless except for putting Priest out of his misery.

"Stroud, come in, Stroud." Cage tried desperately to let Abe know the outcome, but he was too far out of range.

He could barely make out a signal Stroud was trying to send.

The other two choppers followed suit, dropping their gas into the lower tree line, trying to better target the fleeing mass of brown-backed creatures below. Cage felt the helicopter turning in a wide arc. "Take us back to the rendezvous point. We've got to get our people out now." Cage stared at the disappearing sun in the horizon.

"Yes, sir!" agreed Dave at the controls.

The other helicopters responded to this order with so much enthusiasm that they didn't circle the field of destruction below as did Cage, who desperately hoped to see that Priest was far from his misery now.

Behind choppers two and three, Cage moved ever closer to the rendezvous point, trying once more to hail Stroud, whose broken words could not be understood.

" . . . double-cross . . . Kerac . . . bastard . . . knows . . ."

"Stroud, come in, Stroud. What're you saying?"

" . . . put down . . . rendezvous . . . rendezvous point . . . safe . . ."

"Finally, they're ready to listen to reason!" Cage told the pilot. "Rush us to the rendezvous, Dave."

In the dusk, seeing had become impossible. It was too dark for ordinary eyes to penetrate the thick blanket of grays and greens below them from the helicopter, and it was too light to switch to infrared visual aids. But something was clearly amiss up ahead on the long ridge where they'd planned the pickup. Cage saw the smoke of gunfire first, and then he saw one of the helicopters spinning madly out of control, several of the enormous, hairy beasts hanging like maggots to its skids.

"Stroud, Stroud! Come in, come in!" he hailed Stroud anew.

But now Stroud was not answering. Cage looked over the monitors on all those below. Every one of them had racing heartbeats, their pulses screaming. The cameras showed Cage that the others were in another dogfight with the enemy, for possession of the rendezvous point, and instantly Cage knew what Stroud knew—that Priest's abduction was a feigned attack designed to draw defensive action away from Kerac's intended target.

"Cunning bastard," said Cage to himself. Cage now saw the red fire of a bazooka shot explode a plot of stones, sending several of the beasts flying like toys off the side of the ridge. Another of the gas bombs exploded, but these were the smaller, hand-held ones, their efficiency questionable.

As for Cage's lending support, chopper one was out of gas canisters. So Cage rushed to the cargo bay and pulled a high-powered rifle from the wall. It was scoped, and it had infrared sighting as well. He'd earlier placed silver bullets in its magazine, and now Cage opened fire.

Stroud had tried desperately to stay on the radio, attempting to warn off the helicopters before they made the fatal mistake of setting down here. But the beasts had seen the approaching foot soldiers, most likely smelling them first. Now they turned and cascaded down the ridge in swarms, coming directly for the small party of humans who dared open fire on them. Stroud had to forgo the radio long enough to fire at those coming directly at Anna and him.

"Lay down a barrage of the gas first!" shouted Saylor. "We're running short of the good bullets, damn it!"

"Damned smoke just makes it harder for us to see!" disagreed Blue, who grabbed up one of the bazookas and with Tulley's help began firing mortar shots with deadly accuracy. Saylor continued throwing out the gas grenades. Stroud killed two of the beasts who'd almost gotten to Saylor's position. Anna More lay down a fire line that kept others at bay.

Yet, there remained a dangerous contingent of the beasts at or near the ridge. Stroud prayed the fire display would dissuade the pilots from landing, but he couldn't count on this. He tried to fight and send warnings at once, but this proved futile. The things were everywhere, falling around them from trees, leaping out from bushes and from behind every rock.

"Come on! Come on!" Blue was shouting over the den. "Come and get this, you big apes!"

"Fire away!" Tulley shouted, and another bazooka blast did its deadly work. But the shrapnel-wounded beasts were dragging themselves away, their wounds healing within minutes. Stroud saw some of these same ones launch a second attack. And Saylor was right: the useful ammunition was running dangerously low.

The throng of *were-people* seemed to fly through the undergrowth, and from a distance others were coming to join the fight.

"We've got to take control of the ridge!" shouted Saylor.

"Push ahead!" Stroud agreed, pointing to the movement in the waning light at the crest of another hill in the distance that now silhouetted the army of creatures coming for them. "Kerac's band!"

"Come on, Blue! Blue!" Tulley tore at Joe Blue. "We've got to scale the ridge! Now!"

"They're trying to flank us on all sides!" shouted Saylor.

In front of him, Anna More fell to the earth and Stroud heard her scream and saw that she was being tugged along by something on the ground. It was one of Blue's walking wounded. It'd lifted up a claw and wrapped it around Anna's ankle, and was dragging her into the undergrowth when Stroud pumped several shots into the brush, the claw releasing Anna. He helped her regain her feet, and together, they raced for the summit, dirt and rock cascading underfoot.

"Cage! Cage! Don't bring in the birds! Unsafe! Kerac set us up!"

Then gunshots came from overhead, striking a beast within inches of Stroud, instantly killing him as Cage's bullet found the creature's brain. As they got over the crest, Stroud saw that the other two helicopters were in trouble. One was wheeling like a drunken animal as nine or so of the beasts hung from its skids, while the second machine was sitting stationary, the pilot dead at the controls where a horde of the monsters was feeding on him in the cockpit. The bubble glass was splattered with the pilot's blood.

"Get them off the chopper in the air!" Stroud shouted.

Anna kneeled, aimed and sent one of the beasts to the earth. Stroud brought another down. Saylor and Tulley did likewise.

The beasts were falling like flies from the helicopter, but it was in serious trouble, tilted blades cutting the branches of trees, when the blade was suddenly stopped by a large oak.

"Take cover!" cried Stroud as they all dove for safety.

The helicopter plummeted into the stationary chopper like a stone, sending up a flume of smoke and fire that lit the surrounding darkness. Several beasts ran about, their bodies inflamed. The roars of those trapped in the explosion became silent, and it became apparent that most wanted nothing to do with the raging fire.

"Everyone here?" shouted Saylor. "Sound off!"

"Tulley!"

"Stroud!"

"More!"

"Blue! All accounted for, sir!"

From above Cage had continued to fire on the fleeing beasts. But he now communicated with the survivors. "We're sending down a rope ladder. See that you use it!"

The remaining pilot was having trouble keeping his craft steady, the rising waves of superheated air from the wreckage causing a sure disturbance here. Still, Cage was determined, and so down came the ladder. The roar of the helicopter drowned out any chance they might hear the stealthy creatures all around them. Only the light from the fire which singed their eyebrows helped them to see those among the wolf-people who were foolish enough to continue the attack.

Blue held them off, shouting for the others to take the ladder. "Go on! Go!" Blue's AK-47 stopped suddenly, and he grabbed Tulley's away from him. "Go! All of you! Go!"

Anna More went first up the rope ladder, followed by Tulley, as Stroud and Saylor argued who would go next. All of them had torn away their gas masks, and these dangled about their necks. They had also thrown aside the encumbering camera equipment on the race for the hill.

"Go, Earl! Now!"

"Don't be a fool, Stroud. You're the brains here. You get killed, and what's left for us to do? Me, I'm paid to stay. Now go! *Go!*"

Stroud stared for a moment, but then began the ascent to the helicopter, seeing that Anna was already climbing into the cargo bay door. He saw Cage waving him on madly between shots he was taking with the infrared-equipped rifle. Stroud climbed for his life and crawled in just behind Tulley, who had taken up a position the opposite side of the helicopter and was firing down on a party of the creatures coming in on Blue's blind side. Stroud took up a position alongside Tulley with a second infrared weapon, making each of his shots count.

Below them Saylor was yanking at Blue to get onto the ladder. Blue fought him, insisting that Saylor go ahead. Saylor started up, firing as he did so. Blue's gun quit on him and he threw it, raced for the rope ladder and caught it in midjump, scrambling up just behind Saylor when one of the creatures leapt up and held Blue by the legs, making him scream. Saylor threw down his rifle and pulled out a Beretta automatic, firing into the creature's head, but this one was replaced by another, and the weight of a second one sent the helicopter gyrating, with everyone aboard spilling about in its belly. Cage had been sent out the door and was holding on to the frame, with Anna trying desperately to help him. Stroud crawled to them and grabbed hold of Cage's hand, holding firm as Anna helped pull him back in. Then the machine swerved the other way, threatening to send them all out the other door.

Saylor fired past Blue's nose, but as soon as one creature dropped, it was replaced by another and another until Saylor was out of bullets.

They ripped and tore at Blue's legs, one suddenly coming away with his boot and his foot inside it.

"Blue!" Saylor screamed as Joe was torn away, and he fell into the waiting mob below the helicopter. The helicopter, released, careened skyward with Saylor dangling below it, the anguish in him at odds with the sudden realization he was free and alive.

Moments later, at the top of the rope ladder, the others helped Saylor onto a stable platform. No one asked him, but he said, "Blue almost made it . . . but they tore off his leg . . . loss of blood . . . couldn't hold on."

Tulley trembled at the thought. "Earl, we ain't getting paid enough for this gig . . ."

Saylor went to Stroud, saying, "We're not done with these mothers yet, are we? Well, are we?"

"Cage estimates there are between a hundred and a hundred fifty left. We've got infrared spotting on the chopper, and now we've got fuel enough back at our base . . . now the other machines are gone."

"Along with two good pilots," added Tulley.

"I'm for resuming the fight," said Anna More. "Stroud was right from the beginning. They must be exterminated."

"We need more help," said Cage. "We can't do it alone."

"That's right," said Tulley.

"We do this my way, Tulley!" said Stroud. "Bringing in more people would just get more killed. Can't you see that?"

"Earl, tell him! Tell him it's over!" shouted Tulley.

Saylor shook his head. "You didn't see what they did to Blue. I came to kill these bastards, and that's what I will do, Tulley, with or without you."

"We've got to prepare better," said Anna. "We need to ready more ammunition, do something."

"I say we put it to a vote," said Cage.

"No, Lou!" shouted Stroud. "This isn't up for a vote. We do it my way. Those of you who want out can wait for us at the base camp where we first dropped Kerac. As for me, I won't rest until Kerac is dead, along with all of his kind! And that's the end of the discussion. Anna's right. We've got to start using our heads. We've got to prepare. Priest, Nails and Blue didn't die in vain."

"Hell, we've killed almost half of 'em!" said Saylor. "Now we go back for the other half."

"And they've killed over half of us!" shouted Tulley. "I don't want to die the way Blue died, the way Priest died."

"Get hold of yourself, Tulley."

"This ain't no goddamned army, Earl. If I want out, I'm out."

"Fine! Fine, you pussy! Do just that while More here does your job for you. Sick, man!"

Tulley went for Saylor's throat with a bayonet knife. Stroud grabbed Tulley's hand just as Saylor's booted foot hit Tulley in the testicles, doubling him over. "Get hold of it, Tulley! Nothing to be ashamed of. We're all afraid. So am I. So's More over there, aren't you, Chief?"

Anna More gritted her teeth and nodded, saying, "Of course. Only a fool would be unafraid." She said it as if to Stroud, whom she stared at now.

"We're going back in at dawn. All of you, get some rest," said Stroud.

Stroud found a corner and nestled in it. His mind imagined a one-armed Kerac far below, baying up at the receding aircraft, secure in the knowledge that he had beaten Stroud.

Anna More joined Stroud. Exhausted, she slid down the bulkhead to sit alongside him. He looked into her dirt-smeared features, riveting her eyes with his own. "We are doing the right thing, Anna."

"The only thing," she agreed. "I'm sorry I ever doubted you, Abe."

"We've got to stay in the air, Stroud," said Cage. "We can't win on their level, not so long as they have Kerac as their leader."

For a time, Stroud dozed, exhausted along with the others. Anna put a finger to her lips, indicating that Stroud was asleep.

Cage squinted at the scene beside him. "Is he really asleep? Or is it another of his blasted blackouts?"

"He's exhausted. We all are."

"Exhausted, bleeding . . . bruised, all of you," said Cage.

They were soon approaching the base site where additional provisions awaited them, and where the pilot could refuel. Meanwhile, Cage opened a second vat of silver nitrate in liquid form for the new ammunition supplies. As soon as they touched down, he would have to begin work on additional gas bombs. As they drew nearer, the helicopter about to set down, Saylor and Tulley nervously watched the perimeter. They were a good fifteen miles from where they had exited the forests, but they must never again underestimate the enemy.

"Wake Stroud," Saylor said to Anna.

"Let him rest," she replied.

"We don't know how safe this area is."

"He needs rest. We all do!"

"It's all clear according to what I can see on infrared," said Tulley. "I think we can all breathe easy, for the time being."

"Thank God," said Cage.

"We've got munitions to load, partner," said Saylor to Tulley. "You with me?"

Tulley, considerably calmed by a few drinks of whiskey that Saylor had offered him on the flight, nodded and took Earl Saylor's hand, apologizing for what he called his bad behavior.

Saylor said to think nothing of it, and then the two men were away, leaping from the helicopter even before the rotor blades shut down.

Anna, savoring the moment with Stroud, took his hands in hers and quietly cried for those who had perished.

Kerac now knew that he must act before his kind were systematically exterminated by Stroud. He fought for control of the remaining numbers, his roars of warning telling them that the thing called Stroud would return to wipe them all out. The others led Kerac away, deeper and deeper into the forest, indicating they knew of a safe ground. Kerac went willingly. The others brayed about him, encircling him. With the others he was safe from Stroud.

He no longer thought of his former self. Kerac was no longer even a vague memory, and yet something about the Indian woman disturbed him. Seeing her again had stirred something in him, making him recall the other self, ever so indistinctly.

One of the were-women took Kerac's one good hand in hers, making him tear it away and howl at her. She howled back and was pushed off by a second of the females, who bared her fangs to Kerac. The first one leapt on this one's back and they began to rip and tear at one another.

Kerac and the other males watched the fighting with a mixture of admiration and lust.

A third of the females in the pack tugged at Kerac to come away. This one was older, silver-haired. She might have been as old as the leader Kerac had killed. She bellowed and howled and the others stopped instantly in their fighting. All of them started moving on again, on toward the safe ground.

Kerac tried to emulate the sounds made by the older one. He must learn to effectively communicate with all of the others, short of killing those who disobeyed him.

Several more of the women of child-bearing age came closer to Kerac, surrounding him in a mist of their musk. All about the fringes of the herd, Kerac saw the little ones who'd fairly well been kept in hiding during the battles.

Kerac thought of fathering such a child. Only a monster called Stroud stood in his way.

—20—

It was an abyss, the darkest, deepest hole he had ever seen, as if Stroud had fallen into the blank blackness of a computer screen. He felt nothing, no sensations of touch, only sound and smell. The deafening sound was a mixture of rushing water, wind and the howls of creatures hidden here. The sickening, overpowering odor was of their defecation, decay and rancid meat, intermingled with the unmistakable animal musk of the werewolf.

The bowels of this underbelly of earth that Stroud had lost himself in were enormous, long and winding; it reminded him of the treacherous vampire cave in Andover, Illinois, where other creatures of the night had kept their lair, feeding on other animals and people they had dragged down into it. The vampires in Andover that Stroud had vanquished from that place had used a method of cocooning up their victims, keeping them just barely alive, so as to produce for the monsters an endless supply of blood to feed on time and time again.

But there was none of the vampire stench here.

This place, wherever he was, reeked of the freakish wolf-people, the dank hair and hide smell of a mammalian-human aberration, almost ratlike in its bodily odors.

Stroud realized only now that he was defenseless, without a weapon. He wondered where the others were. He wondered where Anna had got off to. He wanted to run, but which way? Every direction was unfathomable via normal eyesight. He found a pair of huge infrared binoculars around his neck. His fingers went to binoculars, lifting them without feeling them, and he hesitated before putting them up to his eyes.

He heard clearly now the rushing water, but it was not water after all, but *breathing*. All around him, hundreds of breathing animals in the dark. He sensed them there behind the wall of darkness that denied him vision. Did he dare lift the glasses to his eyes?

He steadied his hands and lifted the glasses, pressing them to his eyes, but they were working improperly. He could see nothing but dense grays. He tried to adjust the infrared dials. Nothing. No change. He stared again through the binoculars, feeling he was taking an inordinate amount of precious time with the damned things when he saw something before him, yet not before him.

It was the image of a woman.

There came a distant whine, a human sound of a dazed, semiconscious woman, plaintive and pleading. Was it Anna?

According to the binoculars, she was right before him, standing close enough to touch him, and yet her features remained indistinct. He put out his right hand toward the apparition, but touched nothing. In a moment, he realized she was part of a kaleidoscope forming *inside* the binoculars.

From the frayed gray matter that created her, like images in smoke, deep inside the binocular darkness, Stroud made out the features of the dead woman, Nells. She was pushing the dead air ahead of her as if waving him away, as if warning him off from this place. Then she vanished into the mist of the world inside the oversized binoculars in Stroud's hand, to be replaced by Priest— or an image of Priest—as he was before they mutilated him. Priest spoke but could not be heard. Stroud tried to read his ghostly lips, coming up with the words "down and below." This, moments before Priest faded, and with his fading, Stroud heard the distinct scream of a woman. Her screams riffled through the cave and through the binoculars and through Stroud's brain. It was the horror-filled scream of terror and pain he most feared hearing in the world. It was Anna More's screams.

Suddenly the infrared capability on the binoculars was operational, and through them Abe saw in the red glow of the underground world Dr. Louis Cage, Tulley and Saylor—all of them, bent over Anna, stripping parts of her flesh away, feeding on her. All of the men had become werewolves, and the walls and ledges of this place were filled with other werewolves looking on, howling in a chanting fashion at the display before them.

"No!" cried Stroud, who suddenly saw Kerac's one good claw come down at his eyes, taking half his head away.

Stroud's scream turned into a gurgle for breath and he came suddenly into consciousness, sitting upright on the cold, hard metal of the helicopter's cargo bay. The others were filling the bay with provisions, and all of them looked at Stroud now, staring. Anna climbed in and rushed to him, taking Stroud's hands in hers.

"It's all right, Abe . . . it's all right," she assured him.

Shaken, sweating with fear, Stroud tried to gather in his breath. He felt as if he'd been crushed by a great weight, as if Kerac's nightmare claw had indeed cut him in two, as if Anna had been killed and all the others had been changed by Kerac into what Kerac had become.

Cage came to him with a cool, wet rag, placing it over his forehead and giving him a shot. Stroud objected, "No barbiturates, Lou! Nothing that's going to—"

"Just a little energy boost, Abe," Lou assured him. "I gave it to the others as well."

"Must've been *some* dream," said Saylor from the cargo bay door.

"Yeah . . . some kind of dream," Stroud said. His head was pounding with a horrible physical pain, and it was filled with the image of the cave where they had all died. He thought better of telling them a word of it. If it was a premonition, he must change the course of history, he told himself. He prayed it was just a nightmare . . . yet, it was so real. He feared telling the others that he had just been visited by the ghosts of Nells and Priest.

"He'll be fine now," Cage assured Anna.

"Are you all right?" she asked Stroud.

He nodded several times, but his eyes were on the overhead ceiling of the helicopter where the predawn light danced in from the doors on either side, making Anna look up as well. She could not see the images of Blue, Nells and Priest that danced also in the light.

"*Down . . . below*," Stroud repeated the words of the ghost.

"What?" asked Cage.

Anna, seeing nothing on the ceiling, looked back into Stroud's eyes and once more saw there the odd, near-human-faced shadows, like dots on his cornea, moments before they simply disappeared.

"We must again locate them, Cage!" shouted Stroud suddenly,

getting to his feet, ignoring Anna's protests.

"What?" said Cage.

"They'll disappear for good if we don't find them now! Now! That's what the dream was trying to tell me. We must get aloft! Now!"

"But we haven't got all the supplies," complained Anna.

"Do we have plastique, Saylor? Did you load any plastique aboard?"

"Plenty of it, sure."

"Good, then we'll have to make any other preparations en route, do you all understand?"

Stroud rushed past them like a man on speed, going to the pilot and ordering him to ready the helicopter for flight. "Come on, hurry!" Stroud was shouting.

"Coming," shouted Tulley, dropping a last crate of ammunition and grabbing Saylor's hand to be pulled up just as the helicopter got away.

"What the hell gives, Stroud?" asked Cage, certain his sudden strange behavior had to do with his dream.

But Abe waved him off. "We've all got to do some spotting. Are there enough infrared binocs back there for everyone?"

"These people have to get some rest, Abe."

"No time for that now, Cage. It's crucial we know where they are. Look at this! Look at it!" Stroud had snatched up the complicated geodesic map of the region. Anna More and Saylor came closer to hear and see what was going on between Stroud and Cage in the cockpit.

"What am I looking at, Abe?"

"This region is dotted with limestone, and where there's limestone, there's artesian water, and where there—"

"—there's artesian water, there's underground caves."

"Exactly, and should they retreat to these caves, we've lost them for certain."

"How did you figure this out?"

"Earlier, I was looking over the map . . . must have stuck in my subconscious," he lied.

"They may already have gone underground in that case," said Saylor.

"Perhaps not," countered Stroud. "This area right here"—he poked the map—"is a goodly distance even for them to go. If we're lucky, there'll be stragglers."

"What makes you think they'll go for that area?"

"According to the map, it's the likeliest place for a large underground cavern. And if my hunch is right, this lair of theirs has to be large. They've probably used it for generations, living out most of their lives there."

"You don't think for a moment we're going inside *with* them, do you?" asked Tulley, who had come closer to hear the plan as well.

"I hope it won't come to that. I hope we can place charges at the entry, seal them up."

"And any other exits they might have," said Saylor, enjoying the idea now.

"Whatever we can locate," agreed Stroud.

"Who's going to set the charges?" asked Cage.

"Tulley and me," replied Saylor. "We can handle it."

"We've got to first determine what needs blasting and where. We'll have to do a thorough recon from the air," said Tulley, who had had a great deal of experience with plastique explosives. "If a second blast team is needed, Stroud, you and one of your friends here is it."

"I don't want everyone in those caves," said Stroud. "Prepare the stuff, tell me exactly what to do, and I'll be the second team. Anna and Cage stay with the helicopter."

"I'll go in with you, sir," said the pilot.

"Forget it, Dave. The others need you to fly this thing out of here. Aside from me, you're the only one who can handle the controls."

Abe got up from the seat he was in and started handing out the infrared binoculars. "I want you all on watch. We've got to spot them again, follow their movements."

Abe went among them doling out the field glasses, and Anna More shouted over the rotor blades, "I'm going with you, Abe."

"I said no, Anna! Not this time! Nor you!" he said, lifting a finger at Lou Cage.

"It's something you saw, isn't it?" asked Anna. "Something in your dream."

"Nothing like that."

"Don't lie to me, Abe."

He looked away. "We have a right to know, Abe," Lou said to him. "We all of us have a right to know . . ."

"It was just a nightmare."

"Your nightmares have a way of coming true," said Cage, "and it was something in your dream that told you about the caves, wasn't it?"

"Priest told me about the caves."

"What?" shouted Tulley. "What'd he say? Priest?"

"And the others."

"What others?" asked Saylor.

"Blue and Nells."

"This is nuts," said Tulley.

Saylor shook his head. "Can't buy this, Abe."

"Buy what you like. But under no circumstances go into those caves. Do you understand?"

"Then how in hell're we supposed to set charges that will bring them down? We've got to clear at least the threshold."

"With every step you go inside, you assure yourself of being trapped there forever," he warned them. "All I'm saying is that we must do this thing with every caution, and then some."

"And you really expect us to believe the ghosts of our buddies came to you and warned you about all this," said Tulley with a snarl. "You're nuts, Stroud . . . nuts."

"Just the same," said Cage, "the advice is good and worth heeding."

Saylor took Tulley aside, cooling him down, saying, "These choppers are about as effective as they were in thick brush in Nam, you know, Tulley?"

"Yeah, you got that right."

"Smoke?"

"Sure."

"Tell you what, I'll go out with a grenade before I let those bastards do to me what they did to Blue," said Saylor. "How about you?"

"It'd take more than a grenade to kill you, Earl. Maybe some of that stuff." He indicated the plastique.

"Best get to work on bundling it, huh?"

The soldiers soon went to work on preparing the explosive charges. Stroud, Cage and Anna, along with the pilot, kept a sharp eye out for movement below. In between, Stroud hung up the geodesic map on metal clips to a wire on the gunwale. He frequently studied it, going back to the bubble of the chopper, studying the ground, returning to the map and back, until suddenly Anna More shouted, "I see movement!"

"Where?"

"Three o'clock! Lots of movement down there."

The werewolves were in the area exactly as Stroud has predicted, and this made Tulley even more uneasy about Stroud.

Cage took up the trail. "More on that east ridge," he said.

Stroud, staring through the red glow of the binoculars, saw the movement clearly as well. He tried to calculate the numbers, and the number of locations where they seemed to be disappearing. Each such location might mean another entryway into their underground world.

"They'll post sentries at the entrances," said Saylor, who was now also staring down on the scene.

The light was playing havoc with the infrared at this distance, the sun trying desperately to lift over the horizon.

"Posting sentries would be Kerac's next move," said Cage. "Cunning bastard."

"That won't help them," said Tulley, saddened by the fact Blue wasn't there to take up the chant.

"I count three, possibly four key points where we should explode the stuff," said Tulley to Stroud.

"Show me on the map."

Tulley worked quickly, and what he said seemed to make good sense to Stroud and the others. "Let's do it," said Abe.

"Can we put down, Dave?" asked Saylor, anxious to get started.

The pilot had spotted a place to set the helicopter down, and they buzzed around to this location. In the cargo bay, Stroud took two bundles of prepared plastique off Tulley's hands. Tulley took the other two, indicating that the explosives were wired. All that Stroud had to do was place them. They would be detonated from the safety of the helicopter.

"Let's go, soldier!" shouted Saylor to Tulley, and they were away as the chopper was still settling to land.

Anna More stopped Stroud. "Wait, you need someone to cover your back. I'm going with you."

"I said no, Anna."

"But Abe!"

"Do I have to tie you up, knock you out, what?"

"All right, all right!" She said it like a curse and he was away. Moments after Stroud left, Anna More rushed out after him, Cage unable to stop her. Cage's eyes met those of the pilot before he cast them to the earth.

"We've got to protect the chopper," Dave said to Lou Cage. "Right?"

"Right," Cage said feebly before turning, grabbing up one of the weapons he'd used so effectively from the air, and went out after Anna More.

Saylor and Tulley moved quickly at a crouch like the trained soldiers they were. Stroud watched them go in the direction of the supposed front of the caverns which could not be seen from here, so covered were they with thick brush. Stroud himself was pushing around to the west side of the hillock. Every outcropping of granite, every ledge, looked like one of the beasts. With their uncanny ability to camouflage themselves, Stroud could not be cavalier. He remembered how the trees had come alive in the fight in the forest. Then he heard something in the brush behind him. He wheeled and almost fired when he saw that it was Anna. She had waited until they were at some distance from the helicopters before allowing him to see that she had followed him out.

Angry with her, he motioned her to try to keep up, turned and continued.

"You'll need a lookout while you're setting the explosives," she said to him when she caught up.

"I didn't want to endanger you any further."

"Just like a man."

"Why, because I'm worried about you?"

"Assuming that you can make all my decisions for me, based on my sex."

"Anna, my decision for you was based on the fact that I care deeply about you," he said, stopping in place. "If anything should happen to you—"

"We're a team now. You're stuck with me."

"Just be certain you stay well within my sight."

"Yes, sir."

They made their way around to the other side of the rocks. There was a natural mound here that went on for perhaps another fifty yards. "We've got to get to the end of this ridge," he told her.

"I wonder how Saylor and Tulley are doing."

"I think we'd better concentrate on what we have to do. Worry about them later."

"Kerac and the others must feel safe down below."

"I'm sure it has been a safe haven for them for generations. Someday, maybe, after all this is over, I'll come back with an excavating team, dig up the ruins, see what we can tell about these beasts from an archeological point of view. There's no telling how long they've inhabited this area and these limestone caves."

"Great idea, Stroud. Why don't you wait until we've buried them before you begin to dig them up?"

Seeing some movement ahead, they went to their knees and fell silent. A loosely organized group of werewolves was straggling into an opening in the rock face ahead.

"There's one sure place for a detonation," whispered Stroud.

They waited for what seemed an interminable amount of time as the last of these stragglers moved into hiding. Among them were child-beasts.

"Just as the old Indian said," Stroud whispered. It was the first they had seen of any of the creatures' progeny up close. Their dwarflike, chimp features masked their ferocious nature and flesh-rending fangs.

They had lost the darkness, save for the long shadows of dawn. Stroud now moved on, Anna keeping close to his heels. In fifteen minutes they had found the place where the small band had disappeared into the rock. The crevice hardly seemed large enough for the big ones to enter, and yet they had squeezed through.

"I need to go in a little deeper, attach the plastique to the ceiling table," he told her. "You wait here, and don't dare enter behind me."

She stared into his grave eyes. "I'll just guard against any of those things coming in behind you."

"In the nightmare, we were all trapped inside this enormous cavern, Anna. We must do all that we can to avoid the interior."

"All right, now go—go and hurry back."

Stroud pushed his large frame through the crevice to find that it opened wide once he was past this point. He had shouldered his weapon and reached deep into the pocket of his khaki jacket to find the plastique he carried. Instantly his nostrils were assailed by the awful odor that had so overpowered him in the dream.

He could see nothing but darkness ahead. Only a pinpoint of light from the shaft where he entered illuminated the slick walls where water bled from the rocks, sending down spirals of color. It did not appear to be a deep cavern, but one eaten out by time, water and wind. The right charges, timed at the right moment, could seal them all here and they would starve for oxygen before they began to cannibalize one another.

Stroud feared using a light, feared making a rock tumble or letting the sole of his foot come down with each step toward the interior. He needn't go far in, but far enough that the blast would not be consumed completely by the entryway. He knew that Saylor and Tulley must be having the same difficulty with their work about now.

Stroud reached up with the plastique, pressing its gummy surface into the bald, dry ceiling of this awful-smelling place, when something grabbed his wrist in so powerful a grip he thought it would be broken. He felt and smelled the hairy thing that had him there in the dark, felt its breath coming into his face as it was about to bite his head off, when a gunshot rang out and Stroud felt the enormous weight of the beast fall over him, knocking him into the stony earth.

Anna rushed to where he lay, helping him to his feet. "Are you all right?"

"Damn it, I told you—"

"I just saved your life!"

"And that shot's going to bring others. Come on, we've got to get out of here."

They started for the crevice when they heard a roaring from the other side and they saw more creatures closing in around it.

"Come on," said Stroud. "We've got to find another way out."

"Christ, I hope Saylor's having better luck than we are."

They raced past the dead gargantuan, finding a choice of several tunnels in the beam of Stroud's light. The fat, smooth walls were slick with droplets of trickling water that reflected back the light. They could hear the roar and den of the werewolves coming toward them from all directions.

"Choose one," he told her.

Anna rushed for the one tunnel that seemed to be going in a northeasterly direction, if Stroud could count on his bearings down here. Behind them, a horde of the wolf-people approached at a frightening clip. Stroud wheeled around, knelt and fired repeatedly into the onrushing beasts, sending their leaders to the ground, dead. Anna yelled for him to hurry on. Stroud got up, raced to her position where she now knelt and fired on a second band of werewolves that arrived through another tunnel.

Stroud flashed his light round for an escape route, snatched Anna's arm and raced down another stone corridor that seemed only to lead them deeper and deeper into the black prison.

"Christ, it's my nightmare," he said, "and it's coming true. You should have stayed at the helicopter."

They ventured deeper into the dark.

—21—

Earl Saylor and Wil Tulley had encountered no resistance, and they had made good time. They had placed the first charge at a smaller entranceway, and now the two veteran fighters slipped into the main hole where the werewolves had gone. "In and out," Saylor whispered in Tulley's ear.

He needn't have bothered. Tulley wanted to be as far from here as possible, but he did believe that Stroud's plan had merit. If they could only pull it off.

The fact they had met with no resistance bothered both of the soldiers. It wasn't what they had expected of their enemy.

"Strange," Tulley said as they made their way down the mouth of the main entrance to the underground lair of the creatures.

"Yeah," agreed Saylor. "Best keep still."

Tulley nodded, recalling how sensitive the monsters were to sound. The cave smelled bad, worse than any bear cave Tulley had ever been in, and he had been in a few.

Saylor indicated he would keep watch, but it was so dark the only way he might see was through the infrared binoculars he'd brought along with him. He dared not flash a light. Tulley went to work, placing the last of the plastique, having some difficulty finding a stable place for it. He wanted a clean surface to press it into, but could find none readily available. Crumbling dirt fell into his face where the twisted roots of vegetation from outside and above them sprouted tentacles that hung here suspended in air.

"Come on," said Saylor.

Tulley found a niche in a solid stone where one of the roots had forced open a hole. He shoved the plastique in, but as he did so, he heard Saylor scream.

From out of nowhere, it seemed, various bones and parts of a body were thrown at Saylor, and among the parts were the remnants of Nells' head.

Saylor opened fire, screaming. Tulley felt for his weapon, but at the same instant he felt himself lifted off the ground. One of the cursed creatures had him in its grip. Tulley screamed for help, begging Saylor to do something. Saylor hesitated, knowing he'd have to kill Tulley if he were to kill the beast that had him in its grip.

The hesitation was enough for those creatures who now covered the entryway to come in on Saylor. Saylor grabbed one of the grenades on his belt, popped the pin and rushed at Tulley and the thing that had him in its grip. Tulley's arms were locked in front of him by the monster, but he grabbed on to Saylor's hands, which were wrapped about the grenade.

A second beast reached them just as the grenade should have gone off. Tulley was screaming in the iron grip of the creature. Saylor gave a war-whoop, expecting the explosion to silence them all and likely set off the plastique overhead as well.

But the grenade didn't go off.

"Oh, Christ!" shouted Saylor, who reached for a second grenade, ripping it from Tulley's belt, but he was slammed to the earth, the second grenade rolling away from him as he felt the fangs of the wolfman atop him sink deep into his throat.

Tulley's scream was the last thing Saylor heard.

From the shadows, from behind the safety of a huge boulder, Kerac came forth, looking over the two captives. Kerac's followers had done well in not mutilating these two as they had the others. They had instead stunned them into coma, the venom making them prisoners within their own bodies. How much they sensed, heard, felt or saw around them was anyone's guess. Kerac's only concern was that they be kept alive—at least for now. This time, he had enough followers to protect the bait he would use to draw Stroud to him.

Kerac and the others howled at the success of having lost only a handful of their number in gaining the prize of these two. Some of them were salivating over their prizes, however, fighting the desire to rend them apart and feed on their flesh.

Kerac tore these away from the two humans, roaring and snarling at the others.

Kerac then saw a light far and faint, deeper within the catacombs of the tunnels, and he roared at it, pointing, knowing somehow it was Stroud.

Kerac, with his one good hand, lifted Saylor with little effort, standing the stiffened body upright. The others began to help him, and Tulley was stood erect. In the blackness all around them, the beasts disappeared, a pair of them holding onto and dangling the bait.

Kerac backed off to a point of greater safety, a snarl of gratification curling his lip, baring his fangs.

Dave T. Michelson didn't like the sounds he heard coming from out of the distance at the rock ledge. Gunfire had erupted, which meant trouble, and the others had been gone for almost an hour, and he was getting edgy. One of the rules of working for Dr. Stroud was that absolute allegiance must be given the millionaire, and every pilot working for him had to take an oath never to divulge anything he deemed a "secret" mission, such as this one.

Dave would like to tell his father about this mission. He'd like to blow a hole in the old geezer's notion of the world, of good and evil, of man and angel. This werewolf thing, this the old man couldn't explain away with his Bible or anything else in his small-minded catechism.

Dave was born a minister's son and raised in a stifling, strict and frustrating environment in Oklahoma, just outside Tulsa. He ran away from home at seventeen, bummed around for a time and then joined the army, where he learned to fly. Dave had some Seminole blood in his veins, and this had made him very much in tune with Chief Anna More, the goings-on here, the old legends of wild men that roamed the darkest areas of the continent still, and maybe he was even in tune a little with Dr. Abraham Stroud. Dave liked Stroud very much, and he meant to do his duty by standing his post, staying with the helicopter . . . and yet, those cries he heard welling up from the earth . . . Maybe they needed his help down there. Maybe he should rush in.

Then there was a strange, sickening silence and Dave wondered if all the others were dead, and if he was alone—completely— except for the beasts.

Every bird in every tree made him turn. He smelled the werewolves all around. He sensed their eyes on him.

Dave had wandered closer and closer to the caves but he took up the binoculars again and stared and stared and saw nothing. The quiet all around seemed suddenly unnatural. He turned and looked back at the helicopter, clutching the AK-47 in his hands tightly. The chopper was one of the finest he had ever flown, and he enjoyed being employed by Stroud Enterprises for the very reason that Dr. Stroud allowed his pilots to believe they owned the machine they flew. Stroud left all flying to his pilots. He never interfered.

Dave had heard stories about the strange Dr. Stroud for a year now, one about his having uncovered and destroyed a vampire colony in Andover, Illinois. Dave no longer doubted the authenticity of the story, not anymore. He wondered now if Stroud lay down there brutalized and dying, alongside Anna More, Cage and the others. He trembled at the thought and silently cursed Cage for having left him alone.

Dave then heard something below him in the brush, and his quick turn detected the movement of leaves. "Dr. Cage! Cage, is that you?"

There was no answer, just an uncanny silence again. Something was in that brush. Dave lifted his gun to fire. "Announce yourself, or I'll fire!"

Still no answer. Dave stared at the place where he had seen the movement. It was perfectly still. Perhaps his eyes were playing tricks on him.

"I will fire!" shouted Dave, opening up on the brush, tearing it to pieces, feeling like a fool, when suddenly one of the beasts lifted in a roar of pain and fell the distance from the brush to the bottom of the ridge.

"Sonofabitch," said Dave in response.

He turned and started to scale the hill, going back to the helicopter. He'd get her ready should the others show; and if other beasts began to come for him, Dave might have to simply save himself.

He heard the stones beneath his feet cascade down as he stepped up his pace for the chopper. But he also heard other sounds, other stones, and suddenly, all around him, what seemed like boulders and sand and bush lifted up and started toward him. He was surrounded by the beasts. Dave knelt and spun round and round, firing and firing, bringing down one after the other of the attacking beasts, but there were too many of them, and they were too close. They overpowered Dave, and his screams were instantly stifled by a massive claw that replaced his throat as it was ripped from him.

—22—

Abraham Stroud and Anna Laughing More heard the screams that seemed to well up from the earth below them as it traveled the walls of the cavern. They heard the deafening gunshots. Anna thought she recognized Tulley's voice in the screams.

"It's impossible to tell from what direction it's coming," said Stroud, "but I think it's that way."

She followed his lead. The noise resounded off the walls, the ceiling and the earthen floor. Still, Stroud pursued the sounds, inching along the wall, having doused his light.

"They need our help," she whispered.

Stroud said nothing, pushing on faster.

Saylor's shouts and rancor had barely been heard above the automatic gunfire. Stroud came around a corner too quickly and a spray of bullets sent him diving back, shoving her down when a spray of gunfire bit into the stone all around them.

"Saylor! Tulley! We're on the other side!" Stroud shouted. But there was no answer and the guns were silent.

"Saylor! Saylor! Answer me, damn it! Saylor!" cried Stroud to no avail.

Anna took up the shouts, but it was no use, and Stroud shushed her, holding her, feeling her tremble in his arms. "We're going to die in here, aren't we, Stroud?"

"No."

"That's what you dreamed."

"No!" he denied it.

"Saylor, Tulley, me and you . . ."

"And Cage," he said, "but Cage isn't here, and I tell you, I'm not ready to die. Are you?"

"Do you think Tulley placed the other two charges?"

"We'll know pretty soon. Cage has orders to detonate if we don't return within the hour."

Stroud now took the last of the plastique from his jacket and found a place for it over his head. As he turned from this, he saw Tulley and Saylor coming toward them at the end of the tunnel, and he pointed.

The two men looked strange, as if stricken, and their movements were not animated. They looked like cardboard likenesses of themselves. Something was moving them. Something was behind them.

"What's the matter with them?" asked Anna.

"They've taken the venom. They're in a kind of suspended animation. Sometimes these beasts, for no apparent reason, don't feed on their victims, but turn them into werewolves instead. My guess is that they want to use Saylor and Tulley against us."

"What should we do?"

"Do for them what you wanted to do for Kerac, Anna. Do it . . . now!"

They both opened fire on Tulley and Saylor, instantly killing them, along with the monsters holding them up and moving them along toward Stroud. From behind these leapt others; one of them displayed a missing forearm.

"It's Kerac!" shouted Anna, firing anew, wasting bullets in the sudden pitch.

"They're gone, Anna! They're gone for now."

"We've got to find a way out, Abe. They know every rock, every crevice. We're blind down here."

Stroud backpedaled, taking her along with him, when he saw a light some distance behind them. "Could it be a way out?" he asked her.

"Dunno, but it's our only hope."

They rushed toward the moving light, Stroud's own flash beginning to wane when he saw Louis Cage at the end of the flashlight ahead of them.

"Lou!"

"Abe! Anna! Is that you?"

"Yes, yes!" she cried.

"Hurry!" shouted Cage. "This way."

It looked like Cage, and it sounded like Cage, but after the frightening use of the bodies of the soldiers, Stroud was suspicious and unsure. Suppose Cage had been bitten, as was the case in Stroud's dream. And suppose Cage was suckering them into a trap at this moment.

"There's a way out, here!" Cage called.

Stroud watched Cage's body language as they approached. He was far from stiff, and his animated gestures seemed a sure sign of his being free from the contamination of the beasts.

"Thank God I've found you. They got Tulley and Saylor, saw the whole thing, but there wasn't anything I could do. Fired and fired into them, but it was useless. Abe, it's madness to be here."

"Which way?"

"Follow me."

They traversed a series of boulders strewn in their path and made for a patch of light in the distance. One of Kerac's kind might be behind every rock, pressed against the sides of the cavern, ready to pounce. One or two were suddenly in pursuit, and ahead the light was blocked by a third. Stroud took careful aim, fired, and suddenly the light was back.

"Hurry! Run!" Stroud shouted to the others.

Anna fell, scraping her leg badly, but she fired from a sitting position, police fashion, and brought down another of the pursuing beasts. Stroud turned, fired and brought down several more as Cage helped Anna to her feet.

Cage went through the opening first, followed by Anna, as Stroud staved off the others coming at him. He pulled a grenade pin and tossed it at the remaining pursuers, leaping into the opening and rolling away as the blast sent up rock and dirt and shrapnel.

The three of them, supporting one another, rushed into the thickets around the mound. Cage radioed back to the helicopter to detonate the plastique. There was no answer.

"Dave! Dave! Michelson! Where are you? Come in!"

Still there was no answer.

"We've got to blow those charges, Lou, before Kerac figures out what we had in mind, and why we risked going in after him and the others."

They raced for the chopper, seeing some of the beasts beating about it, tearing things apart, certain that Dave Michelson had been killed by them. Stroud's long legs placed him ahead of the other two, and when he came up on the rise, he was facing six of the beasts, who stared back at him, most with their hands filled with this object or that. Beneath the chopper were the remnant parts of Dave Michelson. They had fed on his body.

Seeing red, Stroud opened fire, riddling the monsters with the silver nitrate carried into their systems by the bullets. They charged as he fired, the last one falling at Stroud's feet. Stroud then raced to the machine for the detonation device when suddenly one of the beasts that had been cowering inside leapt out over the top of Abe Stroud, sending him to the earth, rolling wildly away from the helicopter.

Anna More and Louis Cage arrived at the same instant, seeing the beast fly over Stroud. Anna took aim at the rolling, moving target, Cage cautioning her. She threw down the rifle and went for her Smith & Wesson, holding it firmly with both hands. At the instant the creature was about to chomp down on Stroud's throat with its salivating fangs, she fired and it was instantly killed. Stroud threw it over and watched it roll down toward the caves where others of its kind, including Kerac, stared out at their enemy.

"Fire on them. Pin them back inside!" Stroud shouted to Anna and Cage, who promptly began a volley at the main entranceway to the cavern. Stroud raced once more for the helicopter and found the detonator which Tulley had set to simultaneously set off all four of the plastique charges they had placed inside the cavern.

"Blow that thing!" shouted Cage.

But Stroud hesitated, coming toward Anna and Cage with it in his hands, studying the situation below. There were still any number of the creatures at the breach before the cavern.

"We have to frighten them back inside," said Stroud, "before we detonate."

"What?" Cage was incredulous. "Abe, they may disperse at any moment now! It's better we take out some of them with the explosives as none of them!"

"Just keep them at bay with the gunfire!"

"What're you going to do?"

"Both of you, get into the helicopter. But keep shooting."

"What?"

"Now, Lou! Now!"

Stroud got into the cockpit and ran a finger quickly over the control panel. He was an experienced flier. He took the helicopter up as several more tenacious beasts scurried to latch on to the skids. Stroud took these with him, wheeling toward the cave mouth.

"Drop some of the gas reserves, Lou!"

"Gas, now?"

"Don't argue! They've been conditioned to fear the gas, so give them gas. They'll all crawl back into their damned holes and then we hit 'em with the plastique."

"Of course," said Anna. "It's got to work."

"You know, Stroud, I must never underestimate you," said Lou.

The gas was dropped, and it had the desired effect of sending all the rampaging beasts back to the supposed safety of the underground world they inhabited.

"Bombs away!" shouted Stroud, pressing the lever for the explosives. Below them they watched the gases and dirt cloud cover the entire area of the mound built upon the limestone ledge. It caved in as if held together by matchsticks. Most of the beasts must surely be crushed, and those remaining alive were buried alive.

Anna began to cry, her fears and all of the anxiety of the past twenty-four hours rushing out of her in a cascade of relief. "Finally . . . finally, Kerac is dead."

Kerac had watched the fight at the helicopter, and he stood firm as the bullets rained around him there at the cave's mouth. He was angry that Stroud had escaped with the Indian woman, and him left with two dead Stroud followers, killed not by Kerac and his people, but by their own kind. Kerac thought that Stroud's kind were vicious and ruthless and would stop at nothing to destroy his kind.

As these thoughts passed through his mind, Kerac had watched the helicopter rise again and begin to dust the werewolf's world with the deadly toxic gas once more. Kerac had bellowed and howled and warned and shoved his people back into the safety of their caves, but rushing back inside, he saw something odd like a red flower at the top of the ceiling.

Kerac did not know what this was, but he knew it had to be Stroud's and therefore harmful. He dared not touch the red thing, but he feared doing nothing either.

He grabbed hold of the older female who had shown so much wisdom, and his eyes told her of his fear. She led him deeper and deeper into the cavern to the very center, where there was a large, underground reservoir. She pointed to it and suddenly the walls were caving in with an ear-shattering blast, followed by another, and another and another.

Kerac leapt into the water in an effort to save himself while the old mother was crushed by falling stone. A handful of others who had followed Kerac down here, trailing behind the old woman, also leapt into the water. Huge boulders began to cascade toward the water, and Kerac, taking a last breath of air, dove for the bottom, where he saw a strange, magical light. He swam and swam for the light until he was certain his lungs would explode.

Kerac surfaced outside the caves and the first sound in his ears was the *whirr* of the helicopter as it moved off into the distance, circled and came around. They were looking for survivors, firing on any of the creatures that ran or crawled from the rubble. Kerac dove beneath the water with the return of the helicopter. When he did so, he came face-to-face with another of his kind who had escaped by following him. She was the female who had fought for him and won. Kerac took her to the surface with him, cautious of being sighted from above, but the helicopter was concentrating on the other side of the hills.

The hideous gunfire rumbled to where they bobbed in the water. Kerac hurried her from the water and into the safety of the dense foliage nearby. Here, amid the clamor of the searching helicopter with the victorious, hated Stroud, and all his guns, Kerac held the female until she stopped trembling.

When the helicopter was away and peace came again, it was nightfall and Kerac made love to his new mate. As his lust overtook him, he thought of the son he would one day have, and he thought of the many others he would bring into the world.

Kerac shoved the wolfwoman onto her face again, roaring his fetid breath at her, fuming at her. It made him feel better to do so.

The woman-wolf had hung on Kerac for hours now, whimpering, overwhelmed at the loss of all her kind. They'd made their way to safety of a kind, nestled amid boulders in the side of a hill thick with brush. The female was getting on Kerac's nerves, the whimpering driving him to distraction. She clawed at him and mewed and mewed, as if he could do anything to lessen her pain. She had several gashes in her legs and one at the rib cage but was still fit and hale.

Kerac's rage had taken all his attention, threatening to entirely consume him; his blood was afire with hatred for the thing called Stroud. Stroud had, with one fell swoop, wiped out Kerac's kind and it had been Kerac's own fault, having led Stroud to them. The female at his side tried to soothe his pain and anger and frustration but this only served to enrage him further.

He had growled and swiped at her, and at one point he pushed her so roughly that she fell over a rock and was gone some time before she found her way back up to him. When she persisted, he attacked her, beating her horribly with his feet and tearing at her with his single claw. He stared at her now where she had crept off, whimpering. Something even in her cowering and whimpering further excited Kerac, and he came at her again, sinking his teeth into her. She fought back, tearing at him, drawing blood. Kerac tore away tufts of fur and made her screech in pain as he dug in deeper with his teeth, completely cowering her once more.

Kerac loosened his grip and she turned over for him, and Kerac felt a violent lust for her. He was so violent in his lovemaking that she was beaten beyond submission. When he lifted from her, she was in an unconscious state. Kerac left her like that, vowing to return.

He had Stroud to deal with. Whatever else might happen, Kerac knew he must kill Stroud. Kerac also believed that he knew where Stroud would be. He began to make his way back to the place where Stroud and the others had given him his false freedom.

Kerac's color, the way he moved and blended in with the surrounding blue to brown woods, made him a ghost here. Stroud wouldn't be satisfied until he saw Kerac's body. The vicious creature that he was, Stroud would simply stay on forever or until he was sure. Stroud would be there, recuperating, renegotiating with the others, planning a morning reconnaissance and another after that until *he was sure*. In the meantime, Kerac would see that Stroud's last sure thing was a quick death.

Stroud's evil image was burned into Kerac's mind along with that of Stroud's female, the Indian woman. Kerac would like to infect her with his venom and make her his new mate.

Kerac hurried, tearing at the thick branches that attempted to stay his march back into the foray. It was a long way back to where the helicopter would have taken them. They would be searching here where Kerac was now. They wouldn't expect him to go on the offensive; they would not be looking for him to be in their own backyard.

I want Stroud, he kept telling himself as he fought his way through the darkness. *I want Stroud's blood.*

—23—

Anna Laughing More poured the last of the coffee into Stroud's cup and the two of them looked at the dancing reflection of the firelight in one another's eyes. They had had a long discussion, another "fight" as it were. Stroud wanted Lou and her to take the chopper straight for Merimac, to remove her from any further possible danger. She was all for it, but not for leaving him here alone.

Stroud continued the argument as Lou puttered about the tent beside the helicopter. They had returned to the site where they had first let Kerac go free. It seemed at a safe distance, and it had been a good place to drop the bird the first time.

"Will you please just listen to reason?"

"Me? You want me to listen to reason?" she asked.

"Is that like hard for an Indian or something?" he snapped. "Look, sweetheart, in all probability Kerac is dead. He died along with the others. But we've got to be dead certain. Short of digging up the bones, we've got to do a few day's reconnoitering hereabouts—just to be on the safe side. Lou knows enough about the helicopter to get you out and—"

"Forget it. If you two stay, so do I."

Cage shouted in an exasperated tone from where he stood. "You're both fools, you realize! We're short on supplies and ammunition, Stroud. We don't have any more to give than we already have given physically and mentally, or don't you get it?

And honestly, if I flew out of here, Abe, I'd be hard-pressed to come back."

"Then do it, Lou, but take her the hell with you."

Stroud got up and walked off, disappearing into the surrounding darkness. He was agitated and his agitation worried his two friends who looked at one another now.

"God, he's a stubborn man," she said.

"Runs in the family, I understand."

"You know Abe better than anyone, Lou. What's troubling him, besides the casualties of war we incurred?"

"He's a very intuitive man. Deep down, he must think Kerac is still alive."

"But that's impossible."

"I would've thought so."

"Has he ever been known to be wrong?"

"Not once."

"There's always a first time."

"He's gone to think it through, I guess. Who knows, maybe by daybreak, we'll all fly out of here. God knows we deserve it."

Kerac fought with the night. He didn't want Stroud to see another sunrise. He pushed himself to the very limits. He raced through flatland, scaled rocky passages and dug in like the wolf he was on the higher ground. He smelled his own scent along the line of his earlier passing. He saw the heaps of bodies lying fetid and rotting among the foul meat that the evil mind of Stroud had provided for his race. He saw others of his kind in this nightmare landscape lying in rigid poses, killed by the gas that Stroud's devils had concocted for them. His hatred for Stroud doubled and redoubled as he neared the man; his hatred became a palpitating lump in his breast. It must be released; his hatred must be appeased or it would kill him.

As Kerac drew nearer and nearer, however, his mind conceived of a worse fate than death for Stroud. Kerac thought of letting Stroud live, but not as a man. Kerac thought of how Stroud would like life as one of Kerac's kind, doing Kerac's bidding, being subjugated daily for the rest of his life by Kerac and Kerac's woman.

The idea had merit; it certainly appealed to Kerac. He would do the same with Stroud as with the Indian woman. He could use them to repopulate his race. A keen irony in that for sure. Perhaps killing Stroud outright was *too* easy and *too* kind.

As Kerac approached he began to pick up a scent on the wind, the scent of humans. In the far distance he saw a campfire. Now he had a beacon and he went straight for it, still toying with the idea of making Stroud one with him. With Stroud's cunning on Kerac's side, perhaps whole new worlds could be conquered . . .

Alone for the first time in days, Abraham Stroud tried to get in touch with his feelings. Something like fuzzy tentacles played along the coils of his inner ear, trying desperately for his attention, but in all the commotion and heat of battle, it was impossible to know exactly what it was that bothered him so. Now, staring out at the moonless night, lights blinking from a million constellations, he tried to understand his reservations about leaving this horrible place. Was it possible that Kerac *was* still alive?

"*Yes*," came a whispered voice from deep within him.

Stroud recognized the voice as that of his deceased grandfather. The old man's ghost had saved his life before in just such a fashion. Why should he not listen now?

Stroud opened his mind up to the suggestion, opened his being up to his grandfather's ghost. Ananias Stroud did not disappoint him.

Stroud, cross-legged on the earth outcropping that overlooked the heavens, sensed the truth. Kerac lived. Kerac was near and getting nearer. Kerac was bent on Stroud's destruction.

More than ever, he wanted Anna Laughing More away from here. More than ever, he knew that it would come down to a fight to the death between himself and Kerac. Kerac knew this, his grandfather's ghost knew this, the entire cosmic world seemed to know, except for Stroud's two innocent friends behind him at the campfire.

Stroud got up and went back slowly toward the fire. He sensed that Kerac was dangerously close and closing in, driven by hatred of him. Stroud moved in on Anna and Lou and their eyes grew wide with fear when they saw that he held up a gun to them.

"You two will take orders from me and do as I say! Do you understand, damn you!"

"Abe, this is unnecessary," replied Cage.

"Do you really expect us to believe that you would use that thing on us?" she asked, calling his bluff.

Abe said flatly, "Just leave me what ammo we have left, leave me some of the gas, the equipment I need, and both of you get the hell out of here. *He's coming for me*."

Anna was shaking her head but Lou took hold of her and said, "We'd better do as he asks, Anna."

"No!" She pulled away and fell toward Stroud, who grabbed her and pushed her toward the helicopter, saying, "I'll hog-tie you if I have to, Anna, I swear it. He's on his way here, and he only wants me."

"So, you just provide yourself for him? That's madness! Let us help!"

"You can't help. Not this time. You'd only get hurt, badly hurt."

Stroud put her aboard the helicopter, calling for Lou to take it out of here. With the helicopter roaring off, Stroud looked around at his puny arsenal and the campfire. These were the only things that stood between him and darkness. He knew that Kerac did not want him completely dead; he knew now that Kerac wanted to make of him what Kerac himself was, and that it was an idea that hatched in the mind of the monster as he neared. One bite and Stroud was a lycanthrope, a werewolf.

A rustle in the bushes at the base of the hill made his insides stir. He wished for light and looked around to locate the flares that Lou had left behind.

He prepared for the contest, securing his position, seeing to his weapon. One of the vats of silver nitrate stood in the compound, as did several high-powered weapons loaded and ready. A small canister of gas, the last of it, was nearby, but Stroud hadn't had time to get the mask and oxygen unit necessary to use the gas. Still, as a last resort . . .

Stroud quickly worked to organize as many booby traps as he could, relying on what he had learned in the military. He set out a trip wire around the perimeter of the camp. He placed the silver nitrate concentration nearby, sloshing the shiny, mercurylike material onto his hands as he wheeled the open container closer to the fire. "I'll dip the sonofabitch in it," he told the reflection of himself in the pool of silver-black liquid once it was in place. He placed the gas canister close by as well. He loaded the three weapons at his disposal and he prayed for light to come before Kerac did.

The last thing Stroud did was to locate a thick, felled branch. This he took to the campfire with him, placing one end in the fire, allowing it to burn while he sat on the other end.

He sat before the campfire now, listening, ready for anything, when Kerac suddenly appeared opposite him as if from nowhere.

Kerac's size seemed enormous silhouetted against the firelight. Kerac rose up grizzly fashion, and with a roar, believing he had Stroud completely by surprise and cowered, he dove straight over the fire, singeing himself to get at Stroud. Stroud lifted the long, burning branch into Kerac's midsection as he came over, setting the beast aflame and jamming the fiery wood up and up, toppling Kerac within inches of the silver nitrate drum, shaking the thing and causing it to slosh its contents over onto him. The liquid scalded Kerac but not enough to do serious harm. It must penetrate deeper to be effective. Kerac beat out the fire at his breast.

Stroud had rushed for the barrel of silver nitrate, toppling it now. The contents spewed forth but Kerac leapt back and out of sight, beyond a tree, swerving and coming straight for Stroud again. Stroud rushed for his rifle but Kerac got there at the same instant and snatched and hurled it away. The other two weapons were nearby but Kerac stood between Stroud and the guns.

Kerac's enormous claw swiped at Stroud, making him fall away and wheel toward the gas canister he knew to be to his right. Stroud grabbed for the canister and got hold of it, but at the same instant he felt Kerac's firm, painful grip on him and knew that Kerac was about to sink his fangs into him.

Just then a flare burst overhead, lighting up the entire scene, and Stroud realized it was Lou and Anna from above. She was likely trying to get a shot at Kerac this instant, but was unable to do so without fearing for Stroud's life. The sudden flare disoriented Kerac and in that second's hesitation Stroud lifted the canister of gas to ward off Kerac's attack. Kerac's ferocious fangs came down on the slender canister, sinking into it, spewing gas into his eyes as Stroud pulled free and rolled down from the hillock and away from the dangerous cloud beginning to form.

Kerac stumbled into the fire once more and a shot rang out from above, a shot that exploded the canister jammed in Kerac's mouth, sending parts of Kerac flying down over Stroud where he lay at the bottom of a ravine.

Stroud saw an animal of some size fleeing through the darkness from where he lay, but he couldn't make it out. It appeared, however, to have only two legs and it could be another of Kerac's kind, but then again, it could have been just a deer. Stroud got to his feet and rushed from the widening circle of gas created by the explosion.

• • •

"We've got to be sure," Stroud told Anna and Lou Cage. "We must be absolutely sure that we did indeed destroy them all."

For the past twenty-four hours, Stroud had flown the helicopter in ever-widening circles around the site of the destruction. Where the table rock had collapsed, seeing it from the air, one might think a UFO had landed there.

"We've done all that is humanly possible, Abe," said Lou Cage. "And we've seen no activity down there in all this time. I think it safe to say our work here is over."

Stroud continued with the infrared equipment in the night, searching, obsessed with the idea that some of Kerac's pack had escaped the destruction below. Anna More was asleep on a cot in the cargo bay. All of them had become depressed and extremely upset over the loss of life, the final deaths of Saylor, Tulley and then Dave Michelson like a hammer blow to the heart. Cage also found that the recording equipment had been smashed and the film ripped away and missing. All of their "evidence" for the existence of Kerac's kind was gone, all but the film from Stroud Manse, and this, Cage knew, would be ridiculed if brought before other scientists.

Stroud assured him that someday they'd return here with an archeological team, and all the evidence of the wolf-people would be uncovered and catalogued properly.

Anna More, hearing this, got up and went to Stroud. "No, you must never disturb the site . . . never!"

"You're not suddenly going superstitious on us, are you, Anna?"

"Leave them to their graves, Stroud . . . please."

"She may have a point, Abe," agreed Cage. "We still don't know enough about the properties of their body chemistry, the venom they carried, their blood. Suppose their decaying bodies carried a dormant, transferable seed of some kind? Opening the crypt we just made for them could be very dangerous."

"Perhaps you're right."

"Let's go home, Stroud," said Anna.

Stroud nodded, turning the bird toward Anna's home of Merimac.

EPILOGUE

Saying goodbye to Merimac, Michigan was easy, but saying it to Anna Laughing More was difficult for Abraham Hale Stroud. But there was no staying, and from Anna's perspective there was no leaving her home. Not even for him. They had had a final passionate time together, a time that Stroud would remember for the rest of his life, and then he said his final goodbye to her at the airport, vowing that he would return to her some day, even though both of them knew better.

The Lear jet banked once and circled about the small community where so much had happened. Abe thought of home, of Andover, but he knew he must postpone going home long enough to stopover in Chicago to see how Cage was doing, and to hand over a final report to Commissioner Burns. Once these chores were done, he could think of home.

He returned to Chicago several days after Lou Cage had arrived in the city. Cage had quickly settled back into the routine duties of his job as Chief Medical Examiner of Chicago by the time Stroud had wandered in to see him. Lou was fine and hearty, back to his usual jolly self, but there was something troubling him, and he kept telling Stroud he shouldn't have come back to the city, that he should have gone elsewhere.

"Where else?"

"Anywhere else," said Lou, slapping a newspaper in front of Stroud. The absurd headlines had only worsened during their time in Michigan. "You're going to have reporters all over you if you don't get out of here soon," he warned Abe as they shook hands.

Of course, Lou had accurately gaged the interest of the newspapers and the public in Abraham Stroud, and so had Stroud. He had wisely used no limousines, traveling across the city by cab, drawing no attention to himself. He made his way to Commissioner Burns' office next.

Stroud read about himself in the back of the cab. The photo was one taken during the manhunt for Kerac, a not too complimentary likeness, in which he was grimacing like a madman. There was enough innuendo in the story to lynch him if this were 1924, but nothing in the way of solid evidence, nothing one could quite call fodder for criminal proceedings in a modern court of law. Yet, he knew Lou's concern did signal a very real danger. He knew there were going to be several unhappy days spent here in the city which he had helped save from the likes of Kerac and a long list of killers and rapists. He'd be hounded by the press and disparaged by other cops, Phil McMasters in particular. As for Burns, he was unlikely to be anything but the politician he was, only wanting to distance himself from Stroud.

Stroud saw himself a virtual prisoner in his suite at the Palmer House, his newfound infamy and celebrity a curse from which he knew he must run; yet he doubted escape was even remotely possible.

Stroud saw Commissioner Aaron Burns, detailed the entire incident for him and handed him all the documentation they had on Kerac and the existence of hundreds of werewolves in the forests of Michigan, showing how Stroud had, with the help of his team, eradicated them. Burns could do with the information what he wished, and apparently he wished to bury it. He had contacted Stroud soon after receiving the film in which Perry Gwinn was killed by Kerac, along with the affidavits from Cage, More, and Stroud himself. Burns suggested that Stroud keep any further information on the case to himself. Then Burns buried the file, but not so far that Burns himself could not get his hands on it when he might need it. He told Stroud that he would like to call on him in the future for any "unusual" cases.

Stroud replied that he wouldn't be interested. He was weary of things "unusual" and weird. Burns warned him that Phil McMasters and others had spread some misinformation about him, and that he might be reading about himself in the *Star* or the *Enquirer* in the near future, but that they'd gotten no help from Burns.

"What kind of rumors?" Stroud asked, although he didn't really want to know.

"For instance, that you are such a bored millionaire that . . . that . . ."

"Go on."

"That you held a man captive, released him into the forests and hunted him down like an animal."

"Nasty enough."

"Your place in Andover'll be a hotbed for reporters for a while. I suggest you take a trip abroad."

"I'll take that under advisement, Commissioner. And thanks for the warning."

The following day the tabloids featured Abraham H. Stroud as a mad millionaire, onetime war vet with a steel plate in his head, a psycho cop and now a "playboy" of the bizarrest order who, like Vlad the Impaler, enjoyed seeing other men suffer. There was a list of employees in Stroud Enterprises who were on the missing persons' lists of several major cities. The old story of how Stroud was at the center of controversy in his native Andover, where a strange case of mass disappearances was somehow linked to a terrorist raid on that town, was rehashed. It linked Stroud with the strange disappearances of literally hundreds in Andover—which only Stroud and a handful of faithful friends knew as the vampires they were. The story called him a disciple of the fictional vampire hunter Van Helsing from *Dracula* fame. It said that Stroud was insane enough to think himself a modern-day vampire hunter and killer, except that what he killed were other men.

The fools didn't even know that Van Helsing was indeed a real flesh-and-blood man that Bram Stoker had written about, that *Dracula* was a nonfictional account of diaries and letters compiled by Stoker, and that Van Helsing was the predecessor of the Stroud line, that Stroud's father and his father before him had all been vampire hunters. All facts too bizarre even for the *Enquirer*'s editors.

Burns had been right. The tabloid press was having a field day with Stroud, undermining his reputation as a serious archeologist. The Chicago papers took up the case of the missing Perry Gwinn, whose body had never been found. They laid his disappearance at Stroud's doorstep, a warrant was gotten up and the manse was visited by FBI agents serving papers. They had found nothing, and could not locate the central chamber where Kerac had been kept and where Gwinn died, not without Stroud's cooperation, and he gave them none.

Andover was crawling with press. Stroud flew out, escaping the madness in search of peace, and he found as much as he might at the Cahokia dig. A new chamber had been discovered at a stratum that no one there even suspected. That night, Stroud telephoned Cage from the field to gloat over the fact, and to again thank him for all his brave assistance in Michigan. Cage was angry with Stroud for being lucky enough to be back at the dig, complaining about the amount of work that had piled up in Chicago during his absence. He also complained of his assistant, Ira Howe. Howe had not let Cage rest since the day of his return, pounding him with curiosity about Kerac and the outcome. Cage said that Howe was relentless about it.

"Take him to Burns," said Stroud. "Ira deserves to know the truth. Show him the film. That'll shut him up."

"Like it did Burns."

"What do you mean?"

"Burns isn't your friend, Abe, believe me."

"Meaning?"

"He sicked the press on you, Abe, to hang you out on the media line. I thought you'd have figured that one out on your own."

"I thought it was McMasters."

"Bet he told you to leave the country, didn't he?"

"Something like that, yeah."

"Bet he told you McMasters was behind the accusations, didn't he?"

"Yes . . . yes, he did."

"The whole thing was too much for Burns to handle. Maybe it's too much for any of us to handle, Abe. You included, along with me and Ira, and Anna More."

The mention of Anna's name slowed Stroud's heartbeat. "Have you heard anything from her?"

"Abe, I know you love her. Why don't you go see her; talk to her."

"No, not now . . . not with all the hullabaloo following me these days."

"Understood, and as for Ira Howe seeing anything in Burns' files—forget it."

"Bastard Burns."

"Abe, if any man deserves better, it's you. You should be a

goddamned national hero. Instead, they're frying your ass in the press, making you look like . . . like—"

"Like a fiend and a ghoul, like a sadist, a modern-day Marquis de Sade, a man-killer who likes to bathe in blood."

"Maybe you ought to heed Burns' suggestion, Abe."

"What? Go abroad? Turn tail and run? Admit to the world they're all right?"

"They'll find you at the dig; disrupt things for you and everyone there."

"I left a false trail."

"When they can't get any information from the Ashyers about you, or from your friends and enemies in Andover, they'll dig up the fact you've been spending time at Cahokia, and they'll be on those people there like ticks."

"Goddammit, Lou, what in hell do you suggest? The French Foreign Legion?"

"I have a friend who's involved in a fantastic find in Egypt."

"Egypt? A dig?" Stroud was instantly curious. "What sort of find?"

"The best sort, in the city of Nazlet el Samman, at the foot of the great pyramids, where they've found an archeological site below the city. It was uncovered during the excavations for a goddamned sewage treatment plant that the Egyptians asked the Americans to help build. All construction has stopped for the time being, until they can determine just what they've got."

"Sounds intriguing."

"Why not join them?"

"Can you arrange it, Lou?"

"Can a duck swim? Of course, and you won't regret a minute of it. You'll be as content as a hog at the trough. Meanwhile, everything here will cool; it'll all be placed in its proper perspective, and you'll be vindicated."

"Wouldn't go that far . . . vindication's a lot to ask of people. I'll settle for silence."

"Least people'll learn you don't have blood dripping from your walls, maybe."

"Maybe."

"Egypt it is then, and I'll get back to you with the particulars. You can fly over as soon as you hear from either Mamdoud or me."

Stroud almost choked. "Dr. Al-lulu Mamdoud? The curator of the Cairo Institute of Egyptian Antiquities?"

"That's him."

"This must be something big . . . really big. . . ."

"Like a dream come true, isn't it? But believe me Mamdoud'll work your tail off. There's a time limit on the dig before the Egyptian authorities'll come in and close it down so they can get on with their damned plans for a proper sewage system there."

"Then I'd better hurry."

"Exactly. As for Cahokia, the place doesn't need you, Abe."

"Yes, well, my friends here are still my friends, but you're right. Once the place is descended upon . . . Did I tell you, Lou, what we've recently found here ties in with the Wendigo belief?"

"What's that?"

"The new chamber revealed some new information on the Cahokia's so-called mythology about a half-man, half-beast that roamed about the fringes of their world. The cryptologist and linguist and pictographologist are treating it as curious, arcane and quaint information about the folklore of the Cahokia."

"Yes, well, between the wolf-people and Abe Stroud, it would appear there is something in common in that thread."

Stroud laughed lightly. "How so, Lou?"

"You're something of a folk tale yourself now."

"You sure Dr. Mamdoud will want a fearsome legend working for him?"

"Mamdoud is his own legend. He won't let it get in the way of his dig."

"Sounds like as good a hiding place as the world has to offer a celebrity like myself."

"I'll set it up, Abe. And, Abe . . . for what it's worth, thanks . . . thanks from me for every goddamned one of us."

Lou hung up on that note and Stroud felt strangely alone, and yet strangely at peace. He knew that he had taken each step in his fight against Kerac and Kerac's kind with the intention to safeguard human life; he knew, as Lou and Anna knew, that he was not the fiendish architect of evil, but the demolition expert of evil; he trusted firmly that his visions and his actions were right actions. Stroud thought of the incredible heritage of his family, brought to his attention not by his father who had been killed by a vampire's conniving, but by his dead grandfather's spirit which he had inherited along with Stroud Manse; he now invited visitations from the benevolent ghost of his past which continued to guide his steps.

Finally, Abraham H. Stroud was beginning to accept his "aberration" and his difference. He accepted even the fact that he had somehow survived a battlefield in Southeast Asia that no one else had survived. He accepted the fact that he survived the Andover devils that had infested that place for generations before he had arrived, kept at bay all those years by his ancestors. He also accepted his fate in regard to Kerac's attempts to destroy him, and in doing so destroying almost everyone around him. He had been spared to finish out his life, to encounter again and to struggle again with evil.

Stroud now knew beyond any doubt that this destiny was ordained by a higher power, a power that had implanted a psychic gift from nature, and a power that had crowned this gift with a melding of mind and minerals in the steel plate in his head. All to stave off the satanic, the horrific and the abominable in this world.

If you enjoyed *Curse of the Vampire* and *Wake of the Werewolf*, then you'll enjoy reading the next Abraham Stroud novel by Geoffrey Caine, *Legion of the Dead,* coming from Diamond Books in January.

The following is an excerpt from that book:

Manhattan on a cold April 13, 1992

Anton Weitzel did not know what he was doing here in the night, standing before the pit opened deep in the earth by Gordon Consolidated Enterprises. He didn't know how he had arrived here. He couldn't recall the traffic lights or buses or trains—none of the particulars—but he did recall the sounds he heard daily, weekly, *now stretching into the second month* . . . the sounds that had cost him his job and his sanity.

The sounds had begun when the old Maramar Hotel had been demolished and the planned Gordon Towers was begun, just after the deepest foundation holes were dug, far below the former foundations. The noises sounded like straining, muffled voices, the cries of people sometimes. They pleaded with Weitzel for understanding, but the voices were in some strange language he did not know or understand. The cries came from deep within the earth below street level. Either that, or he was indeed mad, and the sounds came only from his addled brain.

Either way, he was drawn here like a somnolent zombie to its lord.

"What in God's name am I doing here?" he asked the empty, mud-packed pit below the towering buildings on either side of him. "What am I doing here again?"

There was some small similarity between the voices and the

electrical pulse of Manhattan all around him with its ominous and resounding *mmmmmmmm* beating into his ears. He had always had a horrible fear of losing his hearing, and now he wondered if he ought not to pierce his own eardrums and force himself into deafness to rid himself of the cursed sound that welled up from below to drown out the city's heartbeat and Weitzel's own.

Weitzel stood just outside the periphery of the construction site, his nerves quivering with anticipation and anger and frustration all at once, a mix that threatened to send his already high blood pressure off the charts. His doctor had told him no more, Weitzel . . . *No more can you do this thing to Ida . . . to yourself . . . No more can you go down there and look and look and wait for this thing to happen. It will kill you.*

Yet Weitzel was drawn to the construction site like an addict to sense the *ommmmmmm* of it all, the sounds no one else heard, the voice no one else heard. It was all here, going undetected in the middle of New York City, an ancient wonder that these fools that worked like automatons over the supports of yet another tower to the sky could not sense. Only Anton Weitzel could sense it.

It had begun on March 14 of the year when he was walking past from his job at the travel agency. Like many others on lunch break that dreary day, he had stopped to examine how the work was going at the construction site of what would be the next tallest monument in the city, a twin towers complex of offices and condominiums being built by one of the richest men in the world, Sir Arthur Thomas Gordon III. Sir Arthur's monstrosity was said to require the deepest set pylons that had ever been sunk into the earth, as it was to be made earthquake-resistant as well as extremely tall. At the top Gordon would have a suite that he might come to whenever he was not world-hopping.

Weitzel and others were taken with the sheer, cavernous size of the hole in the earth, in the heart of Manhattan, that these men had dug. It seemed to him that the ugly insult to the island might be the final straw, that something terribly wrong might come of it. It had been just a passing thought, and yet it festered and festered, bringing Weitzel back again and again to stand for hours staring down into the maw of the enormous hole the machines were digging. He did so by means of little windows cut from the restraining boards of wood and metal that formed an efficient barricade.

It became an obsession. Weitzel's employer packed him off after tardiness had become absences for days at a time.

His wife hammered at him to stop talking about the hole in the ground, and his children and grandchildren ignored his concern, thinking him odd. Anton began spending more and more time at the construction site, so much so that he became a regular fixture and he got to know many of the men working the site. He began to warn them that they must not go any deeper into the earth. They laughed at him.

Then one day Weitzel found a way down into the pit. He didn't know why he climbed the barrier fence. It was foolish by day to do so. He didn't get far before he was grabbed and held for the police, who escorted him away. The trouble and embarrassment and expense were almost unbearable for a man who had respected the law all his life and had not before seen the inside of a police station except on TV and in movies.

Weitzel spoke to his doctor about it, confiding for the first time to someone outside of the family that he heard strange noises coming from the pit.

"It's the sound of the heavy machinery," said Sydney Baen, his doctor and friend of many years.

"No, nothing like mechanical."

"Echoing from off the metal girders, those pile drivers, Anton . . . Anton—"

"No, no, it's alive this sound, and it's much more disturbing than anything mechanical, Sydney."

"Anton, have you ever lain in bed on a perfectly still night, say around midnight when the city is asleep—that is, the people are off the streets—yet the city *hums* as if it has a secret life of its own? You can imagine all sorts of things. Even the electrical hum of the house, Anton, as if it had a pulse, is enough to drive me . . ." Dr. Baen stopped to consider his words. "I mean, this *thing* you have with the hole in the ground, it could be like that, a simple explanation, say a generator or a pump down in that hole that you can't see from where you are. Anton? Are you listening to me?"

"God, God, goddammit, Sid! It's not me! I'm not crazy, Sid."

"I'm not suggesting for a moment—"

"I'm not suffering some sort of break-up! The sounds are real . . . the voices are not all in my imagination, Sid. The voices are coming from inside that pit! Not from inside me! Do you understand?"

"Calm down, Anton. How can we talk if you are so agitated."

Weitzel paced the room as if possessed. "It is no time for calm. Sid . . . no time for calm. There's something wrong out there in that hole and nobody is listening to me, nobody! And now you . . . you don't believe me."

"Oh, but I do believe you, Anton."

"You have a strange way of showing it."

"I believe that . . . well, that you believe—"

"And you believe that I am ready for a rubber room and a head shrinker. I know what it is you believe, Sid."

"What is happening to you, Anton, I am just not equipped to deal with, my friend, but—"

Anton began talking as if to himself. "In my head? You think it is in my head? Something down there is trying to tell me something—a warning, maybe? I don't know. Can't make it out clearly. But the begging, whining sound of it, can't anyone understand? Can't anyone else hear it?"

Dr. Baen could only stare at his old friend now.

Weitzel broke off his gaze, continued to pace and speak. "Sometimes I stand there and I think I hear a thousand voices all crying up at me at once . . . other times, it's like two voices . . . one warning, the other enticing."

The room became silent as the two men's eyes met again. Dr. Sydney Baen felt helpless in the face of what was happening to Weitzel. His hands opened, closed, and opened again in a gesture of supplication as he fought for words. He cleared his throat and finally spoke. "Anton, I have a close friend, an associate at the hospital, a fine doctor."

"A head doctor?"

"I would like you to see him."

"A shrink . . ."

"A psychiatrist, yes."

"You think I'm crazy, Sid?" Both the way that he asked it and the desire behind the question told Sid that Weitzel was sincere. "If I'm going out of my mind, Sid, I want to know, and I want to know what I should do."

"Then you'll see Dr. Marchand?"

"I'll see him, but I got to tell you, I don't have a lot of money."

"For me, Marchand will reduce his rates. Not to worry."

What Weitzel got from Marchand was the same advice that he had gotten from his wife: stay away from the source of irritation. Stay completely clear of this pit. But here he was, and he was unsure just how he had gotten here, by cab, by train, by foot? He didn't remember leaving the house, and it was pitch-black outside and his watch read three A.M. He didn't understand why he was here, but he knew he had been drawn back, just as before, only this time there was no one else around.

Anton found the entryway, on his guard for anyone who might be watching the place. There was a trailer some hundred yards off with a light in it, a watchman inside with coffee or cocoa, no doubt, as the air was chill, near brittle. Anton ignored the ache in his legs, ignored the unreasonable action he was taking and the cold as he scaled the fence. Some power source had drawn him here from his home in Brooklyn. It was so powerful that it had somehow lodged in his brain and had gotten him up and dressed—*had Ida been witness to his leaving?*—gotten him across town and was now getting him over a rickety fence covered with construction signs that seemed more permanent than the barrier itself. Some power beyond Weitzel's control drew him down into the pit.

Weitzel moved forward feeling he had no choice. Whatever this thing was, he must see it through. No one on the other side of the fence had been the least help to him. As he moved ever closer to the deepest level of the construction area, Anton Weitzel passed silent machines that stood like sleeping bovines about him; he passed layer after layer, finding it mind-boggling that they'd persisted in digging so far, so deep. Architects must have required the pylons to be fitted at something like 650 feet, if not more. Far below the sewer lines and the underground rail lines, and even the tunnels that ran between Manhattan and the mainland.

Weitzel found the blackness closing in all around him, but in the distance he saw what seemed like some strange, green firelight. It was the source, he told himself . . . the source of all his months of grief. He heard the *ommmmmmm* of life here, like the pulsating electricity that would one day run through the building those fools proposed to build over this . . . this thing. He heard the voices in his head struggling for dominance.

"*Oooommmmmm*, a-way . . . go/no . . . here to-stay . . . a-way . . . *commmmmmmmme* for-ward/a-way . . ."

Weitzel did not know anymore what he should or must do, but he did know that there was only one way to get an answer to the mystery plaguing his life. With the will and determination that had always characterized his forefathers, Anton Weitzel moved toward the green glow at the very deepest trailing of the tunnel, passing concrete posts already embedded in the bedrock as he did so.

When he reached the light, it had disappeared, sending him into total darkness. He stood, shaking, fearful and trying to ward off the incredible odor with a mere handkerchief when the light reappeared, diffusing all around him and entering him through every pore and fiber of his clothing and his being.

Now in his head he heard laughter, dizzying, bantering and then teasing laughter like that made by a man in the throes of sex. The laughter was in him and it came out through his throat. It was loud and brazen now and Weitzel's body glowed in the cavern like a green lantern, until suddenly something shouted that was *not* inside him, but outside and coming toward him. It was the watchman.

"It's you, you old bastard! I've called the cops and this time, you're really in trouble! Damned old fool! I ought to shoot you dead for trespass!"

Weitzel's body collapsed before the watchman's eyes, the watchman shining a powerful beam on the old man's form. "Damn it, damn it, no!" But at the same instant, the watchman saw something skitter from the heap that Weitzel had become, rush to the dark corner of the tunnel and begin to burrow like a large rat.

The watchman's light tried to follow the thing, but each time it darted out of the light until suddenly it was gone, beneath the earth.

"Damn . . . damn. What was that thing?" the watchman asked himself when suddenly he saw that Weitzel was in some distress. He went to the old man, who was groaning, and roughly got him to his feet.

"Come on, you old fool. We've got a date with the cops."

Weitzel said nothing, his blank expression and dead eyes registering nothing. The zombielike appearance in the man's eyes startled the watchman for a moment before he said, "Drunk as a skunk, aren't you?" But smelling no booze, he amended his assessment of Weitzel. "Got into too much Geritol, or bought into some coke, huh?"

Weitzel said nothing and only moved along if directed and helped. When together they took a few steps, the watchman realized that he was surrounded by a strange, green fog that was somehow luminous. "What the hell?" he asked himself, dropping Weitzel, who felt like a weak kitten, to the earth while the watchman looked down between his feet at the peculiar two-headed, six-legged rodentlike creature between his legs that seemed to spit forth the green light. The watchman heard this thing talking to him deep within the coils of his brain, saying that in time he would be called upon to act, but for the time being, his power, his synergy, was required by the thing at his feet. As it ripped its way from the earth, it attached itself to the watchman's leg, and from there it began to drain him, not of blood or bodily fluids, but of his mind.

Nazlet el Samman, Egypt, the same day

The working conditions were dismal and filth-ridden, a former stone "hut" of one of the city dwellers that happened to be situated above the dig; it was a place that seemed to have accommodated thousands of years of dust and sand flying through the door, seeping in through the cracks and the tiny, single window. Abraham Hale Stroud and the others on the archeological dig who worked at this terminus of the site had to do so under field lights and a generator brought from elsewhere. The lights illuminated the work and the stark environment. You could almost see the fleas in the sand that filled the cracks in floor and wall. Then they had the further inconvenience of the slag heap piled in the next room, filling it; shovel porters with rickety, noisy wheelbarrows went in and out all day long making room for more until the find was had.

Dirt and dust had long before taken possession of his lungs, and the marvelous and recent discoveries of Cheops' most secret, most hidden and most treasured of treasures had taken possession of his imagination. But at the moment, Abraham Stroud felt a wave of fatigue flushing through his veins, threatening nausea and dizziness. He'd topple if he didn't get rest, and it was foolish to push himself to such a state, yet he felt a sense of urgency as if some great power beyond his control might at any moment snatch the prize of these days from him.

The discovery here at the foot of the great pyramids was the most significant find since the opening of Tut's tomb. He was very proud to have played a part in the new archeological endeavor which would dramatically call the world's attention to the Egyptian forebear of Tut, Cheops. Stroud's own fascination with the bevy of skulls fashioned from crystal and other minerals led him to already make calls worldwide to inform colleagues around the globe that it appeared to be genuine proof that there existed a definite link between the Egyptian pyramid builders and those in Central America, as the Central Americans had been, to date, the only ones in possession of the mysterious crystal skulls which some believed to be psychic antennae.

Of course, there remained years of study, painstaking documentation, cataloguing, all the burdens of science, and yet Stroud knew he would not be allowed anywhere near the treasures of Cheops much longer. So, working with Dr. Al-lulu Mamdoud and Dr. Ranjana Patel, both of the Cairo Institute for Egyptian Antiquities, and both fine archeologists, Abe Stroud had furiously worked through the last seventy-two hours to finish his abstract on the Crypt of Skulls, an impressive collection of crystal, onyx, gold, silver, balsite and other minerals fashioned into the likeness of the human skull, an entire room full.

This portion of Cheops' burial chamber had had an instant attraction for Stroud, as the ornate skulls *spoke* to him. He heard lives—past and present and future—speaking through the incredible skulls, saw life in the iridescent, jeweled eyes of some and the simplicity of the completely crystal ones, which by all accounts could not possibly exist, either then or now! There was and remained no technology that could create them. Yet here they were in his hands.

Staring into the depths of such a crystal-fashioned skull, Stroud saw and felt the time of Cheops, whose twenty-three-year reign ended in 2657 B.C. He marveled at the basalt skull, too. Basalt was rare, expensive and one of the most difficult stones to cut, reserved typically for the flooring of temples.

Now, here they were, skulls of basalt and crystal . . . in Abraham's hands, dug from the grave of Cheops, whose great pyramid was the largest ever built, and truly the only other thing known about Cheops. Where did he get all the skulls? Why did he collect them? Had he chosen to be buried with his collection? Was there some reason why?

Burial was an elaborate ritual in his day, to ensure that neither the pharaoh nor Egypt should ever die. The journey to eternity began in the nearby Valley Temple, where the pharaoh's body was taken for ritual purification and a kind of embalming that modern science still could not duplicate. For the final rituals, the body was carried up a long, cavernous causeway to a mortuary temple next to the pyramid.

The discovery in March 1990 of Cheops' Valley Temple at the

foot of the pyramids in Nazlet el Samman had confirmed theories about the layout of Giza Plateau for the seventy years in which Cheops, his son and his grandson built their three pyramids and monuments here.

Nazlet el Samman lay at the foot of the plateau, facing the Sphinx, and for decades sewage from the village had been thought the chief cause of the Sphinx's deterioration. A U.S-financed sewage project worked in close accord with Egyptologists, who, because of the proximity of the monuments and the probability of uncovering antiquities, were paid well to monitor construction of a modern system.

They were soon unearthing mammoth granite and limestone blocks, flint knives, Roman brick walls and other relics. By the middle of the first month more artifacts and remains were turning up, and finally the main prize—a 59-foot-long row of basalt rocks. Dr. Mamdoud immediately identified it as the floor of Cheops' Valley Temple, and Dr. Patel gave her instant agreement. Basalt was reserved for royal use as flooring in sacred places.

The Egyptian Antiquities Organization moved in quickly, taking charge, overseeing every detail. By the time that Stroud had become involved, the dig was out of the hands of Mamdoud and Patel, yet they remained for their own reasons and as a go-between with the Americans on site. When one American left abruptly, Dr. Abraham Stroud was asked by the University of Chicago Museum of Antiquities if he would care to fill in. He had jumped at the chance, turning down a trip to Russia in the bargain.

Stroud had come on the scene rather late in July and now it was almost nine months he had labored under the close scrutiny of the Egyptians. This alone was enough to drive a man insane, but the way that Drs. Mamdoud and Patel withstood the assaults on their integrity was inspiring, and each in his and her own way kept the prime objective clearly in view at all times. It was harder for an American, Stroud knew, to work under circumstances in which your expertise was being paid for, but your advice and motives were constantly called into question. Of course, Egypt had been robbed and plundered by archeologists in the past, and if Egypt had anything beyond the great monuments of the pharaohs, it was a long memory.

The newly found ruins lay some fifteen feet below street level and had been partially covered with sewage, which had had to be pumped out and disposed of. The dig had gone slowly, bogged down at first by the sewage and later by red tape, not to mention the fact it was in the center of a thriving Egyptian city in which two earlier digs were going forth for Roman-era artifacts. In Nazlet el Samman they worked in an alley only a few feet from the doorsteps of houses. Archeologists had had to contend with children at play, passing carts and donkeys, as well as angry, suspicious villagers worried that antiquities officials might at any time invoke their legal authority to evict them and begin excavating below their homes.

When Stroud had arrived, one such home had already been confiscated for the purpose, with plans for a second. The stress and pressures these kinds of incidents applied to the dig were tremendous and nothing like Stroud had ever dealt with in the typical, rural dig he was used to. He had expected tents and desert winds and sand; what he got was an alley reminiscent of the worst in any Chicago hamlet where he had once been a policeman for some thirteen years, earning rank as detective before returning to his first love, archeology, gaining his degree from the University of Chicago.

The field laboratory here was a confiscated warehouse with only half a floor. The other half was sunken to thirteen feet, a ladder going down into Cheops' secret burial place. The place was dirty and the light was horrendous. They'd brought in a field generator to improve the situation, but the bright light only showed Stroud just how horrible the conditions were, and now he worked with a directed tensor lamp at the wobbly, wooden table that'd been provided him—his desk.

Cheops himself, his mummy, along with most of the richest artifacts found, had been removed for "security" reasons long before, each as soon as the archeologists had claimed, cleaned and catalogued it. There might be some truth in the security measures nowadays, because the community was getting rather noisy lately about their rights, and about allowing peace to the dead and buried. Superstitions abounded, and the archeologists often found symbols written in blood on the door when they entered in the morning.

In the field laboratory where he had labored the entire night, not stopping for so much as a cup of coffee, knowing that his presence in the country was no longer required or needed, Abraham Hale Stroud documented what he could of the final cataloguing of artifacts to come out of the greatest archeological find perhaps in the century. He looked closely again at the ancient find he slowly turned in his massive hands, cradling the onyx skull of perhaps three centimeters in diameter and less than three pounds in weight. The jeweled eyes stared back at him like two flaming embers, the red rubies mocking him with their mastery. The find was by no means the most important to come out of the exhaustive dig at Nazlet el Samman in Egypt, but for Stroud it held in its curves and smoothness and essential mystery all the world's wonders. It was the reason he was here, living in a strange admixture of dirt and fascination that made him both cough and catch his breath in the same instant.

Both Patel and Mamdoud were nearby, but when Stroud lifted another of the skulls, a beautiful crystal skull, he knew they did not see in it what he saw. In fact, he doubted that any two people on earth would see the same thing in the crystal skull, that somehow it radiated back some subconscious core of stored information, perhaps aspirations, perhaps wonders, perhaps a man's fears. It was impossible to say for certain. But now, in the myriad pools of dancing light, Stroud saw a stranger to him, a man standing poised on the brink of an enormous pit that seemed to surround and engulf both him and something else. He saw an iridescent green light rise from the earth to engulf the man. He didn't know who the man was, but he saw him turn around and look out of the crystal into Stroud's eyes, but the man had blank eyes with no life whatsoever behind his gaze. Stroud sensed that he was some sort of lost soul . . . a zombie of some kind. And then beside him stood a second man with the same blank stare and careless eyes. And then they were both gone. It had occurred within the space of an instant.

Stroud didn't know what this represented or what it meant. He only knew he could not write about the event in his scientific journal. But while it had been the only time that he had seen two men in this particular skull, it had not been the only time that Stroud had seen the face of the first man, a man he somehow knew was named Weitzel. None of it held any particular meaning to him, yet something about the man—the way he stood, the way he moved and the way he looked but *did not see*—it all cast an overwhelming sense of panic and plague in Stroud's mind, so much so that rather than sleep or eat, he had worked, thinking work would stave off the panic he felt creeping into his being.

The others, particularly the sensitive Dr. Patel, felt his recent change, the obvious no-longer-at-ease stance he had taken. The others believed that he was beginning to worry about the locals, rightly afraid for his life, and, too, they were likely wondering why he, an American, and a wealthy one at that, had come here and exiled himself in this way from his homeland.

"Dr. Stroud, you must get some rest," Ranjana said to him, making him look away from the skull and into her jet-black eyes. She was a small woman, middle-aged, always a smile of reassurance on her face. "You must be tired."

There were a few cots at the back, but he could also go to the Hilton on the other side of town where he had kept a room that he had used very little in all his days here.

"Yes, perhaps you're right. I think I will take some time."

"The work will be here when you return, I assure you," agreed Dr. Mamdoud, a lusty, well-built Arab who was lighter-skinned than most Arabs; the Egyptians often treated him rudely, even those in the Antiquities Organization. He had had an American education, and he was considered by the Egyptians as an American, since it was Mamdoud who had organized the U.S. financing of the sewage project at the outset. Consequently, the Egyptians didn't trust him much more than they trusted Stroud or other Americans on the project. Mamdoud wore soft-soled oxfords and the coat and tie of a professional, even in the Egyptian heat at noonday. The locals considered him quite mad.

Stroud said at the door, "I'll be back."

Within an hour after arriving at the Hilton, showering and shaving and having a light snack tray sent up, Stroud knew he would not be back. His door was knocked on and men with guns stood outside, the Egyptian police. They held him at gunpoint while searching his room, ostensibly for stolen artifacts. Some earlier people working on the dig had made off with a few incidentals—knives, stone pieces, jewels—or so the Egyptians claimed. His sudden departure from the warehouse had worried someone high up in the Ministry of Antiquities, Stroud supposed. He let them search. And they did so with abandon, angering Stroud, who stalked and shouted at the police when they began to toss things about.

"Come on, take it easy with that!" he yelled when they hurled open a briefcase filled with papers.

"Here, here it is, Captain," shouted one of the young officers to his commander, holding up a small, bejeweled bracelet.

Stroud knew instantly he was being hustled, and that the bracelet had not come from the Cheops' burial temple. "All right, so your boss wants me off the dig."

"You are in serious trouble here, Dr. Stroud," said the smiling Egyptian commander, a curl lifting his cheek. "I think very bad trouble for you."

"What is it you want?"

"I think it will save the state some difficulty, Doctor, if you were on the next flight to your country."

"I thought so."

"We will, of course, escort you to the airport." He ordered his men out as Stroud tried to clean up the mess they had made. Then the officer said, "I will give you time to dress and pack your belongings, Dr. Stroud."

"Thank you ever so much."

"Not necessary for thank-you." He was gone, but began knocking for Stroud to rush before a few minutes had passed. Stroud packed, attempted to contact Mamdoud or Patel at the site, and failing this, he went with the authorities to the airport. Over the police radio he heard that the field laboratory had been the scene of street violence when police and locals clashed there. There were reports of gunshots and wounded. Stroud silently prayed for Patel and Mamdoud and the beautiful skulls of Cheops.

On the flight that would take him to New York, Stroud leaned back in the seat and fell asleep, the face of a stranger to him, a man named Weitzel, crystallizing in his mind. A face . . . just a face . . . sad and empty and devoid of all emotion . . . just a face . . . yet something deep within the mind of the emotionless face, buried but striving to climb to the surface . . . a hunger or thirst or longing, or all three: a hunger to be destroyed. But this death wish was also opposed by the same source. The dual nature of the longing to live and the longing to die represented a powerful life force. Bizarre, perhaps; perhaps unnatural. Either way, the abject sadness of the little man and the force that kept him alive seemed shrouded in a mystery that Stroud would never unravel, for the impressions and the vision wrought in his brain were fleeting, giving way to oblivion and sleep.